In This Delicious Garden

Garden

or, Les Enfants du Paradis

Seth Thomas Pietras

ISBN (paperback): 978-1-7344466-0-9
ISBN (ebook) : 978-1-7344466-1-6

Library of Congress Control Number : 2020901190

Any reference to historical events, real people, or real places are used fictitiously. Names, characters, and places are products of the author's imagination.

Cover design by Jay Fletcher / jfletcherdesign.com
Map and collages by Lindsey Dolan / @lindsey.dolan
Additional design work by Cole Townsend / @twnsnd
Author image courtesy of *The Wall Street Journal*

For additional credits, see "Acknowledgements."

First printed in the United States of America.

First printing edition 2020.

Mediastopheles, LLC
Rue du Purgatoire 1
Geneva, Switzerland 1204

Mediastopheles.com

In memory of Aurélien Capelle

and all those who fly on the wings of black crows

Contents

Author's Note..ix

1 : Kanchenjunga
Summer 2

2 : Les Chevaux des Bossons
Autumn 57

3 : Sex, Drugs, Rock & Snow
Winter..123

4 : Les Chocards
Spring 221

Acknowledgements..295

References..297

About the Author 317

Author's Note

I once served as a public relations consultant for a small island nation, whose economy was tourism based and whose politics were hostile and divisive. One day I received a call from a local colleague informing me that a mental patient had escaped a hospital, found his way onto a luxury resort, broke into a room, sexually assaulted a woman, and used a machete to lop off the hand of a man who had come to her aid. The deranged attacker had been caught. All was fine.

All was fine? Based on my experience, I knew this would cause an international sensation, a perfectly lurid opportunity for the political opposition to make claims of poor regulation and use the bad news to call for change. No, I was assured, no one would hear of it. Even the opposition knew not to mess with tourism and external perceptions of their island paradise.

Sure enough, only small, separate items appeared in the local papers: one notifying of an escape and capture, and another of an injured tourist sent home. Everything had been reported accurately, except the dots had not been connected.

Years later, after having moved to the other side of the world, a fresh personal tragedy evoked that earlier island experience. A friend of mine died while skiing in Chamonix, France, where I now live. His loss, while confounding and devastating to me, hadn't warranted even a mention in the local news. I only learned of it from another friend. But why was he there? Who was with him? How did he fall? Nothing. The only answers I got were from "Cham'radio," the gossip shared by the mountain guides in the bars. Even then, no one could tell me what my friend had been thinking when he climbed up to ski the Whymper Couloir. "C'est ça à Chamonix (It's like this in Chamonix)," was all I got.

Mourning my friend and piqued by my lack of understanding, I continued to dig and found, sadly, that this is indeed how it is in Chamonix. My friend was just one of dozens of people who died that year on Mont Blanc. In fact, dozens die every year— due to falls, accidents, avalanches, or because they simply vanish into the ice. Most go unreported. Just the famous or strange deaths get attention.

Struck by this revelation, I spent days searching for death notices on the internet and in publications in local libraries. I sought closure. I found something more: The deaths of Chamonix are the easiest thing to explain about this place.

Across time and in between those losses, my searching revealed many stories about people and events in this steep, secluded valley—peculiar items that seemed to faithfully report facts but offered little in terms of context or follow up. Only by pouring over decades upon decades of news clippings did they collectively become difficult to dismiss: bizarre animal behavior, tragic crimes treated as happenstance, courageous acts left uncelebrated, and more—so many unconnected dots comprising a mortal tapestry of mountainous proportion.

Chamonix isn't isolated by ocean waves or reefs, but its massive rock walls and hanging glaciers make it an island unto itself, a reality emphasized by the elusive nature of the locals, the Chamoniards. In demeanor, they are the opposite of friendly islanders. In practice, however, they are the same: welcoming to those who wish to appreciate their home; fiercely protective and secretive of the undercurrents of their society and culture. The former shapes outside opinion with warmth and charm, the latter with a cool indifference. Both approaches make good commercial sense: creating enough intrigue to encourage a visit, yet enough unease to prevent outsiders from staying too long or asking too many questions.

I, however, have stayed. I knew there was more to the story of Chamonix than has been told; more to the people who have long made this inhospitable environment their home; more to anyone's death than the idea that they were an "addict of the extreme" or an "adrenaline junkie." To make sense of life in Chamonix—I have found after asking maybe too many questions—it must be looked at through a lens that is sometimes surreal, sometimes magical, often times both.

The result is a novel about a place. It is a novel because some of the names have been changed and some assumptions have been made to connect a few of the dots. But the rest, it is told exactly as it occurred.

— STP

"Well everyone knows Custer died at Little Bighorn.
What this book presupposes is…maybe he didn't?"
— *Eli Cash*

1. Kanchenjunga
Summer

The sight of several monkeys—small, gray and spectating—evoked no surprise from the American as he ran past. It was summer in the Alps, and the runner, Cody, had just arrived at the grassy summit of Bellevue, a ski station located in the Chamonix valley of France. After a glance, he wiped the sweat from his brow and kept on down the other side.

For the most part, primates don't live in Europe, or in France specifically, and haven't for more than 9 million years. The Ice Ages that once expanded across the continent pushed them all south. And Chamonix, tucked way up in the mountains, has been, for much of its history, barely inhabitable even for humans.

Mont Blanc, the highest point in Western Europe, generates tongues of ice—massive glaciers—that unfurl thousands of meters from needle-like peaks into the Chamonix valley below. As recently as 150 years ago, the ice flowed seasonally into towns and villages and demolished whatever was in its way: houses, hamlets, roads or farms. A Catholic congregation in Chamonix once summoned a bishop to exorcise an errant glacier threatening to consume their church. He did, and it didn't.

Today, the ice barely ventures into the valley. The glaciers now serve more as a pernicious playground than as a curse from above. Their retreat over the last century has coincided with their growing allure to outsiders, as Chamonix has increasingly attracted climbers, hikers, skiers, BASE jumpers, trail runners—like Cody—and many other types of outdoor adventurer and holiday maker.

Still, it remains no place for monkeys.

Cody was nonplussed for two reasons. First, it was the hottest day in the hottest month in the hottest year on record. Second, he had just run 105km as part of an ultramarathon, and he still had 15km to go.

Should I have included more electrolytes in my drinks? Methodically, Cody recounted his race preparations, and questioned each decision—all while continuing to run. He added up the calories he had eaten. The amount of potassium, sodium, calcium and magnesium he'd consumed. He second guessed his endurance training. Even his choice of hat brim: *Maybe I should I have covered my neck better?*

Hallucinations among athletes are not uncommon. Had not Pheidippides visions of Pan during his run from Athens to Sparta? The effort required to maintain a winning pace over 120km while climbing more than 7,000 meters begs for some grand mental breakdown: high body temps, dehydration, hyperventilation, nutrient depletion, sleep deprivation, sensory overload. Visions are taken in stride—a test of the very limits of one's capacity for pain. And at that point in the race, Cody was just off the lead.

I'll dunk my head in the water trough at the Les Houches check-in, and drink an extra cup of Coke.

His calm evaporated at the sight of more monkeys. There they were again.

This time he didn't ignore them. He tried to get a look while running. The trail descended steeply from Bellevue, a contorted single-track of roots and washed out drop-offs. The monkeys, too, were on the move, making it hard to determine exactly what they actually might be. Then they vanished.

For the next few kilometers, Cody tried not to think about them, or to think about anything at all. He "meditated," as was his habit, chanting: *Feeling good, doing great, you got this.*

His stomach churned with nausea; he experienced intermittent blood sugar spikes; his left calf flickered with muscle spasms; his right knee tweaked with sharp pain; his head was cloudy; and sweat and dirt burned his eyes. Basically, all normal.

As the dirt trail transitioned to the paved streets of the village of Les Houches, Cody reassured himself the mountains and the monkeys were now behind him. He knew that North American runners don't traditionally do well in the Alps—the conditions are much too steep for too long. *Still, monkeys?*

The Les Houches check-in point was last before the finish. As Cody took a quick swig of Coke and dunked his head, two runners passed him with an "allez" and a "courage." He freaked.

He hadn't expected this. He must've slowed on the descent while preoccupied by monkeys. The 10kms from Les Houches to the finish in Chamonix center were flattish and undulating. Now it would be a proper footrace among competitors whose bodies were ravaged and minds drained.

He set out after them with a new sickness in his stomach. *Damn those monkeys!*

But then it hit him.

All an ultramarathon runner—or really any endurance athlete—has is his or her mental state. You can be as physically fit as you like, but if you're not able to grind through the pain and fatigue, those moments when all importance for completing the challenge has been shed for better sense, when there is just no question that you should stop—if you cannot push through that barrier, then you'll never finish, let alone win.

Yet this goes for more than just the race. The training is isolating and burdensome, as Cody could attest. Going for a drink? *I have to run.* Want to get away this weekend? *I have a race.* Let's stay in, start a fire, open a bottle of wine. *I have to go out into the freezing cold, run 25km in the dark, eat a bland and wholesome meal, then go to sleep, and do it again tomorrow.*

Make no mistake: Regardless of whatever pretense of community may exist before or after a race, regardless of the countless magazines and websites and hashtags that attempt to foster some sense of connectedness, regardless of the product marketing and advertising meant to inspire and coalesce, a runner is a runner is a runner—an individual out on the trail, whose only company are the thoughts and experiences that keep anxiety, despair, and loneliness at bay.

Cody, however, had succumbed. He was now far past hitting "the wall." He had made it across hills and dales, into the hinterlands and the dark forests of the mind, edging ever close to the true sense of "running on empty."

For the next hour, Cody made his way into Chamonix center. In addition to everything else—aches in his knees; a toenail that was about to fall off; blisters between his toes, rubbing like wet sand; and chafing in his shorts—he had monkeys on the brain. Along the pavement, through Les Houches, down the hill, across the river Arve: monkeys. Up the road to Le Coupeau and then on a dirt path along the river, in and out of houses and trees: monkeys. Up the soft trail, through the pine groves, now nearing the lake: monkeys. Into a clearing by Les Gaillands, where climbers climbed, children played, and dogs ran free: monkeys!

He did not see again the runners who passed him at the check-in, and he failed to register one more runner who slipped by him along the final stretch. All he knew was that he had to keep moving forward.

At points, when he'd venture off the path, the growing number of bystanders and onlookers pushed him forward in the right direction—like a drunk at a festival following the noise. As he came into the center of Chamonix, where throngs of people cheered him on, the cacophony of voices and clapping and bells and whistling went from all he could hear to complete silence.

One foot after another. One foot after another. You're doing good. You're doing grea— OK, you're doing good... You're doing grea— OK, you're doing good...

Cody crossed the line in seventh place.

He stopped and stood for a moment. He couldn't hear anything, though every face at the finish was that of a monkey and every hand, every wave, was that of a claw. "Monkeys," he said through a desperate laugh. "Monkeys..."

His eyes rolled back and down he went.

×××

Word got around fast.

Chamonix isn't a big place after all. Maybe 25,000 regular inhabitants, most of whom tend to be keen observers—from the superficial: walk out of the house wearing more than one item of clothing from the same brand, and within an hour you're getting texts congratulating on the new sponsor; to the poignant: when the mayor once mentioned off-handedly at a lunch that the town may play host to a refugee family from Iraq, he found a package of cash and clothing donations along with a formal notice of protest waiting for him by the time he got back to the office. More than anything, the locals just like to keep an eye on outsiders—a voyeuristic tradition that predates skiing and running as pastimes.

It hearkens back to a time when Chamoniards with telescopes climbed the hills around town to assess the efforts of foreigners making a bid to surmount the high peaks—as much out of suspicion of their claims as concern for their wellbeing. It transformed into spectating and became institutionalized as a pastime when Chamonix hosted the first Winter Olympics in 1924.

Now, during the summers, even the eldest Chamoniards will sit at the cafés in the early sunshine, sipping coffee or, more likely, a panaché (beer and lemonade), cheering on the runners who come in all throughout the night during the Ultra Trail du Mont Blanc (UTMB)—the town's biggest annual event.

The race Cody ran, the TDS (abbreviated from its official name, "Sur les Traces des Ducs de Savoie (The footprints of the Dukes of Savoie)," is just one of several foot-races that make up the UTMB. Each circumnavigates all or part of Mont Blanc, passing between France, Italy and Switzerland. To do the full UTMB (170km) on foot, would take an average person 10 days. Most runners complete it in 40 hours. The winner will do it in about 20.

What is classic Chamonix, and unlike the Olympics, is how every participant is afforded equal admiration. While athletes in "traditional" sports may make fortunes and appear on talk shows, the best ultramarathoners—or the best climbers, or the best mountaineers, or the best free-riders—all stand as anonymous celebrities, even in their own communities. Some are only really known for their Instagram pics, Snapchat stories and viral videos. For those watching, the emphasis is on the act, not necessarily the individual, an ethos taken from Chamoniards, who view fame derived from self-promotion as an obscenity.

To be on Chamonix's streets among the walking wounded—those hobbling zombies who have already completed their races—or to look up at night to tiny points of light, headlamps, slowly bobbing in the darkness near the mountain tops—is to be infused with curiosity and wonder at whatever nameless human spirit is before you. It doesn't matter who won, but rather how many people finished at all. From which countries? What adversities did they encounter? What weather? What pitfalls? Or how, simply, did they do it?

So, when a young man returns from his trial having been waylaid by primates, it is a story worth sharing. To come in seventh seeing monkeys is almost better than coming in first without breaking a sweat.

And yet, almost no one was surprised.

Not the 2,000 other runners who maybe at some point experienced their own delusions, hallucinations or exhaustion; not the 5,000 support volunteers who looked after the hoards in the hills; not the race organizers who reflexively sent out extra warnings about the heat and reminded everyone that Americans didn't do well in the Alps; and certainly not the locals—the real locals, the Chamoniards whose handful of names line the cemetery, whose mountains these were, and who said nothing at the news, only made furtive glances at one another and moved on.

Almost no one was surprised.

Only a single person, when hearing the story of the American with monkeys on his back, found himself to be alarmed. A Swede, Harry Nilsson, or Nils as he was known, said aloud to no one in particular, "Yep, all good. Okay...I'm coming—" to the clear confusion of all those around him.

✕✕✕

For Nils, a comparable incident had occurred earlier in the week. He didn't, however, have the immediate cover of race exhaustion. He had been on a training run along the Grand Balcon Nord—a massive boulder-strewn ledge high above Chamonix, where pure granite rises vertically to the icy spire of the Aiguille du Midi, and below forested terrain sweeps steeply a thousand meters to the valley floor.

In this landscape, a human is very small and his or her perspective, accordingly, becomes distorted. The eyes take in too much—depths, heights, distances, textures, colors. The mind works to process and rationalize but is overwhelmed.

Perspective matters when trying to be mindful of the hazards. The simple concerns are ankle twists and scrapes. The more serious issues are being clipped by falling rock or ice, or taking a tumble off a cliff. Rarely are animals a problem. Ibex keep to themselves and large predators—big cats, wolves and bears—have long since been killed off or driven away.

So when Nils caught sight of two gray monkeys dragging a brightly colored *something* across a dry glacier, he stopped more out of curiosity than surprise.

He assessed: two hairy children clumsily tugging a body over the ice—until they realized they had been spotted. One cowered next to the colorful object, the other sat upright and looked straight at Nils.

Many foreigners arrive at Chamonix to roam its peaks with varying levels of skill and displays of fashion, so Nils's first thought was: *Should I call for a rescue?* But, as dark clouds churned and the wind picked up, he hesitated shouting out to them.

While the geological grandeur of the mountains can rearrange one's spatial awareness, and even one's definition of what constitutes imminent danger, no man loses his base instinct in the face of a threat; no man mistakes teeth bared, lips back, for a smile.

Nils froze.

"Fan (Fuck)," he said aloud and began to shake.

He was now no longer in control of himself, guided solely by sympathetic response, that stress-induced hormonal cascade dictating his next move: *fight*, *flight*, or—as it goes with a 19-year old—*photograph*.

Nils glanced down to grab his phone but when he looked up, the monkeys were gone, vanished into the ice.

The wind whistled, water trickled.

He stood alone, below the jagged peaks. Below the hanging seracs. Below the bloated clouds turning purple from an unseen setting sun. And below him, the lights of Chamonix began to turn on, disguising the one light he left on for himself. The glacier emitted a sonorous conk; ice slid and stopped.

Nils shuddered—a violent ripple across his shoulders. The air around him cooled the sweat across his back, and away he ran. Hard and fast, all the way home.

He slammed the door to his dark, empty apartment, and slunk down, heaving for breath. Nils heard only his mother: "Hey Nils, have a good day? Hurry up, dinner is ready." But the voice came from a long time ago.

✕✕✕

Mountains have long rained unexpected torment upon humans. Mont Blanc was known as Mont Maudit—the Cursed Mountain—to Chamoniards, before they decided to establish a more inviting image for outsiders. The peaks of Chamonix were avoided for hundreds of years because they were thought to be damned. They hosted fairies and other supernatural beings that hurled ice and rock into the valley without explanation— enormous, house-sized boulders; sweeping, suffocating snows. They still do.

At the turn of 21st century, one avalanche laid waste to the village of Montroc at the top of the Chamonix valley, killing 13. Houses, buildings, most everything pulverized. Right in the middle of the day, catching off-guard even one of the most experienced local mountain guides as he sat for an afternoon tea at his own kitchen table. Would anyone feel differently if those deaths resulted from a malevolent dragon? Could the losses be explained more easily to a four-year-old in a Superman cape?

When explained as the randomness of nature, such destructive events signal an uncaring world; when attributed to the something mysterious, they at least take on some meaning, as the result of some *thing's* decision. Blame is easier to assign to that which is personified. Or perhaps sinister creatures do exist and most people choose to look the other way.

×××

"Haft en bra dag? Skynda på lite, maten är klar—" Nils's mother said through the bathroom door, which he leaned against, shaking uncontrollably. Fresh blood dripped down his shin. "Have a good day? Hurry up, dinner is ready."

"Ja, allt är bra. Okej...jag kommer—" he replied. "Yep, all good. Okay...coming."

Five years before the monkeys, while returning from cross-country practice, Nils had been walking alone in his neighborhood where the houses and street lights were few and far between. Almost home. A car pulled up. Nils thought nothing of it, though paused when the passenger door swung open. No interior light. "Get in." Didn't feel right. "I said, *get in.*" He bolted across a yard and into the trees. He looked only ahead but could feel hands reaching after him. "Get here boy." He struggled—with the darkness and the branches and the mud. He lost a shoe and his shirt was torn away. He was bruised and bleeding. But he got away, because he ran hard and fast.

"Yep, all good. Okay...coming—" is what Nils repeated to himself in his apartment after encountering the monkeys, his body shaking, his mind racing. He could feel hands unknown reaching through the door, as if reaching through branches.

"Yep, all good. Okay...coming—" is what Nils thought and involuntarily said upon hearing about Cody's supposed encounter. Urgency leapt up within him as his friend conveyed the story—triggering wave upon wave of self-doubt and hurt.

Looking at Nils through a sharp eye, his friend said: "You think there really are monkeys up there? Cody seemed pretty convinced."

Nils's heart thumped. He shook his head as casually as he could. "Nah." He had never told anyone about the man and the car, and hadn't planned to tell anyone about the monkeys. He wasn't going to start right then.

"You distance runners are crazy. Either there's something fucked up in the world, or something fucked up in that guy's head—"

"Maybe they're someone's pets," Nils offered.

"Don't think Chamonix attracts those kinds of celebrities."

"What about the Merlet Animal Park? I heard they had an elephant once—"

"Maybe he was just tired."

All these years, Nils believed that if it wasn't for the scar on his shin, the man in the car might have just been a product of his imagination. How many times had he thought of confessing. "In our neighborhood?" He could hear parents saying. "Never." A persistent anxiety of the hairy unknown plagued him from then on, only assuaged by the one thing he knew that worked: running. But now the monkeys triggered something deep that stopped him dead in his tracks.

Nils's disquiet grew. Once again, he felt trapped between the unknown and the unbelievable. Then it occurred to him: *I'm not alone.*

Cody spent the night in the Chamonix hospital and was released the next morning. That was the last anyone saw of him for a good, long while.

×××

Nils knew Cody, had befriended him on Facebook. But he didn't *know* Cody—didn't have his number, didn't know where he lived. Nils messaged him. He inboxed Cody's Instagram as well, after seeing a post-hospital selfie of Cody with a big goofy grin and Mont Blanc in the background. It was tagged #monkeysee. Nils heard nothing back. After a day, both the Messenger message and inbox went unseen. So while awaiting texts back from a few mutual acquaintances, Nils engaged in a bit of online stalking.

Cody had all the basics: Facebook, Instagram, Twitter, YouTube, Snapchat, a half-complete LinkedIn profile and an eponymous website that appeared haphazardly updated. It was clear that Cody's main sponsor had set him up online to "build his personal brand as an extension of the company's brand"—something Nils's people had explained on more than one occasion. If you want the free kit, race entry fees and travel money, there is more work to do than just run.

Cody's approach to social media was more free-form than Nils's, who had cultivated a tight routine for outreach to his followers. Nils devoured the packet of information that his sponsors gave him on "guidelines for sharing" and "best practices for posting." He also keenly followed other athletes and mimicked what they did: posting daily training updates from beautiful places, tweeting pics of the large amounts of food he ate, feigning fixations with coffee as a drug and representing his sponsor's energy drink as a healing elixir—all in all, churning out running-porn to prove he was out there working hard and living "the life."

There were also a fair number of selfies. At six feet, Cody was on the tall side for trail running, which usually attracted smaller, lighter people. Nils knew, because he too was six feet, though rail-thin. Cody seemed quintessentially American: muscular and typically fit; not the look of a runner, but that of a shaggy-haired frat boy—a perception reinforced by the numerous shirtless selfies and persistent baseball cap.

Cody, irritatingly, had more followers that Nils did. On Instagram, he numbered more than 20,000. His content was more organic and a greater number of people seemed engaged. Cody had an impressive 40 percent like/friend ratio, Nils noted (summing, and summing again, the figures on his phone).

There were a lot of in-jokes with friends, and content not race or brand related: drinking beer, hanging out with girls, time spent with family at a lake. Several of Cody's Facebook page "likes" revealed an interest in the absurd: alien abductions, the Illuminati and something about fluoride in the water system. The races and training seemed to be an afterthought; hashtags didn't necessarily match the content. Even the most carefree people in this sport were deeply disciplined. This guy seemed like a mess.

He scrolled deeper into Cody's life.

Within a couple hours, Nils felt he had a grasp on who this guy was—something of a mindless wanderer, an enthusiastic bro who often succeeded despite himself, someone who insisted on "experiences" and "living for the moment." Cody clearly was the Uber rider to Nils as Uber driver—different sides of the same coin, of the same generation, and Nils felt pangs of both envy and annoyance.

On a more practical level, Nils had sorted out some important details. In the tagged photos of Cody, there was an image of Cody's "new pad," when had he moved to Chamonix—much nicer than Nils's tiny shared space. Nils glimpsed another pic of the "view from my pad yo! #alps #livingthedream." And a response to a comment on another pic—"dude im just across from annapurna"—brought Cody even closer: he lived next to the Indian restaurant in town.

If he didn't hear back from anyone, Nils decided that tomorrow he'd go around and have a look.

While the detective work amused Nils, giving him a type of self-satisfaction for once not related to training or sport—he suddenly realized he was well off his own schedule.

OK, what to post.

Although Nils had done a live update to Snapchat and Instagram that morning during his ride, he opted to take a still selfie from the same workout, which was a particularly good shot: from the ground, focused on him on his bike with the Aiguille Verte blurry but recognizable enough in the background. The light was nearly perfect and all the necessary logos were in view.

He slapped on a standard filter, instead of tinkering with the individual edit tools, then tagged three of his sponsors along with the ever-present #runmohappy—the summer companion to #skimohappy: tags his main sponsor insisted on. Before posting, he thought about adding #monkeysee, but reconsidered.

Immediately, numerous *like* notifications popped up, which made him feel good. He averaged about a thousand.

He checked Cody's accounts again. No updates.

Still invigorated by his research and realizing that he had no food in the apartment, having missed going to the market,

Nils thought it would be good to eat out this evening. Besides, there was one place where he thought he might find Cody. Nils had never been, but knew the name too well: Monkey Bar.

×××

Chamonix Sud, or Cham-sud as everyone calls it, is something of a paradox. It is the neighborhood nearest to the Aiguille du Midi lift—the most important lift station in the valley (if not in all of the Alps, and possibly all of the world)—with superb views of Mont Blanc. It is centrally located in town, near several transportation terminuses, and has plenty of parking. It should be a coveted place to stay, a hub for Chamonix's many social and outdoor activities. Somehow, it isn't.

Faux gingerbread canyons of cheaply constructed condominiums and apartments appeal primarily to the lower end of the holiday and rental markets. The courtyards are dingy, paved over and poorly kept up. The shops, too, are uninteresting: a neon-lit convenience store, a real estate office, unused commercial space and a discount outdoor gear outlet, among others. At times, packs of leadless dogs compete for space with packs of drunken young men on stag dos, a mix of Asian tourists misled by "luxury" as a marketing term, and numerous Brits on gap year.

About the only thing going for Cham-sud are three bars, which sit side-by-side: South Bar, Bighorn Bistro and Monkey Bar, the most established. They have French, American and British owners, respectively, and try mightily to make the most of being tucked away from the main stream of Chamonix's visitors.

When Cham-sud boasts a summer night crowd, as on the evening when Nils arrived, it is difficult to tell where one set of patrons ends and another begins. They merge across three terraces in a raucous swell whose din echoes betwixt and between the thin walls of the buildings, making impossible any poor visitor's sleep and giving second thoughts to any couple who thought they had scored a deal on a cheap room.

It was uncommon ground for Nils. He didn't often eat out—or go out at all for that matter. As an endurance athlete, he consumed a daily balance of proteins, carbohydrates, fruits and vegetables in order to maintain a target nutrient level that enabled a constant and high rate of energy output over a prolonged period. Nils scanned Monkey's menu hopefully for familiar items and ingredients: white rice, eggs, sweet potatoes, beans, avocado, salmon. Fortunately for him, it was "Taco Tuesday."

While he awaited a waiter, Nils looked again at Cody's Instagram, hoping for an update. Nothing. He set an alert for new posts.

Nils scrolled back and came across a post of Cody's in which Cody was sitting in a New Hampshire restaurant, taking a sip from a fishbowl cocktail: *Hard earned margarita! Knocked back a nice and relaxed 30 mile trail run, 4600' of climbing. Fun morning!*

Nils didn't know how he felt about this: envy, confusion? It wouldn't be in his own regime to have a drink after such a run.

Hungry and now impatient, Nils edged his way through the hot, smoke-filled crowd and went inside, where the air conditioning made his skin crawl.

"Bonjour," a young British woman said from behind the bar.

"Bonjour," Nils said.

Nils quickly assessed her as being not-French and said: "I have an odd question."

"OK," she said. "How can I help?"

"Do you know why this place is called Monkey Bar?"

"No," she said, "why?" expecting a punch line. They both waited through a couple beats in which she looked at him and he at her before Nils said: "I don't know. I was asking you."

"Oh," she said. "Climbers, I think. Climbers are monkeys."

This would make sense, he thought. "It's a joke, I see. Have you ever seen any monkeys in Chamonix?"

"Yeah, maybe at Elevation," she said, citing another bar frequented by alpinists. Again they looked at each other. "You gonna order something?"

Outside Nils found an open seat at a mostly occupied, communal picnic table and awaited his order. He flipped through Cody's Instagram feed. An old finish line pic of Cody looking a bit ghostly: *Yes, I puked 5 minutes after this picture was taken. Legs and lungs felt prepared for the race...however fast early pace combined with inexperience, dehydration, electrolyte imbalances led to stomach issues and massive "crash." OK, out of excuses!*

This made Nils feel better about not ordering a beer.

The friendly crowd continued to fill in around him— an increasing patter of languages all discussing the day's adventures over beers and curly fries; sunburns, bandages and crutches betraying minor tales of heroism.

"Excusez-moi, est-il disponible?" a paunchy middle-aged British man asked pointing to the remaining empty seat at Nils's table.

"Yes, feel free," Nils replied.

"Oh, you speak English," the man smiled. "One never knows, you know."

Most anyone who looked at Nils would know, and would identify him as distinctly not-French. Leave aside his clean-cut blond hair and bright blue eyes; Nils's neat, new clothing—hat, tee and shorts—were always emblazoned with either Sweden's flag or the country's triple-crown crest.

If Nils's heritage wasn't obvious, his fitness certainly was. He had the lean disposition and posture of a runner, and, most notably, in the thick heat, he wasn't sweating. This didn't get past the man who was.

"You must have run one of those races?"

"This year, no UTMB," Nils said, putting down his phone to look him in the eyes. "But I have others coming up. You?"

The man laughed—"That's not really my thing"—and rubbed his round belly.

"What is your thing?"

"Skiing. I adore skiing. Unfortunately, it's the wrong season for that!" he laughed again and sat back with a smile. "We've just come, my wife and I, to visit our daughter."

Nils could see what was about to happen, though he recognized he had a choice in the matter. Having nothing better to do: "Does your daughter live in Chamonix?"

"Oh, yes," the man said. "She moved here last winter. We used to bring her and her sister here every winter to ski. She loves to ski. She's always been so good at it. Much better than me. We didn't have the opportunities she's had! But I think she now snowboards. And rock climbs. You know what they say, you come to Chamonix for the winter but stay for the summer. I see that now. We never..."

Nils smiled and smiled, nodded and nodded. This was more than he had anticipated.

"...she met a guy here. A French guy, and she's decided to stay. She found a job at one of the retail shops in town. I don't recall the name. She very much enjoys it. Or so she says. Not exactly what her studies were for, but one has to live whilst young! She..."

Nils looked around for a rescue—maybe this guy's wife was supposed to arrive soon? But then, food arrived and Nils cut him off: "Could you take a photo of me?" The guy looked confused. "Of me with my food. Maybe get Mont Blanc in the background." He handed the man his phone.

Before Nils were 12 tacos on a tray, a small salad and a bowl of sweet potato fries. He handed the man his phone, then scooped up all the tacos between two hands and grimaced as though he was deciding which to eat first. "Be sure to get the salad and fries. Snap as many as you want."

The man complied and, handing the phone back to Nils, said: "You're a runner, what do you think of that guy who saw monkeys chasing him down the trail? Pretty hilarious, right?"

Nils had just taken a bite and could only chew.

"You runners really push yourselves. One wonders how healthy it actually is for a person. The body can only take so much, and the continued punishment. I mean, really. This is no way to live..."

Nils was about to respond when the woman seated next to him said: "I'm sorry to butt-in, but I agree. I've been climbing these mountains for 20 years and I've never seen any monkeys. To push yourself to delusion is absurd."

"You talking about those monkeys?" the woman's friend said. Others at the table perked up at this.

The conversation about the monkeys then burned across the table like a lit fuse—until it reached the end, where an old Swede and a Frenchman sat. The Frenchman said: "But there *are* monkeys on the mountain. The runner, he likely heard about the cage. It was found not so long ago, and, like a dream, he dreamt up real monkeys!"

Everyone turned to look down the table at the Frenchman—a small, tan man with short dark hair, blue eyes, and an un-ironic moustache.

"It's true."

Nils had just finished eating. He now spoke first, asking what was on everyone's mind: "What cage?"

"The ice, it moves, and one of the cages of the monkeys popped out. This was many months ago. It still had the monkey inside."

A single bead of sweat ran from Nils's temple down the side of his face, and just like that he finally felt the heat. *Yep, all good...*

"Where did the cage come from?" one of the women asked.

"From the plane, of course."

Realizing that no one at the table knew what he spoke of, the Frenchman, rather pleased to have an audience where his drinking partner, the old Swede, had failed him, held forth with a clumsy version of the following tale:

On January 24, 1966, at 7:51 a.m., Air India flight 101, about ready to complete a leg from Beirut to Geneva, instead flew directly into Mont Blanc. The plane disintegrated upon impact, creating a massive crater in the snow and rock and scattering debris for kilometers. Letters with Indian postage stamps were found as far away as the Mont Blanc tunnel, some five kilometers off.

A storm had broken out above the mountain. Black clouds boiled up through low cumulus, making the massif invisible to the pilot. If the plane had been just 15 meters higher in elevation, it would have cleared the ridge—no consolation to the 117 people who perished immediately in the crash. It is unlikely anyone on the plane had time to appreciate the fine margin upon which their lives existed, or ultimately to register that they were at their end.

When the storm cleared the next day, wreckage could be seen through binoculars from Chamonix: pieces of metal jutted from the snow and sparkled in the sun between the Refuge Vallot and the Rocher de la Tournette at about 4,750 meters. People in town watched helicopters ferry guides up to the crash. There was, however, little left of the Boeing 707. The rescue was called off just a day later when the rescuers insisted it was too dangerous to continue. Wind tore at the peak. Fresh snow blanketed the victims.

"The ice consumed the people, consumed everything," the Frenchman explained.

Only six bodies were ever recovered from the crash, the most intact of which was the co-pilot, still strapped to his seat, gripping a crumpled cup of tea. Skulls and body parts, teeth and hair were all that was left. Everything else receded into the depths of the glacier, whether immediately down crevasses or frozen into the snow over days, weeks, months, years and now decades.

"But, the glacier, he does not keep secrets forever," the Frenchman continued.

Snow on the top of the mountain gets snowed on. Each incremental layer weighs down the frozen mass. Down, down, slowly, slowly—until whatever was above is ejected into the valley below, many kilometers from where they first came to rest. The snow melts, but that which isn't made of water remains.

For hundreds of years, it's been well understood in Chamonix that if someone or something falls into a glacier at the top of the mountain, it will likely reappear about four decades later. Notices in Chamonix newspapers alert mountaineers to victims who were lost in the past who are likely to reappear in the present.

The fate of Air India 101 was no different.

"I have only ever found scraps myself," the Frenchman said. "Never have I found the jewels or the money—or anything... more valuable."

Others have.

Forty-six years after the crash, a mountain rescue worker found on the Bossons Glacier a type "C" diplomatic pouch, the kind that carries non-confidential documents. The jute bag held mail and office calendars. A year after that, a young mountaineer stumbled across a metal box containing 100 diamonds, emeralds, rubies and sapphires valued at €250,000. A year after that, another climber discovered nearly 50 pieces of jewelry—bracelets, necklaces, pendants, gold chains and earrings. They lay upon a rock as if someone had placed them there to display, he claimed.

These finds stoke the imaginations of opportunists and children. What wonders do the mountains hold? The tales dare those foolish enough to go out onto the glaciers to search for treasure—as if visitors to Chamonix need additional excuses to risk their lives.

The Frenchman, however, dismissed this notion: "What everyone is really looking for is the reason."

"The reason for what?"

"Why it crashed, of course."

"You said bad weather."

"Ah yes, that is what they would like you to believe—"

While there were jewels and government documents on the plane, the real treasure on that flight wasn't material, it was human: Homi Jehangir Bhabha, the father of India's nuclear program. Forty-two Indian sailors flying to pick up a ship in Germany died, along with four members of a Belgian cultural mission, six Britons, two Americans, a Swiss, and a Frenchman; but this one scientist...

Stocky and handsome, Dr. Bhabha was considered a brilliant physicist and an outsized character. He wielded influence through scientific eminence, wealth, family ties, powerful friends, a sharp intelligence and a flair for the arts. Almost singlehandedly, he brought peaceful nuclear power to India, and advocated for its responsible use on the world stage. But at the last minute, for whatever reason, he changed his plans and got on Flight 101 to Geneva.

As word of the crash reached India, Indira Gandhi was being sworn in as prime minister. The news cast a pall over inauguration activities. Members of the government immediately suspected involvement by archrival Pakistan (against which it had fought a second war a year earlier) or the CIA, since India was allied with the Soviet Union during the Cold War.

Adding to the speculation was the pilot—who contributed suspicion precisely because he wasn't suspicious.

Captain J.T. D'Souza had almost 20 years of flying service, with no record of incidents, and stood as one of Air India's most experienced pilots. He had flown the Alps hundreds of times, and had made the trip to Geneva just over a year earlier. When Jackie Kennedy visited India in 1962, D'Souza had sat as co-pilot. As he had for the flight Pope Paul VI took to India in 1964.

"How could such a pilot, so experienced, make such a simple mistake?" said the Frenchman. "Even if D'Souza wasn't the cause, there is more."

As it turned out, Air India flight 101 wasn't the only plane to crash on Mont Blanc on that day in 1966. Although no formal announcement was made, the debris of a Lockheed F-104 Starfighter marked "US Air Force," also turned up.

"Quelle coincidence!"

At the height of the Cold War, as two regional rivals armed with nuclear capabilities stood as proxies for their superpower patrons, the sudden death of a leading figure in the drama caused a sensation.

"For a moment, the world was on highest alert!" And then, the Frenchman added: "Oh, and there also happened to be monkeys on the plane."

A quiet moment followed as if the listeners were taking in the view of Chamonix from the Grand Balcon Nord.

Aboard the plane—besides the atomic scientist and 116 other passengers and staff, besides the jewelry and low-level diplomatic correspondence—were 200 caged primates on their way from India to the United States. When those six human bodies were brought down from Mont Blanc to Chamonix, with them were 15 dead monkeys.

Nils blinked: "Did any of the monkeys survive?"

"Of course!"

While the rest of the table carried on about the conspiracy theories, the old Swede, sitting across from the Frenchman, saw Nils's frame stiffen, almost imperceptibly. Ignoring the chatter from the table about the jewels, the Swede caught Nils's eyes and said: "Det är ingen apa på isen. (There's no monkey on the ice.)"

The old Swede had sun and wind battered skin; threadbare clothing laid on a slender, muscular physique. Elsewhere he would appear homeless, but in Chamonix, he appeared accomplished. So, while Nils wanted to roll his eyes at the old man's pun—a twist on a colloquial Swedish expression that means *there's no problem*—he put up a smile of acknowledgment instead. Then the old Swede confirmed what he meant to say: "Det är ingen ko på isen heller." (*There's no cow on the ice either.*)

Nils smirked and responded with his own expressionist twist: "Jag håller inte med. Det ligger en apa begraven." (*I don't agree. There is a monkey buried.*)

The old guy seemed amused at the retort, bobbing his head. He then finished up his pint in a single swig and got up from the table unevenly. On his way around, he leaned in gently to Nils, but grabbed him tightly just above the elbow, and said: "Var försiktig, annars är det du som kommer begravas." (*Be careful or you will be buried.*) He let go and staggered inside Monkey Bar.

Nils decided it was time to go.

×××

The next morning, Madame Champignon, a petite, silver-bunned beauty in her 80s, sat in her kitchen staring up at Mont Blanc. She woke to yet another day of bright sun, blue skies and heat, and this irritated her. The dryness of the summer so far had made her life rather difficult. Even with the valley's deep shadows and high, protected glades, the mushroom-hunting had been as challenging as any time she could recall. Some of her most productive spots were almost exhausted.

"Les chevaux des Bossons," she whispered to herself—a common expression among Chamoniards when matters seemed beyond their control. *Les chevaux des Bossons.*

At her kitchen table, she plotted where to go today. From her window, she could see the glaciers glistening a thousand meters above. They hung rotted and dirty from fallen rocks and mud. No good. Just in front of her, bees and butterflies jounced desperately among her dried-out flowers.

Today would require a bit more effort than usual, she thought. Yesterday yielded nothing worth selling. She couldn't show up to the market empty-handed. *What would they think!* Besides, she was running low on spending money, and didn't want to ask her son for anything. If she did, he would probably make her take in another tenant. He had already let out one of her rooms without much consultation. It was embarrassing enough to have a renter, but even worse to have one who is not-French. *Airbnb is easy*, her son told her, *and it's just for the summer—an experiment*. But an American!

However, it *was* her idea to offer to do the American's laundry for a small fee. She didn't tell her son about that. It was simple work. All those synthetic shorts, shirts and socks dried quickly on the line. The young man was not very tidy, and she could tell this helped bring a little order to his life, if not for his sake then for hers.

She went into the closet and grabbed her climbing rope and harness. She knew of a few humid cliffs on the backside of the Prarion. They always had something. It was one of her most secret spots, and the trip required a bit of bushwhacking and abseiling.

Having heaved her gear bag out the kitchen door, she looked down the length of the chalet to the back door, the one to the American's apartment. There was a pile of running shoes outside. *This was some experiment*, she thought, shaking her head. Though it did remind her that she needed to drop off his laundry. He hadn't been around in a couple days, so she had forgotten.

When Madame Champignon returned, a skinny blond man stood outside the American's door.

Nils, who had identified Cody's place by the pile of trail shoes and several stuffed-animal monkeys thrown in the mix, was reading a note written on a whiteboard stuck to the door ("Gone up the Jonction, back tomorrow!"—with a cartoon monkey drawn next to it).

A small, strong, elderly woman walked up to him with a basket of folded clothes.

"Bonjour, madame," Nils said.

"Bonjour," Madame Champignon said. "Puis-je vous aider?"

He looked at the old woman, who, although dressed fairly formally, was clearly about to go for a hike. He had also dressed for the trails. He had hoped to get Cody out for a run, if he encountered him. But Nils and this woman exhibited generationally different attire. She wore cotton: khakis and a long-sleeved button-down shirt. He, synthetics: shorts and a singlet. She: sturdy boots and a wide-brimmed hat. He: light trail shoes and duckbill cap. They both thought the other looked ridiculous.

Again, she said: "Puis-je vous aider?"

Nils didn't quite understand her accent. He focused and mustered: "Je suis ici pour Cody."

Putain d'Anglais, Madame Champignon thought—a common sentiment locals have for outsiders, who, regardless of national origin, are identified derogatorily as "English."

"Il est parti en montagne, je crois," she said.

Nils didn't follow. Mountain something. Slow, clearly-enunciated French he could only just make out. This woman's French was awash in her age, rinsing every word. He shook his head apologetically.

A child, Madame Champignon thought, sizing him up. *Just like the American.*

"Cody is out," she said, knowing she could say more, but was intent to get moving so as to avoid others who might be out for a hike along her path.

"Merci, merci," Nils said. "Do you know when he'll be—? I mean, ahh... savez-vous...quand..."

"Je ne sais pas. Normalement, il laisse un message." She pointed to the whiteboard. "Pardon," she said and moved to unlock Cody's door and enter with the laundry.

Nils stood at the threshold as she went in. The place was dark but clearly a mess: dirty dishes, clothes strewn about, papers everywhere—and more stuffed monkeys. A paper cutout of monkeys had been strung across the lights.

On the counter by the door, Nils spied a number of printouts: a map of La Jonction trail, and—he gasped—a couple articles about the Air India crash. He grabbed a pen and made to write a note, saying aloud in English: "I'm going to leave a message, if that's OK."

Madame Champignon waved at him as she glanced around the place, making a mental note to ask if the American would also be willing to pay her something to clean up. She moved on, shooing the Swede out the door. Nils discretely took with him several of the printouts. He hurried, saying "Merci, au revoir!" without turning back.

Madame Champignon, locking up, thought: *Time to climb some cliffs.*

Nils sat on a public bench applying sunblock while glancing over Cody's printouts. *If Cody had gone up to La Jonction, he must have gone to find the monkeys.*

Reflexively, he checked Cody's Instagram. Nothing new. He scrolled back through the feed: Cody with his cross-country team after a race that he had won; Cody leaping into the air atop a mountain in Utah; a video snippet of Cody playing the guitar. Nils listened. Not bad.

Then, a new Instagram post appeared: a selfie of Cody from le Bec de Corbeau, a well-known spot part way up La Jonction trail, which sits atop La Montagne de la Côte, a massive fin of rock that splits the Bossons and Taconnaz Glaciers. The post was captioned "going up! #monkeesee," and it already had a hundred "likes".

Nils tied his shoes and off he went.

×××

The trail up to La Jonction consists of three parts. The first, from Chalet du Glacier to Chalet des Pyramides, is a set of fairly flat switchbacks through a pine forest up the triangular front of the mountain; at the apex, the trail cuts across the side of a ravine toward the Bossons Glacier—whose massive, erratic, glistening white teeth rest on a slope seemingly too steep to keep such precariously positioned ice chunks in place—and then up to the Chalet.

The second part becomes steeper, after passing Chalet des Pyramides (a small house serving bad coffee), which overlooks the glacier. Fewer people go this way. It narrows while climbing the very ridge of the mountain—more like a goat path through grass than a proper walking trail.

Once over the ridge to the Taconnaz side, the Taconnaz Glacier, hanging in just as questionable a manner as the Bossons Glacier, is in full view, often with avalanches or icefalls permeating the quiet that elevation offers. The trail skirts this side of the ridge, now above tree line, and then pops back over to the Bossons side at a saddle called le Bec de Corbeau.

Over the course of five kilometers, the trail rises more than a kilometer in elevation. It is steep.

The third part of the trail, and final 300m of climbing, consists of a scramble up loose rock—a broad slope of boulders and rubble left from glacial activity. No trees, no grass. Just rocks, dust and mud. Metal chains and guide wires offer hikers some protection from slipping, which here could make for a long tumble.

And finally, at the top, La Jonction itself. It is the intersection of rock and ice, where La Montagne de la Côte divides the Bossons Glacier as it flows down the mountain's flanks. Here the wind picks up, coming cool off the icy mass—even on a piping hot day such as the one Nils set out on.

For an average person, it can take up to five hours to get to the top. Nils made it in just under two.

Hot, sweating, and needing shade, Nils ducked into Le Gite Balmat, a make-shift refuge of colossal boulders near the trail terminus. Against the rock he rested. Without a breeze, the heat intensified. How could he have missed Cody? He had expected to find him camped out at the top. There's really only one way up and one way down. Plus, Cody's car—which Nils identified from Instagram—had been in the parking lot when Nils set off. He racked his brains—about missing Cody, about the monkeys, about the absurdity of what he was after.

Tired, Nils emerged from Le Gite and noticed a wooden plaque bolted to the rock:

Le 7 Aout 1786 les Chamoniards, Jacques Balmat et Michel G Paccard ont bivouaqué dans des conditions difficiles sous ce bloc de granit. Le lendemain 8 Août, à force de volonté et de courage, ils atteignirent pour le 1iere fois le sommet du Mt. Blanc ouvrèrent la voie de l'alpinisme moderne.

On August 7, 1786 the Chamoniards, Jacques Balmat and Michel G Paccard bivouacked in difficult conditions under this block of granite. The following day, August 8, by force of will and courage, they reached for the first time the summit of Mt. Blanc, opening the way of modern mountaineering.

Nils looked up to an amphitheater of peaks, the center of which was Mont Blanc's white dome. To the southeast, he could see the snowy shoulder where the Air India flight crashed; he could follow the glacier down to where he stood. Far across the ice to the southeast sat the mid-station of the Aiguille du Midi lift, near where he had encountered the monkeys.

A cool wind whistled, water trickled.

Fan. Maybe Cody didn't go down. Maybe he went up!

×××

To appreciate the implications of what Nils did next, one must consider the nature of a glacier. In the abstract, a glacier consists of accumulated ice and snow that make up a solid, persistent mass. The Bossons Glacier is more than 7kms from top to bottom, just over 1km wide, and varies from 10 to 30 meters in thickness. But what makes a glacier a glacier is that it *moves*, flowing under its own weight, most often unperceptively slow.

This movement, particularly where it occurs over undulating ground, causes the icy mass to crack and contort. Spikes and flakes the size of houses jut toward the sky. And where this particular glacier diverges at La Jonction, it forms what looks like a kilometers-long, hundred-vehicle pile-up on a snowy highway—but the vehicles are the size of houses and made of ice.

The Bossons Glacier behaved no differently 250 years ago when Messrs.' Balmat and Paccard left the relative safety of the rock jetty that is the Montagne de la Côte, where Nils stood, and where they stepped onto the ice. The only difference is that back then there simply was more ice.

The path that Balmat and Paccard took is rarely used today. The glacier has retreated to such an extent to make it a considerably dangerous crossing. (Blame could be assigned to the Catholic congregation that had the Devil driven from the Bossons Glacier in the 19th century to stop its growth. Members of the same church have since asked the seated bishop to return to *de-exorcise* the ice, so it could grow once again. He did, but it hasn't.)

Intent on finding Cody, Nils assessed the risk of venturing out onto the glacier. He would go un-roped and without axes or crampons, just like Balmat and Paccard. They had no sunglasses, and little food or water either. Nils had carbon ski poles, where Balmat and Paccard had alpenstocks. They all had a significant amount of experience being in alpine environments.

What Balmat and Paccard lacked in modern scientific and meteorological learning (Nils had a weather app on his phone), they made up for in better covering: gaiters, lamb's wool stockings, cloth trousers, woolen smock frocks, night caps, handkerchiefs to cover the neck, woolen gloves and straw hats. Moreover, they had brandy. Nils had only organic energy chews.

Balmat and Paccard had stepped into the unknown. Nils had a clear destination: the Grand Mulet Refuge, just the other side of the ice, an unmanned resting point where he could conceivably catch up with Cody. He had come this far, and had done so in excellent time. Even if Cody wasn't there, he could exit relatively easily to the Plan de l'Aiguille du Midi—near where he had had his encounter. Still morning, he had all day.

There is no clear path through a glacier's extending flow. The first step on is a basic one, since the ice meets the rock, like a river meets its shore. But traveling over ice blocks, step faults and crevasses is like climbing through that hundred-vehicle pileup—alternatively easy and impossible, with little view of what lies ahead. Nevertheless, Nils eyed a path, one that Cody likely took, and which offered the respite of a granite boulder floating atop glacial fins about 30 meters out.

The sun-softened ice made for easy going at first, and Nils climbed up and over the giant slabs at a good pace—until his first slip. He caught himself, but discovered concerns he hadn't considered. There wasn't an identifiable bottom between the blocks. If he lost his grip he'd slide deep into the ice, likely wedged into a frozen chasm. Whether two meters down, or 20, he'd be trapped. Here he was now well onto the glacier. He didn't want to look back. He didn't want to go back. He had identified a path, and he just wanted to move ahead.

From one icy fin to another, slowly he inched nearer the floating boulder. His hands, red, wet and freezing, began to shake; his knees started to jackhammer as they held his weight on smaller and smaller ice edges. He caught a waft of his own body odor, the smell of cortisol.

Nils closed his eyes and breathed: *If that dope Cody could do this, so can I.* He breathed in deeply the cool air off the ice. His composure returned.

The fins now became steeper, almost vertical, and the bottoms—which he continued desperately to ignore—receded into inky blue. He could no longer skirt along. He had to straddle the ice and slide.

To get a better grip, Nils cracked one of his carbon poles in half. *This is really becoming a sacrifice.* He could stab the splintered end, knife-like, into the softer ice to gain more purchase. The remnant grip of the pole, however, slipped into the abyss. Nils reached after it, but quickly whipped back to secure his grip on the icy ridge. The piece clacked against the ice and then vanished.

Yep, all good...

Nils threw his leg up over a fin. His legs and bottom grated against the rough cold. His light running shorts were soaked. His gloveless hands were losing color and feeling. And yet his neck and face burned in the sun and glare. The dripping and fizzing and sloshing of the glacier became deafening.

That's when he noticed the butterfly.

With varied yellow and orange wings and a black body, it rested entombed almost perfectly in the ice. *Wow!*

Here in this chaotic wasteland of frozen rubble existed a scene so sublime—all else vanished.

Nils pulled out his phone and with numb fingers took a pic. He took a few more, trying to get the right angle—difficult with wet fingertips. "What are you doing here?" he asked the butterfly. Its delicate features seemed exquisite suspended in the clear, glistening ice.

Before putting away the phone, he rechecked his pics to ensure he had something worth sharing and noticed that here, just shy of the boulder, he had *No Service*. "Oh!" Then, as he shifted his painful, frozen bottom to get a move on, the phone slipped away, clattering into the darkness. "Fan!"

Suddenly, there was no butterfly.

Yep, all good. OK...coming. Yep, all good. OK...coming. Yep, all good. OK...coming. Yep, all good. OK...coming. His breath was fast and shallow.

If he slipped, he would freeze to death, be crushed to death, suffocate, or die from the impact of a fall into an unknown depth. There was now no recourse. No phone. No note left for anyone. Nothing. Idiotic.

What would his parents feel when they heard? What would they say? Would they ever find his body? What would that old Swede say to the Frenchman upon hearing of his demise? Would anyone ever even know he had perished? Had lived?

"Move," Nils said aloud. "You sad, pathetic, fucking fool. Move!"

He scraped along to the rock until he saw that there would be no getting up from the ice without standing. He had to get on the very edge of the fin to reach holds on the rock from which he could pull himself up. He looked up at the massive rock. Then down, and now without hesitation, to the depths of the crevasses on either side of him.

With the forefinger and thumb of his left hand, he pinched a large crystal protruding from the face of the granite boulder. The rock was warm and dry. Delicately, he shifted the weight off his right foot, off the ice edge to a lip on the rock. As he rose higher, he searched for a grip with his right hand. Anything. He felt the pressure of his left shoe melting and slipping. He glanced around for places to jump. *Stop doubting.*

Then he felt it, a pocket in the stone. He pulled himself up onto the top of the rock.

Nils rolled onto his back and stared up at the sky, heaving. Breath. Sky. Air. Sun. The rock warmed his wet and shivering frame. He looked up into the blue, into the sublime.

Then he felt the grip of a hand.

Boiling black eyes stared at him from the side of the rock. Nils kicked and scrambled to the other edge, almost falling off. The monkey sneered and lunged. Nils covered his head with his arms.

Nothing.

He peered out. No monkey. Only a black crow now before him. It hopped up and down on the opposite end of the boulder.

At once both terrifying and playful, the bird seemed to contain the whole world within it. It hopped and danced and made sounds that became, with each and every utterance, more like language, until the black crow said: "Haft en bra dag? Skynda på lite, maten är klar—

Over and over.

Over and over.

Over and over: "Have a good day? Hurry up, dinner is ready."

"Fan," screamed Nils.

Unable to go anywhere, afraid even to stand up—he wept. His body shook with terror. He became the boy in the bathroom. *Yep, all good. OK...coming.*

Then human voices.

At the rim of La Jonction, a number of the people Nils had passed on the way up gathered to look out at the small figure on a boulder above the ablated ice.

These small voices emerged from the wind and the clanking glacier. Nils looked toward La Jonction. There they waved. Nothing they said was recognizable, and after another minute of their waving and loud, unintelligible utterances, he could only look away.

No monkey, no bird. He put his head down and took deep breaths. The shouting continued.

After a minute, the noises changed: a rumbling.

The boulder trembled. He clung to the rock, fearing that it would still tip him into the icy depths below. The rumble turned into a roar.

Oh no, he thought and looked up.

×××

Balmat and Paccard also had had onlookers: Chamoniards who climbed the Brévent—a mountain just opposite—with telescopes to mark their progress. Such observers became increasingly useful and increasingly active, because once Balmat and Paccard opened up imaginations to the idea that

Mont Blanc's summit was attainable, others followed suit. Disaster was not far behind. And so, the first real tragedy of Mont Blanc took place not long after in August of 1820.

With certainty and hubris in the balance, a group of would-be climbers and guides attempted the summit of Mont Blanc and were caught in a wind-slab avalanche, which swept three of the party into a massive crevasse and covered them with snow. Prior to this event, no climber had perished in an avalanche. Now, three local Chamonix guides had gone into the abyss: Pierre Balmat (the cousin of Jacques), Pierre Carrier and Auguste Tairraz.

An avalanche occurred; three men died; and for a moment, there was, among the survivors on the mountain, a distinct silence. Wind whistled, water trickled and black crows came to have a look.

It has been written that an abyss never returns its prey; in Chamonix it does. Sure enough, 41 years later, in 1860, the Bossons Glacier—that massive, moving, icy crypt—delivered forth the remains of two of the guides: Messrs. Balmat and Carrier. The following year, the third, M. Tairraz, also emerged.

Their bodies and memory snatched from oblivion stand as a reminder to every guide and visitor to Mont Blanc that we must look after one another in the mountains. While our understanding of what is possible evolves, the physical capacity of a human versus the size and power of nature remains unchanged.

×××

A mountain rescue worker in a blue jumpsuit dropped down from a helicopter onto the boulder, checked Nils's condition, tapping him in various places. He signaled a thumbs-ups, which Nils returned. The rescuer wrapped a harness around Nils, and the winch plucked both of them off the rock.

No one spoke with him during the flight. No one made eye contact with him. In less than 10 minutes, Nils stood on the valley floor.

×××

As soon as he stepped from the helicopter, the machine lifted back up and disappeared over a forested ridge. A dull thumping remained in Nils's ears, as he recounted his story to one of the ground-based rescue workers. He insisted he was unharmed—just stuck out on a rock.

The rescue worker grabbed Nils by the shoulders, examined his eyes, then pointed for him to sit on a wooden bench outside the base. The rescuer joined a few of his colleagues nearby. Nils could hear the man say: "Il m'a dit qu'il cherche des singes sur le glacier... (He told me he was looking for monkeys on the glacier...)"

A man, clearly the captain, in a blue t-shirt with the letters P.G.H.M. on it, came over to Nils.

"Bonjour," he said and shook Nils's hand, then went back to reviewing what evidently was a report about the situation.

"He says you were looking for monkeys up there. You mean climbers. Did you follow out some climbers onto the ice? You see, I have to have the paperwork to be correct."

From somewhere unknown, anger rose within Nils: "No, he's right. I said I saw a monkey, an actual monkey."

"Did you see monkeys out on the ice?"

"Yes, I did. But I followed a friend out on the glacier. I couldn't find him and I ended up on the boulder, where I saw a

monkey. But then there was this crow that was dancing and…"
He trailed off, realizing his story was getting tangled up.

"Did you see the remains of a monkey, you mean?"

"No, a living monkey."

The Captain forced a smile: "You did not tell the doctor you had also hit your head."

"I *didn't*. I'm *fine*."

"You are not fine," the captain barked. "You should not have been on the glacier as you are. You have no boots. No crampons. No clothes. No tools. No preparation. Nothing. By the looks of it, you are in shock—dehydrated and almost hypothermic. You were lucky people were there to call for help. Tell me, why do you trail runners like to run in the snow and ice? Can you not stay to the dirt? Every day now, we are picking up runners on the glaciers. It wastes our time. It wastes our…resources."

"But you have monkeys on your glacier. Don't you know that?"

"Obviously, today I do! If you continue with this, I will send you to have your head checked. No more business with the monkeys. Now get out."

×××

Madame Champignon felt rather buoyant.

The first spot she went to had entirely vanished—not just the mushrooms themselves, but the entire ground itself. Neither good nor surprising. She knew for years that the wetness of the terrain would eventually undermine its stability. That which made it great would eventually destroy it. It had only been a matter of time.

Tsk, what a shame. The ground was once ripe for finding le bolet pinicole and le bolet royal, two of her favorites. *No more.*

The only redeeming aspect of the landslide was that it had opened up the forest to the view. From the top of the 20-meter mud scrape, above which she stood, Madame Champignon now had a clear view of the entire valley of Sallanches, a thousand meters below.

Although the forest would regrow and mushrooms would return, she knew this would be the last time she would be there. Age was catching up with her. To arrive at this place, she had climbed a long way. It would take a lot to make another trip worthwhile.

The second spot she went to, about two kilometers away, had produced wonders. Cèpes de Bordeaux by the basketful, and she would be one of the few at the market with a wild supply.

She did have to work for them, setting up anchor and rappelling along the near vertical cliff. Knees to feet covered in dirt. Flies buzzed, and leaf edges sliced her delicate skin. She didn't mind. It was worth it, and she knew just where to look. No amateur could have pulled this off. People at the market would whisper in disbelief at her luck. *Luck!*

At work and in a rhythm, she'd make quick slices into the earth and separate stalks from their earthen homes. Before examining a find, she'd tuck her silver hair behind her ear. If she approved of the specimen, she'd make sure to shuck off the spore-laden tissue, then scrape off the dirt from the base. Nice and neat.

She carried on for a couple hours. Back in the day, she would have been able to dispatch with an area of this size in 45 minutes. But what did she have but time these days? That was a good thing, she believed. Up here, she could take solace from the world below. With age, she found that her own company proved to be the best kind to keep.

Upon completion, she yoked two full baskets over her shoulders. Not heavy, but at times cumbersome, the mushrooms swung from side to side—and made for awkward, off-trail walking among the trees and brush.

When she finally came up to a hiking path, she bent down for a couple minutes, took a good look around and stepped into the track. Five minutes later, a couple of hikers passed her by, none the wiser. She smiled to herself.

From the Prarion, she walked down toward the valley. She wasn't far from where Cody had seen the monkeys, though she wasn't aware that he had. She did, however, see something far more exciting: weather.

A high, near-transparent line of clouds—just on the cusp of the stratosphere—and the rustling of leaves from a northerly breeze meant a storm would be arriving.

She bet that by late afternoon lenticular clouds would form over Chamonix's peaks, and by evening, rain would drench the valley. *What a fine turn of events!*

As was her habit after mushroom-hunting, she drove up to Les Bossons to check on her horses, six of which summered in the field below the glacier. They too, she could tell, knew there would be a change in the weather. All summer, they had seemed oppressed by the heat. Lethargic. Today, there was liveliness in their step as they glided between the shady spots in the field.

Madame Champignon inspected and brushed them and checked their food—all in a desultory way. Her son had someone who handled all the important matters.

"A young man visited the house this morning," she confided to one of the horses, as she fed him a carrot. "A Swede. He was looking for Cody. He seemed...wild. Clearly a bit closeted. He took some of Cody's papers. I told Jean-François these renters cause trouble."

The horse nuzzled up close to her as she spoke and chomped away. She patted it gently on the nose and stroked its neck. Others came around for the same tenderness and listened to her story.

Madame Champignon talked often to the horses, more and more these days—among the only company she cared for.

As she left the pasture, she glanced over to the parking lot at Les Bossons, next to the horses' fields, and saw that Cody's car was no longer there. *He must have returned to stay ahead of the weather.*

Upon arriving home to see Cody's car in the driveway, she felt reassured. *Good, good.* Now she would not have to have an uncomfortable conversation with her son. Missing tourists are bad. Missing renters are worse.

She tossed her gear in the hallway, put the mushrooms in the kitchen sink to be cleaned later, and poured herself a glass of Crémant. Quite pleased, she could already see a wispy mushroom cap cloud forming above Mont Blanc du Tacul. She poured herself a second.

After three more pours, Madame Champignon stood up and realized she was feeling hungry.

She reheated some summer stew. With bread, it would be sufficient. She sung to herself: "Nous n'irons plus au bois... (We'll go to the woods no more...)" With a little vin rouge, it would be perfect. She opened a bottle of Côte du Rhône; set the small kitchen table for two—though rarely did her son ever show unexpected; and turned on the radio just to have some noise about the house.

When finished, Madame Champignon poured some of the warm, leftover stew into a bowl and teetered her way out the door, down along the house, again singing "...Non, chacune à son tour ira les ramasser... (No, each one takes her turn to go pick them...)" and knocked on Cody's door. Nils answered.

Without so much as a "bonjour," he began: "I think Cody is missing. He should have returned a day ago. He went on the glacier by himself. I think he might have been taken by monkeys. You know monkeys, right? Des singes. Des singes ont Cody."

Madame Champignon forced a smile. She looked behind Nils into the lit apartment and saw no one else. Only the mess she knew. She handed Nils her stew: "Bon appetit."

She returned unsteadily to her kitchen, poured herself another glass of wine—a healthy glass—and called her son.

It took Jean-François about 10 minutes. He hurried. He knew something was amiss. And without stopping to check on his mother—only seeing her while passing the open door, seated next to an empty bottle of wine—he went immediately to the apartment, whose door remained open.

"Bonsoir?"

Nils leapt up and turned to see a middle-aged man, who after a moment he recognized as the rescue worker who had taken his story earlier in the day—the one who had examined his eyes. Madame Champignon craned around the man, who clearly also happened to be her son.

"I'm a friend of Cody's. I think he's missing."

"But his car—"

"I took it. Keys were behind the wheel."

46

"Wait, I know you," the man said. "We picked you up on the ice."

"I was looking for Cody up there. He's in trouble, I'm sure of it." Nils paused and added: "Possibly because of monkeys." He paused again. "No, definitely because of the monkeys."

"Monkeys, monkeys, monkeys. You need to let that go, this thing about the monkeys. If your friend is actually missing, then he is the priority, no? Not your imagination."

"It's not my fucking imagination!" Nils thundered.

Jean-François froze at the outburst. He just glared. Madame Champignon ducked behind her son.

"I know what I saw," Nils said. "I know what I saw today. I know what I saw the other week. And I know what Cody saw. Little. Gray. Monkeys. Fierce as hell, with eyes dark as night. And you know what else I saw? I saw a crow. A black crow with a yellow beak, and it spoke to me in my mother's tongue. It told me to clean up and get ready for dinner. Just like she did the night I got attacked—chased into the night by some creep. I've had to carry that scar around for too long. Running only gets you so far. Stop ignoring the monkey!"

Jean-François stood mute. Nils searched for some sort of response, any basic acknowledgment that he'd at least been heard, that he had a voice. But again, he found himself denied. He put his head down into his hands and he cried into the silence.

"The scientists," Madame Champignon said from behind her son with a thick accent: "zee see-uhn-teestz."

Jean-François turned and said firmly: "Maman." Nils looked up at her.

"Dites-lui," she said. "Dites-lui." She looked at Nils: "Frankenstein!" though as she said it: "Fronk-uhn-shteen!"

47

"Maman, s'il te plait—"

×××

Those who long ago made Chamonix their home chose the valley not because it was an easy place to live, but because the rigor of life here kept others away. Chamonix has since served as a refuge for all types.

Yet, Chamoniards have conspired to preserve their world. They hush up the ghosts and hide the true goings-on of their small corner of the Alps.

But no such system of secrets is perfect. Children talk out of turn. Some strange deaths can't help being reported. And often the elderly, especially when inebriated, say things they shouldn't. Near the end of their lives, what do they care?

There's also—deep down—compassion, born of perspective: for those in hiding, sometimes the best destination is a dangerous rock amidst the ice while awaiting a rescue.

×××

"They were for biological experiments," Jean-François said as he entered into the apartment and sat down across from Nils. "They're medical research monkeys, destined for a lab in New York."

"So they are real—"

"Yes. I mean, no. They *were* real...40-some years ago."

"Fronk-uhn-shteen," Madame Champignon said, teetering.

"She believes they're monsters. Scientific experiments gone awry."

"You all laughed at me—" Nils said.

"The last time anyone had seen monkeys on the mountain was in '66. When the guides arrived at the Air India crash, my father among them, they found monkeys—alive—wandering on the snow."

"They're up there alive—"

"No, they all should have died in the snow, a long time ago. The storm that took down the plane hindered the recovery. Maybe 15 dead monkeys and some human remains were brought back down. They rest was abandoned on the glacier."

"Zee see-uhn-teestz," Madame Champignon said, now sitting in a chair by the door.

"Merci, Maman." Jean-François shot her a glance. "They— the scientists—confiscated the recovered monkey remains. They showed up from the U.S. They demanded that if others were found that they be incinerated. My father told us this. It scared the hell out of all of us. They scared him, and he wasn't one to be scared by much."

"Where is he now? Do you think he knows more?"

"He's gone. Died in an avalanche."

Nils looked to Madame Champignon, who looked to the floor.

"How could they be hiding for 40 years?"

"No," Jean-François said. "They've been *frozen* for 40 years. The monkeys began to appear only recently. A few at a time, right from the mouth of the glacier—"

"Not possible."

"Yeah, I don't think so either. I believe the monkeys are cursed. It was the Bishop, the one that came to 'de-exorcize' the glacier. They all thought it was amusing. Our valley, it has a complicated history with religion. Did they really believe the Devil would simply do what they wanted? He now lives within those monkeys..."

"Have they attacked anyone—killed anyone?"

"Many people disappear in these mountains for many reasons, Nils."

"The monkeys could have Cody. We have to find him. He hasn't posted anything to Instagram in almost a day—"

"Tomorrow. We will have to wait out the storm."

"This can't wait."

"It can. And it will. Do you even know where he is?"

Nils grabbed his pocket for his phone, and then remembered.

"There's a storm, Nils. You have to wait. It is very dangerous to be on the mountain in weather like this. No guide, no rescue worker will go up in these conditions. They know better."

Madame Champignon was slumped in the chair, now asleep. Her empty wine glass lay on the floor, having rolled out of her hand. Jean-François went over to her and tried to wake her. He gently tucked a long stand of hair from her face behind her ear. He hoisted up her little frame. "Ça va, maman. Ça va."

"I have to take my mother to her place. I suggest you go home. I'm working tomorrow, if you want to come by the base in the morning. We can discuss this further. I'll write up a missing climber report on Cody."

He and his mother left.

Nils sat in silence, surrounded by stuffed monkeys, a bunch of ridiculous cuddly toys. He grabbed one and threw it hard against the wall—though it was an unsatisfying gesture. *Fine.*

He shut the lights, locked the door, and drove off.

Mountaineering, it has often been said, is an easy walk in a dangerous place. Getting to the top of most mountains, including Mont Blanc, does not require immense technical ability. It is about endurance and fitness and a willingness to be uncomfortable—with the cold, with heights, with being alone with your own thoughts.

When the conditions are bad—when the ice is rotten, the snow pack is unstable or when a storm comes in—that's when even the most experienced and well prepared are in for a time. That's when a climber needs to have a bag of tricks for getting out of a spot. It isn't easy to find one's way in a storm on a mountain, when visibility is zero and gravity is out to get you.

The rule, generally, when in trouble is to stop and hunker down. When you can't see where you're going, just make yourself safe, call for help if you can and wait out the storm. Because in the mountains, there be monsters, and in Chamonix, there are more than most anyone dares to admit it.

×××

After going home to eat and pack, Nils drove to the lot at Les Bossons and parked where Cody had before. He popped the rear hatch, took out his bag and finished packing. This time he would have all the proper gear to head out on the ice.

His plan was to go up to Le Gite Balmat, stay for the night and then get going in the morning, after the storm had passed.

As Nils grabbed his windbreaker from the trunk and shut it, out popped a Frisbee. *Of course.*

From the car, it rolled down the hill, wobbling and wobbling, across a little dirt road and under a wire fence. Nils poked his head up just in time to see it roll into tall grass. *Great.*

He walked over to the field and, before he grabbed and ducked through the fence, he saw that it was electrified. Little yellow signs on the wire read *Attention!* and *Ne jamais entrer!*

Nils looked to the end of the line and found a spot where he could step on a rock and leap over. *No problem.*

As he did this, a horse noticed him and made its way slowly over to see what was happening. Nils saw the horse, but didn't think anything of it. He plodded down the line, over to where he thought the Frisbee would be.

The late summer grass was thick and tufted, and he had to kick through it to find the disc. The horse came closer, floating quietly across the field. Nils found the Frisbee and bent over to pick it up. Lifting his head, he bumped against something soft but solid, and he jumped, tripping and landing on his back.

"Fan," he said, and looked up to see the horse standing over him.

Despite the startle, Nils gathered his composure quickly. *OK, not a monkey.*

He and the horse looked at each other for a moment: Nils on the ground, and the equine looming over him. It began to sniff the air and, inching closer, sniffed at him.

Nils didn't really know what to do. He had never been around a horse.

The animal took a step forward and placed its front right hoof right next to Nils's chest, pinning his shirt to the ground. Nils froze. The horse smelled of hay and sweet mud. Immediately he thought the horse might be aroused. He tensed up. And then with a quick glance the horse bit Nils's ear, drawing blood. "Ow! Fuck!"

He touched his fingers to his ear, now red, and the horse kept sniffing at him. It licked around its mouth. Nils began to panic. He didn't know what to do. Then the horse bit him again, chomping his shoulder. It was like lightning through his body. Nils shouted and struggled and grabbed at the horse, catching a bell around its neck, ripping it from the animal.

For a moment, both of them stopped.

Nils looked at the metal bell in his hand and back at the horse. Then all at once he yanked his shirt from under the horse's hoof and made for the fence.

But the horse, snapping, was right on his heels.

The struggle didn't last long.

Wind whistled, blood trickled, and a black crow came to have a look.

✕✕✕

Madame Champignon awoke to a fuzzy head and a clear cool sky. It would be a lovely day. She smiled and hummed at the thought of new mushrooms to be found. "Les champignons, les champignons," she sung to herself. Then she stopped. Someone was outside.

She poked her head out the door. Cody.

"Oh good! Bonjour! I left my keys—mes cles?—in my car. Can you open for me? My door. Open? Op-pen?"

She stood staring at him.

"I'm locked out. J'ai oublié mes cles," he said louder, unsure if he was saying the right thing. "Mes cles?" He pointed to the door.

Madame Champignon disappeared for a moment and cautiously reemerged with keys to let him into the apartment.

"Merci!" Cody said, and went inside.

Madame Champignon returned to the kitchen, called her son, and poured herself a drink—though she just sat with it untouched until Jean-François arrived.

"Knock, knock," Jean-François said, wrapping on the doorframe. The door was open, letting fresh air into the apartment. "Bonjour, Cody."

"Oh, hello! Bonjour. How are you? Ça va?"

"Good, thank you. I should ask the same of you. Are you all right? You were gone for a long time. We were worried," Jean-François said. "Everything...okay?"

"Oh yeah, sorry about that. I decided to go up Mont Blanc. I followed the old route to the summit, up from La Jonction," Cody said bright-faced, expecting congratulations. Instead, Jean-François just stared at him expressionless. "The Grand Mulets route. You know it?"

"Yes, of course. Was that...okay?"

"Oh, yeah. Definitely. It was hard going over the ice, but once you get past the refuge, there wasn't much trouble with the seracs. Didn't look like they'd've calved in a while. But on the way down I spent two nights at the Gouter hut. The second because of the storm. What a mess! Hope I didn't cause you all any trouble."

"You went alone?"

"Oh, yeah. I know. I shouldn't've done that. All good, though," Cody said, smiling.

"Okay, glad to see you're safe. Just thought you might be out...chasing monkeys," Jean-François said, picking up one of the dozens of stuffed monkeys in Cody's apartment.

Cody winced. "Ha, you too? They seem to be multiplying." Cody picked one up and chucked it across the room. "I'm never going to live that down. People keep leaving this shit for me. I've become monkey-man, ha."

"While you were out, did you run into your friend? I think his name was Nils or Harry?"

"Nils? No, don't know him. I didn't see anyone up there."

"Not many people on that route, I guess. Did you see any... animals?" Jean-François ventured, cautiously.

"Just birds. Though I think a monkey stole my red jacket. It was there, and then gone." He winked.

"Right, could be—"

"Well, I better clean up my place before your mother has my head! Thanks again."

Cody walked to the door, shook Jean-François's hand and waved goodbye. Turning back in, he noticed his dry erase board and picked it up to clear off the message. He paused looking at it. *Very clever*, he thought, *someone drew a monkey*.

He wiped it clean and went inside.

2. Les Chevaux des Bossons
Autumn

The most popular rumor is that they're Nazi horses, or at least once were, which explains the evil streak. But the horses aren't so much evil as they are violent—and that, too, is only once in a rare while.

They didn't eat Nazis either. That's another rumor: The horses broke free from their Nazi masters after being treated horribly, and they proceeded to consume their captors before making a getaway. It's allegedly what gives the horses a taste for blood.

Don't believe this version, either, even if heard from low voices in the market or late at night in the bars of Chamonix, or in local lore told to children while putting them to bed.

However, the horses' taste for blood did begin during the war. It was a herd of about 20, and they had been starving, locked in a barn. Their owners had fled when German troops came to occupy the area, near a village called La Gance.

What is known is that the horses consumed a French boy of about 15, who had been killed by the German troops. He had been shot in the fields and ran, as best he could, having been hit in the stomach. He hid in the barn, locking himself in with the horses.

The boy took a couple days to die, painfully, leaning against a post in the barn's loft. He didn't cry. He scratched notes into the floor boards and braced himself with the hope that someone would come for him. Which is why he had propped himself against a post to be seen, and why, when his final breath left his body, he slumped over, tilting right off the side of the loft. His body fell to the floor of the barn.

The horses may have been inspired by an innate tendency, though deeply buried, since carnivorous behavior is not instinctual to most breeds. It was innate insofar that the horses were hungry. Starving, in fact. But after the first one used its mighty teeth to tear away flesh from the small bloody body, the others, seeing what was happening, decided to join in.

There is plenty of evidence to prove everything up to this point, and to prove that the horses, emboldened with a new taste for flesh and thirst for blood, crashed the doors of the barn, breaking them down, securing a temporary freedom.

All of this was ascertained by people who came later to see what happened to the village inhabitants. These visitors already had witnessed the war's horrors; many had experienced the previous war as well. They knew what death looked like. They had an appreciation for final resting poses. They knew fear on the faces of the dying, affixed for all eternity. What resignation looked like. Resistance, too.

And yet, never before had they seen what they encountered at the barn that day, when searching for the people of La Gance. There was no pose. No terrified grimace on any corpse. Just bones, flesh and hair. Something had eaten the boy's body in the barn. *Did anyone know the family that owned this farm,* they asked one another. *Don't you recall this boy?* asked one bold solider. *I do.*

War drives men mad, they reasoned. It brings out the worst, the deepest and ugliest in human nature. It unleashes tendencies and behaviors that otherwise would have been locked up and gone entirely unrecognized for the entirety of someone's life, had she or he not seen the hideousness of combat.

This reasoning is probably why Nazis get tied up with those horses in most versions of the story. All the same, the old men and soldiers who had gone looking to see what had happened to the village of La Gance quickly came across the real reason.

They followed the horses' tracks out of the broken barn and across the burned-up fields. This was easy going as the horses had left behind a trail of blood and gore—other people, and some animals too.

When the searchers finally reached the end of that gruesome path, some kilometers away, they didn't need to raise their rifles.

No, at about dusk on that day, when they came into a clearing, on the opposite side near a gurgling brook were the offenders: a normal-looking herd of horses just grazing.

The group of soldiers and civilians prepared for a battle all the same, not knowing what to expect. How anticlimactic it must have been. These were just horses. Not bothered or wild in any way. When the first of them, that bold soldier, went up to the herd to get a closer look and came back just fine, the men produced boisterous laughs, relieving their intense nervousness. Today, at least, they would not have to battle another enemy.

The men and soldiers cordoned off the horses with a makeshift fence, and decided to stay the night where they were. They'd return in the morning and bring them back, then finish their work in La Gance.

They all got good and drunk that night. They made a small fire in a protected wood and shared thoughts on what might have happened to the village, the family, the boy, and the horses—what freak event had taken place.

One man spoke of King Diomedes of Thrace, who had owned four man-eating horses, which fed on any hapless soul who came upon his land. Hercules himself apparently tamed them, though only after they had murdered his companion Abderus.

Another man spoke of a horse owned by Baron de Marbot, who mounted the mare at the Battle of Eylau in 1807. While long known as a vicious biter, she became enraged during the fighting and in self-defense bit off the nose and all the skin on the face of a soldier that had attacked her. She then chased him down and tore out his bowels.

Yet another man spun tales of horses in Tibet and India that killed tigers, and some in Africa that fed on lions. If these episodes were to be believed, then the aberrant behavior of the present herd was no isolated event. Each man pondered silently on the creatures in their possession.

After these storytellers had gone to sleep, the shooting began. The bold soldier was firing at the horses. In the calm, cool morning in the protected wood, the noise shocked his compatriots into running.

When the firing stopped, about 12 horses were left. They tussled up against the makeshift enclosure. The rest lay dead.

There was another body. It was Petit Henri, who was terribly bloody, smashed, half naked. He lay facedown, ass cheeks bare to the early light of day. The bold man explained that Petit Henri had gotten up to take a piss, and the horses charged him, knocked him down in the grass and began eating away. All the bold soldier knew to do was shoot, and shoot he did.

It isn't good to shoot horses. Apart from the loss of life and the noise it caused, which could have attracted unneeded attention, they were not his to kill. In wartime, the horses held even greater importance and value. He claimed self-defense, the bold soldier. He thought he would be next after Petit Henri.

No one wanted to see a big deal made of this. Already a whole village had vanished. So no one took issue with the dead horses, and no one blamed the bold soldier for Petit Henri's death, even though the other men weren't entirely convinced of his story.

What we do know is that everyone wanted to go home. One of the men volunteered that he had family in a valley not far away, and the strange horses could be sent there. And so, in the year 1945, the horses arrived in Les Bossons.

×××

Madame Champignon awoke to light rain. An unseasonably warm, if only occasionally damp, autumn had followed a scorcher of a summer. Some snows had come in above 3,000 meters (9,800 feet), but nothing like what normally was seen in October. Cody had moved on, flown back to the States, and Madame Champignon found contentment in having the house entirely to herself.

Cleaning the boy's apartment didn't prove as pleasant or lucrative as doing his laundry. It was good to have idle hands again. By the time she got out of bed that morning, the skies had already begun to clear.

This might make for some fine foraging in a few days, she thought.

While overall it remained unfavorable weather for mushrooms, the extended summer lured a number of visitors to Chamonix on the weekends—anyone looking to carve out a few more days of leisure before late autumn set in. The sky was blue, the peaks white, the valley trees yellow. The time of year still had much to offer, so people came, and Madame Champignon benefited.

Parents—for reasons Madame Champignon never quite grasped but definitely sought to exploit—enjoyed bringing their children to see the supposedly murderous horses of Les Bossons. Years ago, Jean-François had set up an attractive pictorial timeline in an open shed—images of the horses since the war, mixed with tales of other carnivorous equines throughout history. It provided an experience superior to being snapped at by testy mares with quivering ears. It offered, she often bragged, more excitement than the llamas at the Merlet Animal Park across the valley. All the same, locals stayed the hell away.

Madame Champignon also benefited from growing numbers at the Saturday market, where she sold her fungi. Road trippers, mostly young couples looking for weekend adventure or a romantic outing, frequented her table, seeking something to cook at home. Since they often were not alert to quality, more interested in acquiring "local" goods, she could push mushrooms that were older or less appealing.

Foraged wild mushrooms are among a chef's most coveted ingredients. But since mushrooms are mostly water and dry up quickly, the ones she couldn't sell to the handful of high-end Chamonix restaurants had to be moved elsewhere. It was turning out to be a good season for Madame Champignon—though she was well aware that the market was a boom-or-bust proposition. This is how it always had been.

For nearly 500 years, people have been coming to the market in Chamonix. You'd never guess it today, since its temporary stalls are placed for only one day a week upon a rather contemporary plaza. But the location has long been central to commerce up and down the valley.

The Duke of Savoy first established the market in 1530 through an order that allowed inhabitants to hold a "free fair" twice a year, in June and September. This was when the valley more or less divided its allegiance between the city of Geneva and the Italian Savoia, rather than to whatever notion of France existed at the time. Commerce grew, and within a few years the duke extended his order for locals to hold a public market in Chamonix every Thursday, which in modern times moved to Saturday, and persists today.

Vendors from all over arrive early, some before dawn, to hawk their goods. Fruits and vegetables sold by women who can give you whatever you want, perfectly ripe, if you tell them the day or even the hour you plan to eat it. Pasta makers from northern Italy sell delicate and delightful dishes that make you question ever cooking for yourself again. Olives and tapenade pushed as if they were tickets to a carnival. Cheese. Coffee. Bread. Roast chickens. Homemade wine and spirits. And, of course, mushrooms.

That's just one side. On the other, people come out to sell clothing, dishes, furniture old and new, fabric, artwork, and—perhaps the oldest and now most-overlooked local good—crystals: quartz and smoky fluorite.

More than 15 million years ago, deep in the Earth's crust, liquid rock containing various elements cooled and formed sharp, beautiful, translucent stones that eventually would be pushed to the surface as the Mont Blanc massif churned among shifting tectonics.

To the chamois hunters and subsistence farmers who happened upon them, they were more than just exotic finds. They represented income. Crystals could be sold in the nearby cities of Geneva or Milan to watchmakers and chandelier makers. As with mushroom hunting, their collection became a family tradition, a well-kept secret, conveyed from one generation to the next. To a tourist, it is just one more treasure of the imagination that might be found high up in the ice, alongside the diplomatic papers and glittering jewelry.

But what is most coveted at the market cannot be bought or sold, only traded: gossip.

Among the vendors, a core of regulars gather informally each Saturday to catch up on the latest valley news—though usually it ends with a discussion of who has died among aging friends or would-be visiting adventurers who tried their luck in the mountains.

So when on this bright fall morning an older gentleman, one known for the bitter wine he plied on unsuspecting tourists, brought up a missing Swede, everyone had a theory to offer. Not because his disappearance was unique or surprising—it wasn't—but because it had been a particularly bad summer for the mountains and all sorts of interesting calamities had occurred.

The heat meant a diminished snowpack, which didn't simply mean less snow. It meant that the glue holding the mountains together was evaporating. Just as crystals will splinter into sharp, clean bouquets, so too will the granite composing the entire range, though on a much grander scale. Without permafrost holding the insides, and glacial ice holding the outsides, whole swaths of mountain become unstable, an unpleasant reality in a seismically active area.

Into those conditions more people went, precisely because the summer's weather was consistently beautiful for climbing. A more than typical number did not return. "If the storms don't get you," the old man said, "the sun will."

A few reflected on his saying, and each tossed out a "les chevaux des Bossons" reflexively, as if the French phrase inoculated them from the troubles above.

Madame Champignon waited patiently for the opportunity to contribute, and when an opening came, she casually remarked that she had met this Swede, and that her son had written up the missing climber report.

You might think the revelation would have piqued the assembled gossips, but Madame Champignon often knew more details than the others because Jean-François frequently shared tales from his work—just about all he did share with her. This insider status did not endear her to an already incredulous group. One especially prickly old woman responded, just under her breath, "les chevaux des Bossons" in a way that might as well have registered "no shit." They both smiled and the conversation moved elsewhere.

This expression, "les chevaux des Bossons," had always irritated Madame Champignon. She was very protective of the horses, and the words always felt like a slight. The story of the horses was well-known from the beginning. But no one could exactly identify when their name had transformed into a verbal shorthand and lodged in the vernacular of the valley. Even Madame Champignon couldn't help but utter it from time to time.

Granted, it is true that upon the horses' arrival—or more specifically, their forebears' arrival—a few people had gone missing without explanation. As had some dogs. And certainly no wildlife could live alongside them. Not even horseflies dared go close. Appropriately, only an occasional black crow could be seen chatting with them—a circumstance akin to crossing paths with a black cat; when it is witnessed, locals spit on the ground and walk away quickly.

There also was a small but dramatic uproar among neighboring villagers in Les Bossons. The horses escaped and terrorized the hamlet, killing a local priest. The mayor had to insist that Madame Champignon's father, into whose possession the horses had come, put bells on the animals, so people could hear them from afar. Her father did without protest.

The bells, however, always angered Madame Champignon—because they were useless. The horses proved intelligent and immediately taught themselves to walk in such a way that didn't cause the bells to chime. Their smooth gait—a glide, really—added to the animals' collective creepiness.

More particularly, it was the cost of the bells that irked Madame Champignon. In all of France, there are but two bell-makers—one in the Pyrenees and one in Chamonix. Both are highly skilled workshops, families that have been in business for generations, and both charge a pretty penny for custom bells.

Only a few weeks earlier had Madame Champignon chanced to buy a new bell for a horse that had gone missing. She spent the better part of an afternoon combing the fields for it. No luck. Even to this day, if a horse is ever found without a bell, Madame Champignon will be fined. "Tradition is tradition," the mayor once told her. *Les chevaux des Bossons.*

×××

All along the valley floor, from Les Houches at the bottom to Le Tour at the top, evergreens grow. Among them, on the north and south sides of the valley, there is a path, soft under foot from the pine needles: the Petit Balcon Sud—the lower-elevation companion of the Grand Balcon Nord, where dear Nils first had seen those monkeys.

Along the Petit Balcon Sud now came another runner, an Englishwoman in her early 30s. She was not an ultramarathoner. Just your common, everyday runner—someone who goes out for a few kilometers a couple times a week for the exercise and fresh air.

For runners, the Petit Balcon Sud is magnificent. In places, like where Le Lavancher descends into Les Tines, the path runs right along the river Arve, which plunges through granite cliffs, and the pines open to a view of Mont Blanc.

In this particular spot, the grove is thick and relatively remote, a good distance between villages. A number of smaller paths shoot up steeply, disappearing into trees. Some are proper footpaths. Others are animal paths. Still others were made by crystal hunters.

The river's gurgle, echoing loudly here, caused the woman runner to stop. She had to pee.

Looking around, she saw no one—in keeping with the time of year. All the same, the woman was uncomfortable going off the trail. It simply wouldn't be a very ladylike thing to do. She feared running into some strange farmer or mountain man who would take advantage of her. A city dweller, she felt the need to be cautious—though she had neglected to pack her pepper spray.

So she continued, taking one of those almost-trails that drill into the wood.

After a minute of hiking along, she stopped to catch her breath and assessed her position. Now she was above the trail, still in plain view—especially noticeable with her loudly colored shirt and shorts, and pink cap.

She went further up the almost-path, which meandered between trees and soft earth, around large granite boulders that at some point had fallen from the rocky mountains above. It helped her to grip saplings, and in places to move with a hand on the ground in front of her. That's how steep it was getting.

Now she was well above the trail and out of sight. The almost-path gave her a certain vantage of Chamonix—one that would improve if she went just a little higher. So she did.

This, she thought, *is the best view I've ever had while peeing.*

Before her the valley floor spread out, entirely flat, and on the far side the granite of the Aiguille Verte rose sharply a couple of thousand meters to pointed teeth. Snow whipped by winds flung a halo on the tips. In the distance, the frozen tongue of the Bossons Glacier rolled out of the mouth of Mont Blanc. So calm, so quiet. *This is why I came here.*

And as she pulled up her shorts and turned around, there stood an older woman.

Birds flew from the trees and deer stopped their grazing to look up, upon hearing the city dweller's scream.

The noise did not faze Madame Champignon in the least. She just stared, wondering what the hell the young woman was doing in her mushroom patch. Had she, Madame Champignon, been followed? And why was this interloper peeing on the toadstools?

Quickly, though, Madame Champignon recognized that this woman had no basket, no tools, nothing that would indicate she was poaching her crop. She smiled.

"Tout va bien?" Madame Champignon asked, after the younger woman stopped screaming.

"Oh, oh, oh, oh," the woman said. "I'm so sorry. You scared me to death. I'm so sorry. I didn't see you there."

Putain d'Anglais, thought Madame Champignon, who now realized she was dealing with a foreigner. Her smile dropped.

"I was just out for a run," the woman said. "And I stumbled up here for the view. I hope I didn't offend you. I've only just arrived here in Chamonix. I don't know it very well. I'm from London. We don't have such beautiful views. You're very lucky. I assume you live here? Are you out hiking?"

Madame Champignon's English didn't ever match up for what was required. She understood the language okay. But not enough to hold proper conversations. In a pinch she went with one of the few all-purpose phrases she knew.

"Yes, do you like that?" Madame Champignon said.

"Yes, very much. I love the wilderness. That's why I came here. To get away from it all. The city's just too much. And I broke up with my boyfriend. And my job. I also quit my job. The mountains help put everything into perspective."

"Oh my, yes, it is so big," Madame Champignon said.

For a moment, the younger woman forgot where she was and who she was talking to and just opened up about her life and situation. The scare she received and the realization that all was okay caused her to let down her guard. This older woman, although they had just met, seemed friendly and caring. It all tumbled out.

Madame Champignon tried to keep up with the woman's tale of woe. Something about a boyfriend not ready to commit, a job she could not advance in, and friends who were all getting married and having babies. Madame Champignon smiled and nodded, until the woman wrapped up with what seemed like a hopeful thought that maybe she might find someone in Chamonix.

To which Madame Champignon, obliged by what might become an awkward silence, replied: "The odds are good. But the goods are odd."

This made the woman laugh, and Madame Champignon smiled.

"The trail is that way," Madame Champignon then said, pointing down the hill.

×××

The British woman wasn't the only intruder in Madame Champignon's patch that day. Signs of other foragers were everywhere: inedible mushroom caps kicked to pieces, pine duff raked clear of promising spots. To her it was just amateurs at work, no one who presented an enduring threat. But still, it all added up.

Anything or anyone that attacked the integrity of her mushroom patches caused her to become sad and then angry and then tired. She had been foraging these ethereal gardens for decades and had seen them through a lot: drought, fire, landslides, Englishmen. Year after year, fewer mushrooms were to be found.

She recalled times when she would leave entire glades of morels because she couldn't possibly carry more. When she returned days later, they still lay there, untouched. The problem, Madame Champignon knew, was more than just man.

Picking mushrooms is like picking cherries—as long as the tree itself is not harmed in the process, fruit can be harvested the following year. Thus, if the mushrooms are the fruit, the mycelia are the body, but one that is virtually invisible: a microscopic, fanlike organism that feeds off nutrients in the substrate and generates mushrooms as a means to reproduce. With fungi, as long as you don't harm the mycelium, there will be mushrooms to forage.

Mycelia can be enormous structures depending on the mushroom to which they belong, and they can have a significant influence on a local ecosystem by attaching themselves to root structures, feeding off other plants and even acting as conduits between different flora, pulling and pushing nutrients to keep them alive, only to slowly decompose them for their own food. Or, as Madame Champignon explained it: "They get the trees all drunk just to take advantage of them."

Did Madame Champignon appreciate the sophisticated and imperceptible interconnectedness of her mushrooms and all else that was in the forest? In fact she did—acutely. She could sense it. In the throes of foraging, she regularly achieved a level focus that enabled her—as she put it—to *hear* mushrooms across the hills, as if they chattered discreetly among themselves throughout the wild: a million little cocktail parties she aimed to interrupt. She also kept up with literature about them.

Because mushrooms, as is widely understood, are to be treated with care.

Roughly 30 species of mushroom have proved consistently fatal to humans. It happens for any number of reasons, but mostly from misidentification: The deadly and the delicious often look the same. Indeed, the difference between a morel and a false morel is a functioning liver.

In Chamonix, as elsewhere in France, people can always take their foraged mushrooms to a local pharmacy to determine if they are safe. In Chamonix, unlike anywhere in France, pharmacies always can go to Madame Champignon.

She knew all of the mushrooms in the valley: which ones bring on headache and nausea; which attack the kidneys; which cause instant death; and which leave people with flu-like symptoms for a week, followed by a coma and total organ failure. Mushrooms, as an organism and an activity, represent yet another of Chamonix's hidden treasures that offer the promise of death, along with the potential for inexplicable pleasure.

While not having collected the amount she sought that day, Madame Champignon still found a number of beautiful specimens. Considering the late hour in the afternoon, she felt satisfied enough to begin working her way back to the car—all the while shaking out the spores from her bags to seed another round of mushrooms.

As she came up over a ridge, while still mulling the bizarre scene of a Brit pissing in her patch, Madame Champignon arrived at a mossy glade, where she found another surprise, this one far better: a near perfect rond de sorcier—in English, a fairy circle.

If mushrooms are coins, a fairy circle is a pot of gold. To some, they can be like finding a four-leaf clover. To others, they are like spotting a black crow chatting up a horse. To Madame Champignon, they merely represented her youth.

Amid all the natural forces she experienced on a daily basis—freak winds, falling rocks, insolent offspring—this one, despite its utter simplicity, leapt into a special realm...because it was so orderly, so irrationally rational. A lightning strike could be written off as random. So could a landslide. But a perfect circle in nature?

As when she'd been a girl, Madame Champignon got to her knees and peered into the fairy circle, thinking maybe this time she would spot one, or that a tiny sorcerer would come to dance onstage. She savored the silliness of the act.

She crouched even lower, cheek to the ground to get a more intimate view. The moss was soft; she lay comfortably for a while. She imagined her horses gliding in and out of the mushrooms. She imagined a ballet of dancing deadly equines, floating in and around the toadstools.

Eventually the daydream carried itself, flowering and morphing, as Madame Champignon faded into sleep.

Light cascaded through the foliage. Leaves rustled in the breeze, birds chirped. A woman in her 80s lay napping.

As she did, tiny fairies, like elegant insects, materialized and dipped and bobbed, inspecting her. Perceiving she was not a threat, they moved on.

Her mind stilled, Madame Champignon woke and drifted back to the car.

×××

"Is it because I haven't been giving you enough attention lately? You tell me. Mother is here now." The horses glided down the field, excited that Madame Champignon had arrived.

"Oh hello, hello," she said to one that came right up to the fence. "I've had quite the day so far. You'll need to be gentle with me." The horse nodded. "You'll never guess who I ran into today: a rambling British woman. Yes, I know. Lost in the forest, lost in life." Madame Champignon stroked its face, while the horse nosed around for a bite, perhaps a carrot.

Madame Champignon, after inspecting the horse's coat, continued: "Are you lost in life? Is that why you keep snapping at little kids?" The horse enjoyed her scratching, and another came over. "You too? Are you getting us all in trouble now? Or just trying to get some attention?"

The horses had lately become a menace. One had grabbed a young man's hair by the teeth and yanked out a small patch. Another had bitten a woman's arm, causing an ugly welt. A third tore a guy's shirt clean off. Jean-François thought the late-season visitors might be overwhelming them. Madame Champignon felt they were still agitated by the summer's persistent heat. The mayor, Luc, didn't give a damn what it was and insisted the horses be better monitored or that a fine would be issued.

"You are just behaving like they think you behave. You need to behave like you do for me. Can you do that?" Now she had an audience of attentive horses. "Same with this Brit. She's looking in the wrong place. Living on someone else's terms and according to someone else's idea of what success is. She sure isn't going to find that here, whatever it is—not by attaching herself to some random guy. She needs to look within."

The horse nodded at this observation. Her lectures usually ended with food.

"If she compromises now, she'll be doing so for the rest of her life. You know she said she was worried about not finding a man in time to have children? She told me this. Right in the middle of the forest. She has the freedom to drop everything and come here to live. Isn't that enough? She's practically begging to be tied down. That's not happiness. Don't we know this? Yes, we do. Children just cause more problems..."

Some of the horses pulled away.

"Not you. Not you. And I know you like Jean-François. He is good to you. Maybe better to you than to me. Certainly spends more time with you. Doesn't he?" Some horses floated back to her and she patted their faces. "Yes, he does."

Madame Champignon felt the day wearing on her. "Okay, mes chevaux des Bossons!" she yelled out to all the horses in the pen. "No more biting! If you must eat something, go find that British woman and put her out of her misery!"

The idea amused her, and she moved on.

×××

About an hour later, Madame Champignon was driving up a pitched incline to a slope-side restaurant in Les Houches.

An old friend had ordered morels, among other things, and she was obliged to make the delivery. He was setting up for a private party and couldn't make it to the market.

Pierre, the owner and chef, greeted Madame Champignon outside as she came up the hill. The restaurant, an ancient stone-and-timber chalet, sat on a bluff overlooking the ski slope. In winter, it was ski-in, ski-out for lunching tourists. The rest of the year it was a hike. In any season, it transported visitors to a rustic era in the valley, in terms of both cuisine and atmosphere.

Madame Champignon and Pierre had long known one another, primarily through her late husband; however, the two of them had long ago separately initiated a silent rivalry. Each was convinced that one foraged the other's grounds for mushrooms, although, even after decades, neither had proof of it. In accepting what she brought, he'd always review it keenly, as if one fungi might betray her secret. For her part, she always kept a close eye on what shoes he wore, thinking a boot print might give him away.

Since she never charged him money when he made an order, which usually came only once or twice a year when he was in a pinch, the issue never took root. Besides, as a family friend, she could never feel true malice against him. He might steal away with her caps now, and once had been the enabler of her husband's wild adventures, but Pierre remained all the same a keeper of spirits, both literally and figuratively.

Because while she readily purchased wine from all over France, Madame Champignon only consumed hard liquor made in the valley. Pierre, a relentless experimenter, had always been an expert at this.

Most notably, during the summer, he and her husband would gather génépi blossoms on their long treks, which would be used to make a light, flowery digestif named eponymously for the plant.

Liquor de Génépi can be found most anywhere in Chamonix, even sold generically in grocery stores. But the quality varies greatly. What a tourist might consume as a shot, a Chamoniard would turn up his nose at. Although simple to make, it proves difficult to perfect. Pierre, for one, only used black génépi, whereas mass-produced versions used the white. The difference may be subtle, but for a drink taken neat, nuance is what one is after.

Génépi, however, wasn't what Madame Champignon ever received.

No, what Pierre gave her, year-in and year-out, was more symbolic—a spirit largely unknown to anyone who doesn't live in the region: gentiane.

Another yellow flowering plant in the wormwood family, its hardy root produces a clear spirit, bitter and earthy. As with many homemade liquors, it traditionally had been used as a tonic for any number of maladies, including intestinal sluggishness, gastric reflux, dermatitis, inflammation, jaundice, even anorexia. Aside from taking it as an occasional sleep aid, Madame Champignon used it to clean windows. In any case, a bottle makes a winter, because only a little should ever be consumed at a time.

The gentiane also evoked far better memories than the génépi. To collect it had always been a family affair. She and her husband would join Pierre, his wife and others on a bright, late summer weekend to dig up roots—a dusty and dirty job, one that always ended with a festive meal and good stories. The génépi, on the other hand, was gathered by the men only after descending from trips to far higher altitudes.

"Same recipe?" Madame Champignon asked.

"Same recipe," Pierre said. "But maybe in this one I added some fruit, dried apple peels, if I recall correctly. You tell me how you like it."

She held up the clear jar to the sun, and the strong alcohol made warped tears against its sides. "Strong," she said. He nodded, then asked about the recent storm.

For a pair like this with a long history, it would seem that the immediate discussion of the weather would be a sign of something simmering. It wasn't. To share insights about observed conditions across the valley revealed a mature intimacy and respect.

The conversation then morphed to what might appear to an onlooker as code: "Have you noticed the number of oyster mushrooms on the hardwoods?" she asked. To which he said: "Yes, as well as the donkey ears under conifers and the pezizes in glades."

"We're done with the tricholomes, and I'm afraid I don't have time to scavenge for les pieds bleu in the forests or les pieds violet in the fields."

"Same," he said. "I've been spending my time cutting back the begonias and gladioli in the garden. I still have to mulch the leeks and celery."

They kissed cheeks and wished each other well.

✕✕✕

That evening, as she went to put away Pierre's gift, she noticed the old bottle sitting in the closet with a little left.

She took it down from the shelf and placed both bottles on the kitchen table at the second setting. She then bustled around, making dinner.

Having finished her meal, along with a half-bottle of Gigondas, Madame Champignon contemplated the spirits, which sat as her dinner guests. *Why not see how they compare.*

She poured a healthy finger full of the previous year's eau-de-vie de gentiane. She could have poured it all into one glass, but that really would have appeared overindulgent, she thought wistfully, though no one ever came to see her.

The earthy taste warmed her while puckering her face. She sat comfortably at the kitchen table. As the feeling subsided, she looked at the second table setting, then poured the rest. *There definitely is something medicinal here*, she thought.

Now, let's see how they differ. She poured a tipple from the new bottle and took a sip. It was fresher, brighter—though still soured her face. *Oh my, this isn't just apple.* She finished it, then poured another.

×××

"Maman! Je suis là. Ça va?"

Jean-François arrived at his mother's around 10 the next morning. She still lay in bed. She felt groggy, and could barely register what he was saying.

"The horses got out of their pen," he yelled up the stairs. "Maman, are you all right?" He kept shouting as he hunted around the kitchen and closets. "The gendarme was called. Oh, what a mess."

She descended the stairs. The daylight crippled her eyes and she had to clench the banister. "Are the horses all right?"

"Yes, they're fine. But it caused quite a panic in the campground."

"They got into the campground?"

"Not really. They ran up into the forest. But it was before an avalanche came down from the Taconnaz Glacier. No one was hurt. But between the horses—these horses—escaping and the snow, it caused quite a scare."

"Oh, they're smart horses. They must have known it was coming. Animals are like that." She rubbed her eyes.

"In fact, they broke free a half-hour before the slide." He chose not to ask his mother why she was still in bed this late, having noticed the empty bottle on the counter.

"These horses are different. They are very smart," she insisted.

Jean-François turned and rolled his eyes. She didn't notice. "Do you know where the spare padlock is? They broke the other one. It's just tied now."

Madame Champignon, suppressing a headache, thought for a moment and then rummaged in the crawl space below the stairs. She returned with the lock, and said: "Have dinner with me tonight?"

"I can't tonight, maman. I have to be with my wife. You know how she is."

"I understand," Madam Champignon said, patting him on the arm. Then she said: "I think I need to take a nap." And she did.

×××

The week went by quickly for Madame Champignon, compressed by her day of rest. On the other end of it, she felt rejuvenated, something she attributed to the medicinal gentiane root. At the market early Saturday, she joined her friends.

"Did you hear of the British woman?" one of the men said.

Madame Champignon's ear pricked up.

"Apparently she was hiking up the Taconnaz couloir by herself, and she was caught in that serac fall. A hundred thousand tons of snow and ice. She had no chance."

"A glacial collapse in autumn, mon dieu," another said.

"You hadn't seen it? That glacier is rotten and keeps getting worse," he said.

Madame Champignon asked: "Did they find her body?"

"No, no. They found a note on her car saying where she went and found one of her hiking sticks below the containment—not far from your horse pen, actually. The slide must have carried them. But no, they haven't found the body. She hasn't returned and it has been five days. Poor thing, she only just arrived from London a month or so ago."

"If it stays warm, she should melt out in a few weeks," another said.

"It is possible," one other said. "But we may get snow soon. I've seen the bees circling..."

At that, the rest of them jumped into speculation of the latest animal sign they had seen and what it portended.

Madame Champignon sat quietly. She thought better of remarking that she might have met the woman. It would seem strange if she knew two of the latest who had died. But her son hadn't mentioned this one.

"Les chevaux des Bossons," one of them said. "Yes," they all agreed, "les chevaux des Bossons."

For a good, long while, Madame Champignon contemplated the death of the woman she had met in the forest. She wondered if anyone would be to blame. There was always someone to blame when these things happened—whether it was deserved or not.

In the Montroc avalanche, the one in which her husband, Michel, and 12 others were caught, the mayor at the time took the fall. He was accused of negligence for not evacuating the area, which had been under threat from weeks of mounting snows. No one expects to be killed at home at 3 o'clock in the afternoon. But that's just what happened, and people needed a reason why.

In this respect, Chamonix is by far the most dangerous commune in all of France, with well over a hundred avalanche corridors that lead directly to the valley floor. It isn't every year that town-reaching slides occur. Some might be once in a hundred years, or once in three hundred years. As with earthquakes, though, the longer the wait, the worse they usually are.

The danger, imminent or otherwise, has long been well-understood. When the first explorers happened upon the valley, they declared it in Latin *Campus munitus*, or "fortified field," which in French became *Champ muni*. While these explorers likely made the declaration based on the impossibly steep walls and ice that isolated the valley, *munitas* also could be taken to refer to munitions—the explosions—that reigned down from above.

Since those early days, churchmen chronicled Chamonix's many run-ins with the forces from above. In the ecclesiastical archives under the heading, "Disasters Caused by the Fall of the Great Snows or Avalanches," they tracked with precision every time the Lord sent malice their way. From the priory in the center of town to the shores of Lake Geneva, the people of Chamonix have been long thought to be cursed.

Madame Champignon could never tell if she was cursed or lucky. She must have been one or the other. She had been away when the Montroc avalanche struck her house. When the gendarmes tracked her down to inform her of the death of her husband, she wept before they even spoke.

"Have you been told?" they asked.

"How could I not know?" she said through tears.

To be sure, they then informed her that a mighty snow had swept down from the mountain and struck the four corners of her house, making it collapse in on her husband. She stopped crying and sat silent for a long while before confirming what she had just heard: "Mon mari est mort dans une masse de neige?" ("My husband died in an avalanche?")

"Oui, Madame."

"Oh, les chevaux des Bossons."

She did not exactly see her husband as blameless and upright. Neither did the churchmen, mostly because of her reputation. But they didn't say "les chevaux des Bossons," though some may have uttered it privately. Rather, they said: "'God thundereth marvellously with his voice; great things doeth he, which we cannot comprehend. For he saith to the snow, be thou on the earth.'" And it was.

Madame Champignon quietly packed up and moved to the other end of the valley. She never went to church. She didn't attend the service for the dead when those words had been spoken. She never made comments against the mayor. She never spoke about it again.

What the gendarmes hadn't recognized is that Madame Champignon had, ironically if inadvertently, paraphrased her own husband when confirming his death. It was, after all, Michel's voice that had come over the radio one November day 50 years earlier to inform his colleagues of another tragedy: "Payot a glissé avec une masse de neige." ("Payot fell with an avalanche.")

In this case, René Payot, the lead guide of a team that had gone to conduct rescue and recovery of an Air India crash had been caught in an avalanche that swept him into a crevasse. Madame Champignon's husband, a young guide at the time, had seen and reported it. He declared that they all should call off the search, right there and then, before anyone even reached the wreckage.

An Air India crash—in 1950. Not the flight with monkeys on board. This one was Air India 245, which also had flown directly into Mont Blanc at almost exactly the same place as Air India 101 would 16 years later.

Just as the roar of an avalanche echoes off the walls of the valley, making the air turbulent like a tornado and shaking the ground as an earthquake, so too did the mortal impact of these tragedies reverberate across time.

Where René Payot slipped in an avalanche and fell into a crevasse, so too had his brother, Léon, slipped in an avalanche and fallen into a crevasse at almost exactly the same spot about 10 years earlier.

So when Michel and his colleagues—among whom was Georges, the son of René—went up to conduct rescue and recovery in the *second* Air India crash, Air India 101 of 1966, the loss of poor René was fully on their minds. As conditions worsened, they again decided to call off the effort due to bad weather—oblivious to the unintended consequences: monkeys running amok and conspiracy theories that would spool out of control.

But you can't save what you can't see.

The same went for that poor British woman. While everyone thought they knew where she was, no one would be going to search for her. She would return all on her own, over time as the snows melted—which would take far less time than 40 years. All the same, she became just one more person who had gone to the mountain and not returned.

All of this weighed mightily on Madame Champignon's mind—not all as immediate thoughts, but as a part of her collective consciousness from a lifetime in the valley.

She poured herself a couple fingers from the bottle of spirits. She drank to the British woman, to René and his brother, to her husband and to many others.

She pictured the dead woman's body decomposing. How long would the snows keep it? Over the years, she had twice come across the old, rotting corpse of an animal swept by an avalanche—once a rabbit, once a chamois. The body in advanced decay was something between soil and creature, all mingled and putrid.

After this thought, Madame Champignon drifted to sleep and dreamt of hiking the avalanche path in springtime to forage. She shuffled through the containment area, around the massive artificial pillars, up along the river and into the forest. She could hear the occasional din of a glacier calving or creaking 1,000 meters above—the sounds echoing down the walls of the ancient moraine.

The leafy trees opened to a forest area completely flattened, as if from the fiery breath of a hidden dragon. Among the remains from this devastation, the dead woman, now fully decomposed. A dark stain saturated the earth and the plants around it.

But within the blackness, small mushrooms—like thousands of impish penises—protruded and swayed in a gentle, invisible wind. *Curious.* She knelt and watched as the phalluses changed color and texture and pattern, at one moment clearly edible items, the next moment poisonous ruin. She reached to pick, then hesitated. Reached, then hesitated.

She stayed long enough for the sun to come over the mountain, flooding the flattened grove with light. The dark stain evaporated. The mushrooms, too, had vanished. Before they did, Madame Champignon grabbed at a few remaining mushrooms, feeling them first as liquid and then nothing. Like her dream itself.

✕✕✕

"Do you sell any *magic* mushrooms," a man asked Madame Champignon at the market a good while later. The Saturday morning crowd continued to be brisk, despite the late November weather. The gauzy glow of the fall sun had everyone in a good mood.

The man had made this joke for the benefit of the woman clinging to him, who play-smacked his chest. "Scott, come on." They both laughed. For the previous 10 minutes, the two of them had been poking, smelling and posting online photos of all of the various mushrooms Madame Champignon had on her table.

While doing this, the man complained, and the woman listened with open, almost patronizing pity for his situation.

"Sweetie, being a mountain guide is all about climbing hard routes and doing steep ski descents. Did you see the video I posted yesterday?"

"Of course. I liked it. I like all your posts," she said. He stood and watched it again while she looked on. "What does it mean if you don't pass the ski test?"

"Not everyone passes the first time. The French have it rigged against foreigners. But I've been skiing my whole life."

"So you'll definitely ace it. You're the best skier I know. Then what?"

"Well, I want to get this whole thing done in like 5 years."

"You didn't say it would take that long."

"For some it takes 10," and he patted her on the head. "Not for me it won't."

"But darling, why do you bother? You don't have to work. Why don't you just do something fun? You know, enjoy yourself."

"Sweetie, I told you. It's for my new idea, the video sharing platform. I can make sick ski videos and generate ad revenue, but I need the credibility. You don't think I actually want clients, do you?" They both laughed at this, but for different reasons.

As they continued to banter and preen for one another, a young, attractive French woman walked up, and the man leered over the head of the woman he was with. She didn't notice. Madame Champignon did. The young woman—petite with large almond eyes and waist length brown hair—didn't care. He, however, continued to ogle her athletic physique.

"Try these," Madame Champignon said in English to the man, pointing to a basket of chanterelles. "Make your cock grow. Make your wife happy."

The younger woman had to turn to hide her laugh; the woman with the man raised her eyebrow and said, "Oh my." The man looked pained and said reflexively: "She's not my wife."

Then the woman smacked the man for real and walked away from the table. The man quickly realized his error and went after her. And the young woman winked at Madame Champignon and said: "Avez-vous des champignons magiques? (Do you have any magic mushrooms?)"

"Bien sur," Madame Champignon said, and the two of them had a good laugh.

Madame Champignon then reached under the table for a Ziploc baggie filled with a 100 grams of psilocybin caps and handed it to the young woman.

In fact, she did have magic mushrooms.

Leola, whom everyone called Lulu, had been raised by one of Madame Champignon's oldest friends, Nicolas, and the two women shared a rowdy, independent streak—the kind Madame Champignon's generation balked at but Lulu's generation celebrated. The cross-generational friendship made little sense to most people, particularly Jean-François; as one of his mother's few recognizable friends, however, she had earned his appreciation all the same.

Sales of the magic mushrooms served as yet another minor source of income for Madame Champignon, though she was extremely careful to limit their distribution to all but a handful of trusted people, Lulu among them. She had got in trouble a few times over the years, but authorities always found it challenging to discipline an elderly woman. Her son, forever embarrassed by his mother, found ways to smooth things over.

For her part, Lulu consumed them just for fun or gave them out to her friends. She didn't need the money—a fact of which Madame Champignon knew and approved.

"How's Nico?" Madame Champignon asked, referring to her old friend, Nicolas.

"He's all right. He doesn't like to leave the house or garden much these days. Just keeps watching his movies."

Madame Champignon smiled. "You tell him hello for me."

"Of course."

"Now who is this new guy I've seen you with? He's okay?"

"He's a good one."

"Not going to hold you back, is he?"

"Ha, no. I'm not even sure how long he'll be around for."

"Getting sick of him?"

"No, wingsuiter." Lulu gave a wink to Madame Champignon, who nodded in return.

"You're not up there with him?"

"No. Both feet on the ground. You know me."

"Yes, I do know you. But what have you been up to lately?"

"Usual: partying, work, climbing."

"Still climbing? Winter will be so late this year," Madame Champignon said, tucking a piece of hair behind her ear. "The ground didn't freeze by the first." She referred to November 1, the day by when the snows should be sticking to ground at lower elevations.

"Tour Ronde fell again," Lulu said, referring to a mountain within the Mont Blanc range that had some classic climbing routes.

"You see it?"

"Jesse and I were up there yesterday. Almost took us out, in fact. Huge section of rock—just cracked in the sun and tumbled...must have been 500 meters down. Just missed us."

Such stories normally left Madam Champignon unfazed. But with all the latest goings-on, she surprised herself by being sensitive to Lulu's news—emotions she certainly did not express openly. In response, Madame Champignon only said: "The permafrost is going."

"Yep. I've been seeing this all summer. Mont Blanc might be a few meters shorter after the year's out. But the weather should be changing soon. The forecasts say a cold front is finally moving in next week—hopefully with some snow. Another Christmas without some of the white will be so depressing."

Madame Champignon agreed, but for different reasons.

"How are the horses?"

"They're well. Causing a little trouble these days. You should take your Jesse over to see them. Does he know the story?" She smiled. "They won't bite."

"Maybe," Lulu said. "Maybe."

×××

Lulu wasn't joking. The summit of Mont Blanc is not a rocky crag. It is snow-covered dome, meaning its height isn't fixed. While everyone thinks Mont Blanc is 4,810 meters tall, that isn't necessarily so. Sometimes it's higher; sometimes, lower. It all depends on the amount of snowfall and the wind. The actual highest point of rock under the "eternal snow" is at 4,792 meters—and that, for the most part, is constant, geologically speaking.

Just to the northeast is the Monte Rosa at 4,634 meters, the highest peak in Switzerland. During a few weeks back in the 1920s, after a particularly warm summer had resulted in a massive landslide from the summit of Mont Blanc, everyone thought for a moment that Mont Blanc might have lost its title to the Monta Rosa. Obviously, even geological constants are relative.

The Swiss would've loved nothing more than to be able to claim possession of the Matterhorn, the Eiger, and the highest peak in Western Europe. But that wasn't to be. Quickly, France determined that Mont Blanc's height was unchanged at 4,807m, as established in 1863, and where it remained until 2011, when officially three meters were added—mostly due to wind-blown snow.

Although Mont Blanc technically had gained height, it remained the highest peak in Western Europe. The highest peak in all Europe is in Russia: Mount Elbrus, which stands at 5,642 meters—considerably higher than either Mont Blanc or the Monta Rosa—a difference in altitude well outside any weather-related margin.

If pondering over who has the biggest what, and where, seems unimportant and arbitrary, it isn't. Merely asking such questions has real consequences.

To begin with, Alexander I of Russia—known to some as Alexander the Blessed—asked these very questions. As emperor of Russia in the early 19th century, he had an acutely prickly relationship with France.

In response to the secular aftershocks of the French Revolution—he formed an alliance to instill Christian values in European political life. Religion, after all, unpins monarchy and therefore legitimacy. But Alexander needed something more and called forth his counselor of state, a man named Dr. Joseph Hamel.

Alexander said: "Dr. Hamel, tell me, what mountain is the highest in all of Europe, whose lands are closest to God himself?"

To which Dr. Hamel replied: "Some say Mont Blanc, which is under the authority of the king of Sardinia, His Majesty Charles Felix—though the land, known as the Savoy, has long been contested with the Kingdom of France."

"The Kingdom of France? Never. What about Mount Elbrus within our Empire?" It must be taller."

"I presume you could be correct."

"Well, is it possible to find out?"

"Yes, with the latest barometric pressure instruments, one would be able to ascertain the exact elevation of both mountains from readings taken while aloft their snowy summits. It would be best to begin with Mont Blanc, since it has been climbed, whereas Mount Elbrus has not."

"Terrific. When do you leave?"

And so, Dr. Hamel arrived at Chamonix in 1820, and hired several guides to bring him to the summit of Mont Blanc.

Whether emasculated by the demands of his sovereign, or simply because Dr. Hamel was a man of ragged temperament, he had little patience for the challenge at hand.

Weather came in and he had to wait in freezing rain, wind and snow atop La Jonction. This grated on him. When the weather cleared and the conditions for climbing were not right, his guides said to turn back. Dr. Hamel, who had traveled all the way from "more civilized" regions of the continent, had had enough. In that instant, his mind was no longer intent on questioning the measure of a mountain but instead on questioning the measure of man. "Cowards," he declared.

Dr. Hamel never made it to the summit. While the party did trudge on in the face of his challenge and he did get part way and made it back down safely, three of his guides did not— our poor friends Pierre Balmat, Pierre Carrier and Auguste Tairraz. This, the first tragedy of Mont Blanc.

As we now know, the people of Chamonix consequently became aware of the great forces among which they lived and had occasion to travel—though at this point such forces were natural, not political.

While some prayed and a good many wept, a clutch of Chamoniards gathered to assert some control over the situation. Within the year, they had filed a petition to form "La Compagnie des Guides de Chamonix," to establish rules for walking into the mountains. No longer would guides feel cowed by name-calling clients.

This petition was approved by His Majesty Charles Felix, the 11th child and fifth son of Victor Amedeo III, Duke of Savoy, King of Sardinia, Prince of Piedmont, the incumbent king of Cyprus and Jerusalem, and of Marie Antoinette of Spain. With that edict and all its regal authority, there was created the very first company of mountain guides in the world. All because three men fell into an abyss after a foreigner insulted their authority while frustrated in his attempt to determine who had the bigger mountain.

×××

"He's just another damned foreigner trying to prove something," Madame Champignon said to one of the horses, though she didn't say "damned" because she was speaking in French; instead she used a more visceral term. Certainly, the horses were taken aback by her tone.

"Pardon me, but it is true." As her voice softened, the horses returned to her. "In more ways than one, that man is looking to put another notch in his belt. We have seen this before, haven't we, my children." The horses couldn't help but nod in agreement. Indeed, they had. "To be an alpine guide, he seeks the wrong validation, because he doesn't understand the sacrifice he is truly making…or potentially making."

For a moment, she mused while giving out carrots. She then said: "Damned rich kids." A few horses leapt back; one glided away. "You achieve a certain loftiness in life and you still need validation. There are consequences. Whatever his intentions, there are always consequences."

Madame Champignon walked around the pen and some other horses came up.

"And her. She has no idea what's she's getting into. He won't be there. When he is, he's elsewhere. When he isn't, she'll never know if he'll return. She'll just sit there…waiting, assuming, all while he's off with someone else. Up there. Or wherever." She smoothed the coat of one of the horses. "In the end, they never really come back to you. Fucking men." The horse turned.

"Ow! Don't bite me. Bite that wannabe guide," she said, rubbing her fingers. "He's the one who put me like this."

She looked across the field to her brood. "You all are very uppity these days, aren't you? Are you excited for another adventure?"

The horses, in their own way, understood, and became excited, like dogs told they'd be going for a walk. "Settle down, settle down. Keep it up and you're going to get us all in trouble." Still, they glided about their pen, floating with their silent gait, and Madame Champignon admired their beauty.

A gentle breeze blew through, cooling the sun's rays on her face. She listened to the muted sounds of valley, and of the fields, and of the mountain. Then her phone rang. It was Lulu.

"Just talking to the horses. I was telling them that you and Monsieur Wingsuiter would be coming to visit." She spoke while nuzzling one of the horses. "You should expect some high-flying visitors."

Lulu laughed. "We will definitely try. But quickly, Nicolas wants me to drop something off for you. Will you be around the next few days?"

"Oh yes, I'm home most every night. It would be a pleasure." Madame Champignon paused. "Lulu, just a question while I have you: Have you ever been with a guide?"

While to anyone, including the horses, this would seem a non sequitur; it was not rarefied nor too intimate a question between these ladies, due to the frank if casual nature of their friendship.

"Sure, I've hooked up with a few. Tough men, easy to have their hearts broken."

"That's it exactly," Madame Champignon said.

"You're thinking about the man in the market this morning?"

"Yes."

"He was a handsome one. A little young for you, no?"

"But why was that woman with him? She should be out doing what she wants, not waiting on him."

"I don't know the answer to that. But if anyone should know, wouldn't it be you?"

"Hm...maybe that's what's bothering me. I'm afraid even in these late years, I'm only just now discovering there are no answers to such questions. There are no solutions, no solutions in life. Only improved methods of coping."

Later at home, Madame Champignon continued to dwell on the aspirant guide. She couldn't shake him, and mulled what Lulu had said over a glass of gentiane. This calmed her. It didn't take much. Every day now, it didn't take much. Just a little. Maybe another for good measure. Maybe a little more.

Now she came back to the British woman in the avalanche, who after all had left her man. *She did pay for that, though, didn't she? Good at reading some signs, bad at reading others.*

Indeed, there would have been signs, plenty of warnings of the dangers in that very deadly ravine. It was, after all, a massive containment area for avalanches. Why would she have gone there? Why did she disregard the signs?

Madame Champignon sipped and sipped. Her mind mellowed, and she walked with the woman up the ravine on that day.

She first would have thought it an earthquake, Madame Champignon reasoned: a deafening rumble as snow and ice cracked off the serac and swept downward, a thousand meters, picking up speed and debris. Other than the initial noise, however, there would not have been much warning for the woman. The snow in the relative warmth of the season would have been wet, moving like a thick river. There's no escape in that ravine. A silent, icy wave would have engulfed her, churning her body in with whatever debris it picked up along the way. Within an instant, once the snow's momentum was spent, the river would then solidify, like cement. She'd be entombed.

Madame Champignon paused, took a sip, then considered also: What stunned silence must have greeted the messenger who'd had to announce to the woman's parents that she died in an autumn avalanche.

She was just out hiking? Yes, it was a beautiful day. *A beautiful day, and an avalanche?* Yes, but not just an avalanche, it was a serac collapse. *That makes a difference?* Yes, the serac, it is an enigma—only it knows what it will do. *And she was on this serac?* No, she was in the valley. *And it killed her?* Yes...very quickly.

Madame Champignon paused again.

A quick death doing something you love. That's how they would have rationalized it. That's what they would tell themselves on Christmas Day, when she isn't there. When they have gifts for her, purchased before she passed.

Condensation slid down the side of Madam Champignon's glass, a substitute for tears that never came.

The past began to percolate up freely. Memories and guilt burned hot in her chest, taunted her, made her flushed and dizzy until she squeezed her eyes shut to block it all out—only to open them before her two ghosts: young men, eyes alive but otherwise expressionless; their faces black with frostbite— Jean Vincendon and François Henry.

★ 1 9 5 6 ★

"Again?" said Eloise.

"Yes, they need guides. These boys are in trouble," Michel said, hanging up the phone.

"No, Michel. It's Christmas."

"It *was* Christmas."

"Let the others go, from EMHM or ENSA. A guide isn't needed."

"No one's going…"

"Exactly, because it's Christmas." He looked at her. "And let me guess," she added, "because no one is paying?"

"It's our duty. If we don't go, no one does."

"It's your duty in the summer. No one climbs in the winter."

"I climb in the winter."

"Then what is the duty you have to your wife—and to your child?" She arched her back to emphasize all nine months of her pregnancy. Michel sat down.

"They've been up there since the 22nd, Eloise. Five days at altitude. Freezing to death. They are inexperienced and need help."

"Michel, I know you're bored. I know you're tired of being in this house with me. With us. You want to be out there. But you're out there every day. This is supposed to be our time now."

Only half hearing her, Michel looked up from the radio: "They have a helicopter."

"See, they have it under control."

He continued to listen to the news report. "Not really. The Army gave them a Sikorsky. From Le Bourget du Lac. But why would they give them a Sikorsky? It's too heavy for the altitude."

"Maybe they don't have a choice. Because of Algeria they don't have any to spare."

"The war. Fuck the war. That's Paris's war. It's not ours." Michel paced the floor.

"Michel, there is nothing you can do. There is nothing they can do."

"How do you know that? Maybe there is. Clearly, no one is trying."

"Damn it, listen to yourself. You are married to me now. Not that damn mountain." Tears came to her eyes. "I've given up my life too, you know. I didn't ask for this. I've made changes. I've given up my work. You need to make changes. Because I need you here for me. I need you to be right here. Not on the end of a rope. Not on top of a glacier. Right here."

He had no answer to this, just watched her crying while the radio rambled on.

"Oh, putain de merde. They can't fly. The weather."

The same weather that had trapped two young alpinists, Vincendon and Henry, high on Mont Blanc, had trapped the rescue helicopter, and had trapped Michel with Eloise. The farthest he could get away from the house was the driveway, which he had to keep clear. Eloise was due in a week, and despite his loud insistence on going to help with the rescue, he knew he couldn't leave her. He also knew he couldn't call on anyone to help. Not his parents. They despised Eloise—a sinner and a whore, they said. So too was he a sinner for impregnating her before marriage. But what choice had he? This is what the Lord had handed him.

Each day they spent in the house brought more tension. Aside from one another, all they had was radio and television. And the media had caught onto the story.

What began as a narrative about "reckless boys climbing beyond their limits" soon transformed into the tale of a disorganized rescue service "martyring two young men."

All of France was rapt with Vincendon and Henry. Day after day, frenzied media reports of misses and false starts kept the country on edge. Chamonix itself erupted into finger pointing and conflict: mountain folk against townies, civilians against the military, Chamonix against its neighbor St. Gervais. Even at home, Michel and Eloise couldn't avoid it.

By the morning of New Year's Eve, they knew enough to shut off the radio once word of hope came: A rescue team had been chosen and the weather looked to clear. The boys, frozen and starving, would be coming home. With that, Eloise and Michel played cards for the rest of the morning, and at lunch shared a glass of champagne, since it was obvious that Eloise would never make it to midnight. For the briefest of moments, their worlds finally aligned. Then, in mid-afternoon, the phone rang.

The helicopter had crashed. No one died, but now six people, some of Michel's friends, were trapped in a storm at an altitude of 4,360 meters. The next day, the rescuers had to leave the immovable boys to seek shelter for themselves, but then one fell into a crevasse and became seriously wounded. Updates became torturous. The day after that, the right helicopters came, but the rescue of the boys was called off. Vincendon and Henry had spent 10 days without food, without water, without protection, without warmth. They couldn't talk. They couldn't move. There was no sign of life when the helicopter flew over. It was too dangerous to land.

"Too many people have risked their lives," the father of one of the young men said to the television crews, which by then had fully moved in on Chamonix. "If my son had come back, his limbs frozen, only to die later, it would have been more painful. He will have died doing what he loved."

The following day, Eloise gave birth to Jean-François. For the three of them, it only got harder from there.

The conscience of a community repairs no easier than that of a single man, who, while removed from any conceivable sense of fault, still may punish himself with a guilt so heavy that the burden is borne not just by him but by all those around.

Michel wept that night and many nights after for lost youth—which remains just one more treasure hidden among Mont Blanc's ice and snow to lure those who gaze upon it.

✕✕✕

In the absence of significant frost, tricholomes continued to flourish into December, especially les pieds bleus and les pieds violets. Madame Champignon found the former too sweet, and the latter had an odor that made her nauseous. They could be sold though. For herself, she sought only oyster mushrooms.

Amazed, she couldn't remember a year like this one. But in a way, she was grateful, since she still could wander the woods to take her mind off everything.

Just the day before, the horses again had broken free of their pen and made their way up the mountain, scaring the devil out of all they encountered. No one was hurt. Incredibly, the horses had crossed the valley and were found in a high pasture below the Aiguillette des Houches.

Jean-François, out on a rescue at the time, convinced the helicopter pilot to help him corral the escaped animals—a unique and daring task he relished. Anywhere else, such a stunt would have been punished. In Chamonix, it was applauded, mostly because it had worked brilliantly.

The horses, however, had to be moved from Les Bossons, for the rest of winter at least. Luc, the mayor, insisted. Jean-François was fine with it, since they would be easier to tend up in his fields.

After filling her baskets, Madame Champignon went down to the pen in Les Bossons and tried to help. She wasn't of much use, but stuck around to tidy up the place while Jean-François laboriously drove the horses, a few at a time, across the valley.

While walking the fence, Madame Champignon noticed something colorful in a clump of high grass. She stepped closer and bent to retrieve it: a pink runner's cap. She held it for a moment before realizing where she had seen it before.

A chill came over her, and she looked up to the containment wall and beyond to the Taconnaz Glacier. *The winds must have blown it down.* She could not but help think that the woman was still up there, buried under all the snow—a body frozen in time. And here now was her cap.

At that moment, one of the horses stole soundlessly behind her, snatched the cap from her hands, and glided away.

"Hey!"

She moved quickly after the horse, but her balance didn't hold and she tripped and fell to the ground. Madame Champignon sat up surprised. Just a bump on the knee, the soreness of which she tried to dull with a quick rub. She then looked to see what had tripped her up: a Frisbee jammed into the ground.

A couple of the other horses started to glide over her way, and she knew enough to get up and head back to the barn.

The remaining horses all seemed agitated, which made Madame Champignon uneasy. She stayed in the car until after Jean-François left with the last horse.

It was in the back of one of the horse stalls, in the corner under some hay, where Madame Champignon again found the pink hat—and with it numerous pieces of different types of cloth, all chewed, a few gloves, a broken shoelace and the remains of another cap, this one with the letters ENSA on it. She threw everything to the ground and left immediately.

At home that night, she finally found the bottom of that bottle of gentiane, along with a deep, dreamless sleep—all that she could hope for after her day's adventures.

×××

"Fell off a cliff, the poor guy."

Madame Champignon looked up. "Come again?"

"Our latest death is a man who fell off a cliff. Or I should say, the cliff is the one that fell off and he happened to be on it. Now he's under it."

Madame Champignon immediately thought of Lulu and her boyfriend. "Was he with anyone?"

"No one. He was a guide trainee at ENSA and had gone out to scout a few routes. When will these young ones ever learn?"

Her hands trembled. That's now three: the Swede, the Brit and the wannabe guide. She looked up to the sky and saw a dozen paragliders rising up the mountains on the thermals, like butterflies.

No more for today, she thought. *I need to get home.* And left the market early.

That afternoon, a storm dusted the valley with a few inches of snow.

×××

When scanning the ecclesiastical archives under the heading "Disasters Caused by the Fall of the Great Snows or Avalanches," you will find more than calamities caused by snow and ice. You'll also find landslides, windstorms, floods—all manner of natural occurrence that has hit the Mont Blanc range over the years.

For several centuries, the churchmen used this list to justify their control of the valley, which regularly resulted in clashes with the Chamonix population when demands were made. To ask subsistence farmers to pray is one thing. To tithe them is another.

Regardless, the churchmen kept at it—though, after a while, the reason for the list changed. Despite their undying faith in the Lord, they continued to parse Chamonix's world for explanations that it all was the work of the Devil below.

And while to themselves the churchmen admitted that the exorcism of the Bossons Glacier in 1644 and the "de-exorcism" of it in 2004 were simply stunts to reassure a nervous populace, they also knew they were playing with fire. If in fact the Bishop of Annecy did have the power to alter natural forces, they needed to make diligent note of what miracles had been performed.

To this day, churchmen still pour over these records—which have been kept to exacting standards—to see what patterns might emerge, what anomalies might be found.

When the latest slides occurred—the rock fall, the serac fall and several other disastrous events—a young churchman recorded them. After making note of the latest, this young man then did a cursory search, going back decade by decade to see what had occurred on coinciding dates.

At about 100 years, there did happen to be something—a number of unusual events around 1920, which included the aforementioned landslide that had called into question the height of Mont Blanc. In the preceding years, glacial and geological activity had increased, with events like they were seeing today. Then, a glacial pocket burst, sending a flood sweeping through Chamonix, causing tremendous destruction.

This was followed by the unprecedentedly large rockfall on the Italian side of Mont Blanc—a half-million cubic meters of rock—which tumbled 3,000 meters to land on the Brenva Glacier. The impact shook houses 80 kilometers away, crushing the glacier so that its terminal moraine spewed down the valley like a waterfall. If an ancient forest had not checked the force of the fall, all of the Italian town of Courmeyeur would have been destroyed.

After this, a drought began in October, further drying out the high-altitude rocks. Never before in November, the records stated, were the glaciers so badly crevassed; the plateau on the summit of Mont Blanc, usually covered in soft snow at that time of year, was instead a solid block of ice.

The young churchman then reviewed a side table of measurements related to the height of Mont Blanc. They had thought that the events had the effect of possibly reducing their mountain's height by several meters—an idea that presented itself as amusing until the young churchman looked back to 1820.

There again was a period of similar events, though slightly less destructive in nature; and again, there was a table questioning whether they had influenced the height of Mont Blanc. In the corner, jotted in a dramatic flourish was the word "inconclusive," which related to a note about the ill-fated 1820 expedition with the Russian.

The young churchman went back another hundred years to around 1720, and there again he found a warm year with "earth tremors" and reports of excessive snows falling from the "needles" above. No records were kept 100 years before that.

He pored over figures and data—charts following temperature lines, snow depths, cloud patterns and more. What emerged from the reading was a crude cycle, which seemed to worsen continuously and irrefutably, though at a sharper rate since the early 1800s.

The young churchman, all alone in the dark with his finding and his fervent belief in the Lord above, grew concerned that all of these facts constituted evidence that he and his peers actually had done something to provoke the Devil. Maybe they did have the power to change things. His world, he suddenly realized, was collapsing all around him.

At the moment the young churchman came to this conclusion, at the other end of the valley Madame Champignon simultaneously determined the same: Her world was collapsing all around her. But whereas the young churchman hurried into the crypt to light candles and pray; Madame Champignon sought another means of escape entirely. She went into the cellar and pulled out her stash of psilocybin caps.

All it really takes for a trip to be bad is a bad perspective. Outlook and emotions can be the difference between the mystical and the mortifying. But Madame Champignon was no newbie to taking drugs. She wasn't seeking visions or deep states. She sought serenity, and knew how to achieve it. In fact, she was micro-dosing before the phrase existed. The presence she attained from ingesting a small, controlled dose of mushrooms had at other times in her life brought much needed clarity and perspective. In the 1970s, for instance. Right now, though, such attributes were exactly what she lacked and she knew it.

Madame Champignon emptied out a baggie of *psilocybe semilancea*, or liberty caps as they're commonly known, onto a tray, sorting them into various sizes. She then organized them into a few doses she would take over the next few hours.

The irony of psychedelic mushrooms was that they didn't require the robust effort of those she sold at market. These she found on the grounds of the golf course in Les Praz. She knew the greenskeeper well and slipped him a bag once in a while. He'd look the other way while she combed the turf in the early hours of the day. As foraging goes, it's plush work—wandering about manicured grounds in faux isolation, only the ragged gray peaks above and the golden, glittering dew at her feet. She loved it, and it paid.

Now Madame Champignon let the warm inner glow of the psilocybin caps consume her while she focused her mind on the—

"Madame Champignon? Madame Champignon? Are you there? Knock-knock! It's Lulu."

Merde.

As she made her way to the door, she realized that some super-light visuals had started to take effect—hazy outlines around the lights—which provided a matter of factness to everything, a calming sense that things just were what they were. That was a good thing.

Lulu stood at the door with a young man and an old film tin in hand.

"Come in, come in. What do you have there?"

Lulu handed it over. "Probably an old sex tape," Lulu winked at Madame Champignon.

"Knowing Nico, it probably is," she laughed.

Without thinking, she walked them into the living room and asked if they would like a drink.

Jesse halted at the table, the tray strewn with *psilocybe semilancea*. "Whoa, are you shrooming?"

"Yes. Yes I am. Would you like some?"

Jesse looked to Lulu, impressed. "Don't mind if I do."

"You sure this is okay?" Lulu said.

"Oh yes, my little owl, this is certainly okay. Just don't mention it to my son, the prude."

Jesse and Lulu sat with Madame Champignon, and the three proceeded to have what would otherwise be a fairly typical conversation for Chamonix—about the weather, their plans for the weekend, and the latest goings-on—except for the fact that they all were consuming a potent, psychotropic hallucinogen.

"The snow that came in today was just a start. I hear another front should be arriving tomorrow afternoon."

Madame Champignon nodded in agreement. "I had heard the same."

"Then I should definitely do the jump in the morning," Jesse said to himself aloud, confirming a decision he had already calculated and made. "Yes, definitely tomorrow."

Apart from the effects of the drugs, this verbalization resulted from a highly methodical and organized mind. Regardless of how it is perceived, whether reckless or insane, wingsuiting requires discipline and care.

There's no use explaining the why, only the what: in BASE-jumping, one leaps off a grounded platform with a parachute; wingsuit flying requires a specially designed suit that catches air and allows a jumper to glide; when performed close to terrain such as near cliffs and trees, it is known as proximity flying, which simulates the movement of a bird carving through air.

In places, Chamonix offers near-perfect terrain for the sport, so wingsuiters abound. Jean-François himself had turned down two BASE jumpers who had wanted to let Madame Champignon's spare apartment the previous summer. She argued that they should get the rent upfront, but then Cody came along.

Madame Champignon, reveling in her newfound calmness and lucidity with respect to her life at that moment, said, "Well, if anyone is going to be next, it's going to be you—"

Odds were, she would be right. Fatalities are high among BASE jumpers, who live by a credo articulated by Jesse in response: "Hey, you know, if I die, don't bother crying for me. I'm doing what I love."

He planned to take the lift to the top of the Aiguille du Midi, ascend further to the upper outside terrace by elevator. He'd climb over the railing toward the Bossons Glacier, and down to a rock outcropping, which drops off for about 2,000 meters.

Jesse intended to proximity fly right along the Bossons Glacier, which drops off at a rate greater than the arcing fall of a wingsuiter. He described the process and his experience to Madame Champignon, who by then had receded into her own head. She stepped aside mentally and assessed a basic proposition: whether there existed a protocol for sympathy for people who died doing "what they love".

A wingsuiter flies, she reasoned internally, which must offer an experience that exceeds the "love" someone can have for other activities, such as hiking alone in a dangerous ravine, only to be crushed unwittingly by falling ice. Though how does that compare with the sublime feeling one gets from skiing an open field of fresh powder, or the sense of presence one obtains climbing a rock crag successfully at a level just beyond one's ability—feelings Madame Champignon actually knew once upon a time. Those experiences were not unlike sex, love being something separate.

But, does the amount of love one is able to feel correspond with the extent to which any activity removes oneself from one's daily experience? If so, should that amount of love then correspond with the remorse people should feel for someone who perishes while undertaking that activity? Or is it a binary proposition, and one must not feel bad at all if someone else passes while living the life they chose, even if that means the person tripped and fell into a bus on the road...

The warmth of Lulu's voice brought Madame Champignon back from this voyage, though now the fabric of her being was being tugged in different directions.

Lulu said: "We went to see the horses the other day."

Madame Champignon stopped, put down her tea, and looked Lulu dead in the eyes.

"You did?"

"We got close enough to pet one of them, but he was a bit snappy. We talked to them, like you always do. Mentioned you had sent us. That didn't seem to work in our favor." She laughed.

A tingling sensation crept up Madame Champignon's spine. She looked to the tray on the table and nonchalantly plucked out two small caps and popped them in her mouth.

"Jean-François has moved them. They're in the high fields now."

"Oh, no kidding." Lulu turned to Jesse, who now was taking in the pulsating pine board walls. "You'll fly right over them tomorrow."

"He'll what?" Madame Champignon said.

"Fly over them. The landing zone for the Midi jump is a couple hundred meters beyond that barn in the adjacent field. You know the one, where the paragliders land in the spring."

"Right, that one," Madame Champignon said, munching another cap.

Jesse was now off somewhere else.

As the warmth and contentment drained from Madame Champignon, it became replenished every time Lulu spoke, and she now yearned for Lulu simply to keep speaking to her, telling her things, being there with her.

"Can I ask you something," Lulu said.

"Anything, my dear."

"Did you and Nicolas ever have a fling? Like, properly."

Madame Champignon warmed even more as all thoughts became replaced with fond memories of dear Nicolas.

"He and I had an understanding, you see. A love, and something more. But it was difficult. It wasn't easy being married to Michel. He was married to something else."

Lulu could see that the question had caused some pain for Madame Champignon, and avoided asking more. "I think I know what you mean." She glanced at Jesse, who sat curled over his phone in a small chair, rocking back and forth while transfixed with a video of one of his proximity flights, watching it over and over and over.

"Do they change?"

"No, they don't change. At least, mine never did."

"All those years?"

"All those years."

"And now that you don't have him anymore?"

"You have to move on." She turned away toward the fireplace, her mood on low. "Besides, if the avalanche hadn't gotten him, I would've been the one to kill him."

Lulu laughed, and Madame Champignon turned back, made a quick smile and winked.

×××

An hour after Lulu and Jesse had left, Madame Champignon's trip peaked. The full weight of fear for the wingsuiter now settled over her. It became clear to her that Lulu was in love with this man, and tomorrow the horses would kill him. She didn't know how, but she knew—with utter confidence—they would.

She sat before the fireplace. Presently, she was joined by dear Nils, the British woman, the wannabe guide, Vincendon and Henry. Around the flames buzzed the pixies from the rond de sorcier. Everyone was silent except for the Swede who asked: "What do you do when you see a black crow chatting with a horse from Les Bossons?"

"C'est les 'chevaux des Bossons', monsieur," Madame Champignon said aloud. "On dit: 'Qu'est-ce qu'on fait quand un chocard parle à un cheval des Bossons.'" She repeated what he said, but in French. She then looked from the fire to the Swede, and as she spoke he and the rest of her visitors vanished: "On meurt. (You die.)"

Madame Champignon had lived a lonely life since her husband died, though she might argue that she was lonelier before that. At that moment, however, she never felt more distant and disconnected from the world. A small figure among the unknown and inexplicable.

"I can set them all free," she said aloud. "Then they will go far, far away."

✕✕✕

When Jean-François arrived to his house, the horses had already been restored to their pen. Only a few had managed to get out in any case, and they didn't try to flee. They mostly stood around confused in the cold evening air.

"Where's my mother," Jean-François said to his neighbor, the one who had called when he saw that someone was disturbing the horses. The neighbor happened also to be a policeman, so he rushed over to check on the situation. He found Madame Champignon, wide-eyed and incoherent, trying to let the horses out into the night. Jean-François and his wife were at a Christmas party.

"Jean-François, I know she's old but she's walking a fine line—has been for a long time now. We had an agreement. Don't let it come to this. Control your mother."

Jean-François said nothing, just nodded. Though he knew some things could not be controlled.

Inside he sat her down.

"Why are you here? What were you doing?"

"The horses are killers. They need to go far away from here."

"Is this because you're lonely? Are you looking for attention?"

"What the hell would you know about that?"

"Maman, vulgar language does not suit you."

"It doesn't suit me? Listen to this," she said placidly. "Asshole. Cunt. Shit. Christ Almighty. Shithole. Son of a bitch. Goddamn." She looked at him squarely. "So, you still think it doesn't suit me?"

"You went mad when he died."

"I went mad when he left me."

"Isn't that the same?"

"He left me long before he died."

"You knew what you were getting into. Or should I say, you knew what you were getting out of, when you married him."

"Now who is vulgar?" She looked at him with rage, and the walls pulsated. "I had no choice. You, Jean-François, were no choice."

Jean-François looked away.

"You live your whole life a pariah, trapped in this valley, trapped in a marriage to a man who doesn't love you. But who you think might someday become again the man you had met. He didn't die in that house. He died on that mountain a long, long time ago."

Silence.

She continued: "He retires and then he dares try to leave me. After all that. Did you know that, Jean-François?

Did you know he was going to leave me, go to live somewhere else—by himself? By himself! He finally comes back to me, and then he goes. He deserved what he got."

"Enough!" Jean-François said, grabbing her by the shoulders. "Enough."

Madame Champignon, exhausted and still hallucinating, wrested herself from his grasp, which quickly weakened. She drifted over to the couch, sat down and promptly fell asleep.

✕✕✕

Bang—

✕✕✕

Madame Champignon's heart pounded and she pulled aside the curtain to see into the light of the next morning. If a boulder had come loose from the mountaintop and hit the house, she would not have been surprised in the least. Across the field, she could see that the horses had erupted into excitement.

Everything swam around her, and with her headache she couldn't tell if the sound had been a gunshot or if something had fallen off the table in the next room. The whole world and all its noises reverberated—a sonic pulsing—in her head, in the room. No, the room itself heaved in and out, as if she occupied her own heart at that moment, its walls beating and beating and beating.

Fear rose within. *The horses. The horses are up to something. What did they do now?*

Out into the cold snow she went, crunching across the yard in her boots and coat, bare at the knees and with a naked head. She felt nothing but heat.

Crunch, crunch, crunch through the snow. Around the corner of the barn she came, and there across the horse pen—bright against the white snow—was a massive stain of blood, saturated, steaming. The horses danced around the carnage, whinnying, their bells jingling, their breath visible as frozen air.

They have killed again! This is all my fault. This is all my fault. I have killed again!

And the proof lay before her, trampled by the horses: the remains of a wingsuiter. Colors swirled before her.

"I did this! I did this," she said, weeping.

From around the corner, Jean-François came running. He looked up to a hole smashed through the side of the barn, the shredded remains of a person spread across the field, the horses gliding around excitedly, and his mother, on her knees crying into a scrap of bloody cloth.

"Maman, are you all right?"

She looked up to him, and put her clenched fists into his open hands. She said quietly: "I'm sorry. I'm so sorry. It was me. It was me. I just had to provide for myself. So selfish. So selfish every day." And she wept: "Every time I go to the market, where the lies...where the lies are sold—oh, and I go full of hope—I get in line with the other sellers, with the other merchants, and every morning they tell me a new one has died. They all keep dying. I can't keep doing this. No more. No more."

"What are you talking about?"

"The young man from the summer, the Swede. He's dead. The British woman in the avalanche. She's dead. The guide trainee. He's dead. Now Lulu's love. He's dead. I knew them all. And all are dead because of me. All dead because I told the horses to kill them…"

"Maman! This is crazy. A reckless Scandinavian? A Brit running away from life? A trust-funder trying to prove himself? A wingsuiter who…who dies? You've just described every foreigner in the valley! Those people you met could have been anyone."

"They aren't," she cried. "I killed them. I've killed before."

He shook his head.

"Your father. I killed your father. I poisoned him. No one ever knew because of the avalanche. I fed him night caps. He was dead in that house the whole night and the whole next morning. I killed him and I fled. It saved my life. It saved yours too. All this time it has been me…and the horses, those fucking evil horses."

He knew she was telling the truth. In fact, everyone knew. As a member of the rescue team, Jean-François had seen his father's autopsy report. Michel died well before the avalanche crushed the house. There were discussions. It wasn't necessarily conclusive. But no one wanted to see a big deal made of it. There was too much going on as it was. A whole village had vanished.

The fresh admission, however, inspired rage within Jean-François. Madame Champignon dropped her hands from his, opening to release psychedelic mushrooms on the snow.

"What! Have you been eating those? Maman, my god, you have been drinking the gentiane and taking mushrooms. Mon dieu. You have poisoned *yourself*."

"I want to go home. I want to go home," she cried. "I want to be a child again."

"I'm sorry," he said and now began to cry with anger. "But you are not leaving here."

Amid the gore and the horses, Jean-François picked up the broken woman and carried her into the house. He changed her from her wet, muddy, blood-soaked clothes. Put her before the fire. Brought her soup and water. And neither of them said a word.

Over the next few hours, as the police and ambulance arrived to handle the scene, Madame Champignon slept. For hours more, when she would awake sweating, Jean-François was there to give her water and broth, until he, too, tired from the long day, dozed off.

Then, sometime well after midnight, Madame Champignon awoke with a jolt, her body suddenly aware of its need for something it was now lacking. The room was so hot. She sweated profusely and could not breathe. She got up and went quickly to the kitchen door. Brisk air snapped at her.

Taking in big breaths, she felt clarity come to her, and out the door she walked into the night.

Crunch, crunch. Her skin felt alive against the frozen air. Crunch, crunch. The world around her was steeped in darkness and rich color: the moonlit blue snow, the glowing orange windows, the smoke from the chimney, wispy with sparks sideways, the darker than dark peaks, a silhouette crowning the night sky.

All of this was just a bad dream, a bad trip. That she'd poisoned herself. Tears froze to her face. She walked far out into the field to take it all in.

Crunch, crunch, crunch, crunch. Footsteps came. Now she felt ashamed. She didn't want to face her son. Crunch, crunch,

crunch, crunch. The footsteps came closer, and then a whisper: "Mother, we're hungry, mother. Send us more food, mother. Tell us where to find more food, will you, mother?" Silence. "Or did you ruin it for us? You didn't ruin it for us, did you? Is that why they all came today?"

To this voice she turned to see the dark outlines of horses in the night. Their bells glimmered silently in the intermittent moon. Though wide-eyed, she couldn't scream. She just uttered: "Les chevaux des Bossons." And with steamy breath, the horses closed in on her.

At that, the new weather front came over the moon and snow fell lightly. The land soon would acquire a new coat—gleaming bright white by morning.

Fire Damages Lab in Bronx

A fire yesterday damaged a research laboratory at the Albert Einstein College of Medicine and hospital at Morris Park Avenue and Eastchester Road, the Bronx. A spokesman said the blaze, confined small, unoccupied labor the third floor of the Research Build injuries.

DEUX PYLÔNES DYNAMITÉS

1 million de dégâts

Dans la nuit de mercredi à jeudi, à 20 h. 45, une énorme déflagration s'est produite sur le côté entre Saxon et Charrat. Un pylône avait été dynamité sur ses quatre supports. Il se coucha sur le flanc avec ses 50 mètres de hauteur, brisant le sommet d'un autre pylône sous le poids des fils d'acier. On met cet attentat sur le compte d'agriculteurs en colère devant le marasme du marché des fruits et légumes. Le pylône appartient à la société EOS et les dégâts se chiffrent aux alentours de 1 million de francs. Notre photo: Le pylône couché sur le flanc avec, dans le fond, la région de Martigny. (photo Valpresse, Sion).

3. Sex, Drugs, Rock & Snow
Winter

SUNDAY

"Excuse me, but what does this mean?" a customer asked of Lulu, pointing to an image on a t-shirt that her son wanted to buy.

"Oh, well, the term 'skiing' in pornography refers to when a woman is in the middle of two guys and she's simultaneously pleasuring them with her hands. Get it?"

The woman turned to her 16-year-old son, snatched the tee away from him and threw it at Lulu. "We most certainly will not. Good day."

As the woman hurried her son out the door, Lulu called after them: "But the term was coined in Chamonix!" And as the door clicked behind them, her voice faded with: "Not many people know that." She looked across the store. "Fine. Whatever."

While the woman's response didn't surprise Lulu—she had heard it all before, much worse, in fact—the negativity added to an already terrible day.

Now alone in the shop, Lulu decided it was time to close up. Her heart just wasn't in it.

She bolted the door, flipped the *open* sign to *closed*, and shut the outside light. As she walked across the floor, she tidied up, refolding a t-shirt here, re-hanging a few hats there. All around her: hoodies, bags, stickers and more, all with the same logo:

CHAM'PORN

The shop occupied a small square building at the bottom of Rue du Moulin next to the river. All the furniture—the shelves and cabinets, a few crooked chairs and a desk—had been handmade in Chamonix over 100 years ago, all bought at the market. It made for a good look against the seedy realism of the marketing, which mostly consisted of oversized posters: black and white stills taken from old erotic films, images of intimacy set in an alpine landscape, cropped to be suggestive, slightly discomforting to most, but just acceptable enough for over-interested authorities.

The store was her store. The brand was her brand. She worked when she wanted to, and skied more often than not— at least when there was snow, which this winter there hadn't been so much of. Today, however, a proper storm had come through, and the fresh flakes covering Chamonix's streets proved to be the only thing that lightened her mood.

It wasn't that Lulu felt sad or angry, or any of the normal feelings that come when someone significant leaves. She just felt numb, dead in the face of those moments when she heard a song she wanted to share, or send a text to remark on how bored she was, or maybe when glancing up at a message-less phone. He wouldn't be there. He was now gone. He wouldn't be in touch.

Jesse left Lulu the week after the accident. The death of his friend in such a freak circumstance was too much for him. Even if the horses hadn't devoured most of the body, there wouldn't've been much left. Just bones, teeth, hair and a large hole in the side of Jean-François's barn. The abstraction of fate, well known to proximity fliers, collided with a gruesome reality, one too vivid for Jesse. He required a change of scene: a full break.

Having gone to text Jesse without thinking, Lulu realized her mistake, took a breath and messaged her friend Melanie instead. As she did, an email came in. She almost reflexively deleted it as spam, but took a second look at the unique email domain: Mediastopheles.com. She read:

Lulu,

I'll be in Chamonix Monday morning, and would like to meet to discuss the "Cham'porn" brand. Would you be available at 930am?

Josh

President & Chief Merchandising Officer
Mediastopheles, LLC

The last time she received an email like this it had been accompanied by a cease and desist order. One of the designers Lulu used had coopted an existing design, likely thinking he could get away with it for such a small mark like Cham'porn. Not the case. The multinationals protect everything, and this latest message could only mean bad news. *Great.*

While they'd likely just slap her on the wrist and she'd be required to destroy the offending product, she figured it would be better to get it over with in person before lawyers got involved. She wrote back, and nearly as soon as the message went, she received a response:

Lulu,

Excellent. Meet me in the breakfast room at the Le Hameau Albert 1er.

Soon,

Josh

Damn, okay. She didn't expect the Albert Premier, one of the few five star hotels in Chamonix. She messaged Melanie.

Lulu: Scratch ski tomorrow, have early meeting
Melanie: Drinks, now
Lulu: Necessary?
Melanie: Not for me, for you.
Lulu: ...
Melanie: You need to get out. He's gone. Move on.
Lulu: I said *early* meeting

Melanie: My place, 15 minutes. Move!
Lulu:

It wasn't until this moment, when she inhaled for a deep and calming breath, that instead she came away with an emptiness in her chest, which she quickly tried to exhale but it only compounded the feeling.

Fine. She trudged across town through the snow, cold flakes falling through the light of her phone as she distracted herself by looking up this Josh. At the train tracks, she stopped. Red passenger cars bustled by leaving a whirl of snow. She watched the wheels turn around and around, and, trying to forget everything, traced the turning of it all. "Okay," she said aloud as the gate finally opened. "Here we go."

★ 1 9 4 5 ★

Nicolas spooled the lengthy filmstrip into a reel package, patiently and gently winding up every inch—and while doing so he looked over the projector, its mechanical parts and their accumulated dust, and out towards the dark theatre below. Click, click, whir. Click, click, whir.

Once done, he tinned the film, and carried the metal canister down the back stairs of the booth and out the door into the alleyway where the trash was sorted. He tossed the tin to the ground. With a flat pang, the lid popped off and the film spilled out.

From his back pocket, he took a small canteen, which was filled with kerosene, and dumped it onto the brown unfurling ribbon, careful not to get any on himself. He then pulled out a package of cigarettes, shuffled one out, and lit it. He took a drag, and flicked the match to the wet ground. Up went a quick blaze. He watched the film crinkle and sizzle and hiss. Dark smoke rose up. "L'Assassinat du Père Noël" was no more.

Nicolas had first seen the film, a catch-a-thief escapade by director Christian-Jaque set in the Haute Savoie, a few years earlier. The Alps of his backyard captivated him. As did their appearance in another film, the documentary "À l'assaut des Aiguilles du Diable" by Marcel Ichac. "L'Assaut" captured actual mountaineering in the high glaciers and peaks, where Nicolas had never been. He wasn't a climber or a skier or much of an athlete of any kind. He knew Armand Charlet, the local alpinist featured in "L'Assaut;" he knew well the exploits of many climbers who came from the valley. None of it, however, represented his Chamonix.

Nicolas was too afraid to scale the rock or go onto the ice. So he stayed in the valley, mostly working, because, from a young age, he had to—his parents, subsistence farmers, had neither formal education nor indoor plumbing. Nicolas's Chamonix consisted of herding animals, shoveling shit, and smoky, dirty clothes. The only ropes he handled held pigs. The only knots he knew drew up his trousers. But at age 13, that changed.

One day, Nicolas's father brought him into town and handed him over to a cousin who owned a photography shop. He had a friend who knew a guy who could use the help of a young man with cleaning at "Le Refuge," one of the two cinemas on Rue Paccard. Although Chamonix remained a relative haven of isolation during much of the war, by 1941, France had been invaded by Germany in the north, with the Vichy government in charge of much of the rest. The men of Chamonix silently began to support the Resistance, and menial jobs opened up.

The initial pay was a pittance, but to Nicolas's father who took the money directly, it mattered greatly. Nicolas didn't much mind the indentured servitude, since it gave him reason to remain clean and indoors. And over time, thanks to this preference and because other positions quickly vacated, he worked his way up, from cleaner, to ticket taker, to usher, to projectionist assistant.

By the time Italian forces sauntered into the Haute Savoie in the fall of '42, Nicolas was doing double duty at both Le Refuge and the Mont-Blanc, the other cinema, all while assisting his father's cousin in the photography shop. The country may have been at war, but wealthy French continued to arrive at Chamonix for their holidays. They demanded entertainment, any distraction from a world in chaos.

The only problem was that entertainment was in short supply. The Italians, under an agreement with Nazi Germany, enforced censorship across occupied territory. The only French films allowed to be shown were a couple documentaries by Ichac, including "L'Assault" and Christian-Jaque's "L'Assassinat," which was the first film the Nazis allowed to be made in France under the Vichy government.

Nicolas played them on a loop, day in and day out, for almost a year. As a result, most people avoided the cinema, which left Nicolas plenty of free time alone in the dark to watch the theatres' catalogs of films and to contemplate the large forces—geologic and geopolitical—playing out just over his head.

If the fascists had sought to control the masses by controlling information, the censorship had the opposite effect on this one young man, who—after more than 100 viewings of "L'Assassinat"—became inculcated by the potency of French filmmaking and its persistent existential questions.

Day after day, the opening scene of L'Assassinat confronted Nicolas—in which a village schoolteacher declares to his pupils that there are only two ways to be successful in life: through proper and clean work, or by taking advantage of others' foolishness. What path was *he* on?

If Nicolas looked to his father, the answer was clear. He believed that none of it mattered and every outsider was an imbecile—the Italians, the Germans, even the French themselves. Because, as he pointed out time and time again, Chamonix and the Haute Savoie were not French. They were not anything, he said, but their own state. The outsiders existed to be taken advantage of.

While his father wasn't savvy to the historical particulars—only the broad gist of being associated with independence—the fact was that the region had only really become French by a sham referendum some 80 years earlier in 1860. Before that, it had been a part of the Kingdom of Sardinia, which would become Italy, and only a part of that entity since 1713, when the alpine lands had been associated with variously with Geneva and parts of what would become France.

Swiss, Italian, French, German, all Nicolas's father knew was that very little changed except the faces on the currency, which he rarely ever had in his hands. He kept the taxman at bay with a pitchfork, and told the churchmen to go to hell. He raised his food. He kept his family warm against the snows. That's what mattered. The latest goings-on would bring nothing different. Nicolas, having spent his youth inured to his father's opinions, received a rapid education in the complexities of the world from his father's cousin, and numerous other whisperers about town. To an undereducated but curious teen, the politics of war and the rationalizations of ideology, of nation states and of ethnic identities, overwhelmed—but one thing brought it all home for Nicolas of Chamonix: death.

In this case, it wasn't due to an avalanche or rock fall or crevasse—or even carnivorous horses, which unbeknownst to most Chamoniards had recently arrived in town. It was the bloody torture and gruesome murder of a man on the streets of Paris by the Gestapo. A man Nicolas had never met, but who he felt he knew intimately. The death of Harry Bauer, the actor who played *Père* Nöel in "L'Assassinat du Père Nöel," got inside Nicolas's head from the moment he heard of it—from an off-hand comment by a passing Parisian tourist exiting the theatre.

"He's dead—the actor?"

The Parisian, who had not realized his remark had been overheard, looked around. Seeing only the young man, said quietly: "Yes. About a year ago. The old Catholic played Semitic roles too seriously. The Nazis thought they had a Jew on their payroll." And the man walked away.

Neither treaties nor flags, currency nor language ever inspired Nicolas to feel "French." La Marseillaise certainly had never been sung at his home. He was a Chamoniard. But in those days, the storm that had broken out above the country that claimed him caused black clouds of rebelliousness to boil up through even the gauziest view of life in a ski station or ardent of familial ties.

Pigs he had slaughtered. Fish he had caught. Acquaintances had died, as they would of circumstance or disease. But this— this murder, and suddenly his awakening to the idiocy of the aggression—triggered some new understanding of the world around him, one detached from the rhythms of life as he appreciated it.

After learning of the gruesome fate of Harry Bauer, Nicolas laid that night on his cot in the backroom of Le Refuge, now where he stayed. Tears streamed down his face. With no schooling and no immediate work to take up his time, the walls of the room closed in on him—a line from "L'Assassinat" endlessly repeating in his head: *Everyone, every day, loses a piece of life.*

Armed with only this empty mantra, he tried to rationalize what had happened, and what would happen. None of it made sense, and so as he could not flee his situation, he became determined to fight, to do whatever he could.

Alas, Nicolas's personal faculties did not make it easy for him, only one young man, to have much of an effect, and he failed miserably at the single effort he made to aid the Resistance just before the end of the war.

And so, the signing of the Armistice in May 1945 simultaneously brought the war to a close and sealed the fate of the film "L'Assassinat:" On the day when all of Chamonix gathered for a ceremony to honor the 37 local men who gave their lives, Nicolas passed the time in a back alley doing what little he could to reassert control over his own situation.

"What are you doing?"

Nicolas, whose thoughts had become lost in the flames, looked up from the sizzling reel to see the biggest breasts he had ever seen on a 17-year-old girl.

The young woman, in turn, cocked her head in quick contemplation upon seeing his face, a common reaction Nicolas received—for his individual features were odd: eyes too far apart; forehead too high; nose crooked; lips too plump. But when taken altogether, they somehow worked, and when combined with good posture from a strict father he could be considered handsome. It just took a moment for people to realize it. When the young girl did, she returned to the matter at hand: "I said, what are you doing? Should I call the firemen?"

"No, no. Everything is fine. I'm just taking out the trash." He looked to the smoldering canister. "Ehh, don't mind that. It'll be out in a minute." He spat on the burning object, then turned and smiled. "Who are you? My name is Nicolas."

She looked at him skeptically. "I'm Eloise."

"I don't believe we've ever met. Do you go to the movies often?"

"The whole town is in the square honoring the dead and you're here lighting trash fires. Why?"

"It, ah," he thought for a moment. "I'm the projectionist. The film had gone bad. Why are you wandering around back here?"

"I..." she thought for a moment. "I was walking by and smelled smoke. Others will too. You'll get in trouble."

He couldn't stop looking at her body.

She cocked her head again. "You know, you sure are funny looking. Did someone punch you in the face—your nose is so..." She drifted off when he looked up to her eyes, staring blankly. She kept at it: "It makes sense they keep you away up there in that dark room. Bizarre looking boy who likes to light things on fire..."

For a moment, they both were silent, while the film reel burned between them. She raised her eyebrow and shook her head slowly.

"Fine," said Nicolas. He unzipped his pants and urinated all over the flames—soaking around and around until they extinguished and the mutilated film smoldered. Cock in hand, he turned and affected a smile: "That work for you?"

He felt satisfied with himself and his gesture, but she just looked at him: "It's as funny looking as your face, like a warped little mushroom, isn't it?"

"What?" He put his cock away. "What do you know about mushrooms..."

"I've seen some big ones."

Now Nicolas raised an eyebrow. "Yeah, right. You know, you have some big ones yourself."

"You like those?"

"Can I see 'em?" She squinted at him. He could see she was going to say no. "You did already see what I've got. It's only fair."

"I didn't have a choice—"

"Please?" he smiled in a way that made all his facial features line up for him to appear handsome, and in a way innocent. What else did she have to do. She rolled her eyes, and flashed him.

"Can I touch 'em?"

"No—"

"How about a photograph?"

This comment gave her pause. All the while they had been chatting she had been wondering why she didn't know him already, and then it clicked: "I know who you are."

"What? Me, who?"

"You're that pervert that works in the photography shop."

"I don't know what you're talking about."

"You do work in the photography shop—?"

"Maybe."

"And you do sell nude photos of women—"

"How do you, how do you know about that? Who told you about that?"

"Everyone knows..."

In fact, everyone didn't know. But, a lot of the men who lived in town and almost all of the Italian soldiers and some of the Germans who had been around definitely did. Nicolas did a brisk trade in amateur pornography.

In the beginning, it just consisted of images he found while developing customer rolls—snaps of lovers or, occasionally, lewder—which he would pawn off on passing soldiers for coins.

For more than a year, it gave him a little walking around money, whereas he never saw any of the rest he earned.

It was all fairly basic, until the day his father's cousin, Monsieur Berger, barged in on him while at work in the photography shop and threw down several nude photos, demanding: "Did you sell these?"

Terrified, Nicolas admitted yes, he had.

"Where did you get them?"

He looked to the floor. "I collected them. Over time. From the customers."

"Where are they? Show me."

M. Berger spent the next half hour examining each and every copy with a keen eye, triaging them into piles, while Nicolas waited, burning with fear and embarrassment. Nicolas could smell M. Berger's old, acrid sweat, which made him nauseous. What would his father say? He wouldn't be let back home. What would he do? He would have to leave the valley. Join the military? What—

M. Berger stood up in front of the piles of photos, three of them, and swept the first into the wastebasket. He pointed to the remaining two: "1 Franc, 2 Francs..." and he leaned over and pulled from under the desk a large file box, which he opened "...and these in here, these sell for 5 Francs."

Disbelief choked Nicolas's words.

"You're mostly selling shit, and from what I understand, too cheaply. Even a fetishist wouldn't buy those." He pointed to the wastebasket. "The Italians are discerning. If you want good business, you're going to need better product." He pointed to the box. "This is my collection. No one has ever seen what's in here. It's of fine quality, but I can barely get my dick up any more and you've stumbled upon a market. We split the profits 50/50. You're the distributor, and I'll show you what's good."

Nicolas nodded, and the old man left the room. From that day, Nicolas's world opened up well beyond the farm of his youth and the films of the last few years—although he remained fairly oblivious of his own slowly growing reputation across Chamonix.

He now leered at Eloise, who tucked a strand of hair behind her ear and said: "So if that's you, it means you're a pervert *and* you're incompetent."

"Who the fuck are you?"

"You're the one Monsieur Tarbot got to run dynamite to the Para ski lift—to blow it up. But you couldn't get it done."

Nicolas went white. He looked around. "Son of a bitch, how do you know about that?"

"Monsieur Tarbot is my father."

To be fair, Nicolas's inability to destroy the Para ski lift station had less to do with his personal competency than it did with the organization of the plan, which wasn't his responsibility.

To limit access to and to assert control of the high ground in the waning days of the war, the Resistance sought to disable the old cable car to the Aiguille du Midi. This would be a significant move both strategically and symbolically—effectively seizing control of Mont Blanc. No one, however, wanted the job.

Aside from the base argument of whether to take out the cable car itself, which could be replaced, or one of the cable pillars, which would cause extensive and lasting damage, there was the question of whether to destroy a cherished element of Chamonix's economy. No volunteers came forward.

In this respect, the timing of Nicolas's political awakening was perfect. He had been known to the Resistance, and M. Tarbot in particular, for a while. M. Berger knew the level of interaction Nicolas had with the Italian and German forces would be suspicious, so he made sure to keep M. Tarbot informed of their activities. Amused, M. Tarbot found M. Berger and Nicolas's work to be helpful to keep the occupiers distracted. Though a pious man, he asked Nicolas to limit sales away from the local men, who should keep focused.

Keen to make his mark—to strike back on behalf of Harry Bauer—Nicolas accepted the Midi assignment, after everyone else turned it down. On the night of February 16, 1945, following a brief firefight at the Col du Midi, and during which another skirmish broke out at the Col du Gros Rognon—supported by artillery fire and planes dropping bombs—Nicolas went to work. The young pornographer set out with a backpack full of explosives and hiked from Les Pélerins all the way up to the mid-station at La Para of the old Midi lift. His objective was to destroy the cable car, and he strapped the dynamite as he had learned. Unfortunately, no one had given him blasting caps. Upon realizing this, well after midnight, he hiked all the way back down, secured them and hiked all the way back up.

Unlike dear Nils, Nicolas was no athlete—yet here he was completing a comparatively exhaustive amount of exercise on terrain not too far away from Nils's afternoon jaunt. By 2 a.m., wasted and a bit disoriented from the up and down and up again, Nicolas simply fell asleep while taking a rest stop.

Ultimately, it didn't matter. The Resistance took the high ground that night anyway, with a single death on their side, and few people were the wiser about the debauched operation at La Para.

Nicolas seethed with embarrassment nonetheless. Bitterness consumed his patriotism. "What good can I do for the French, if I cannot even do right by my own village." He vowed never to get involved in someone else's fight again.

Desperate not to relive any of it, he cut off Eloise, who was saying: "Was it the fear of heights or the fear of death that—"

"So does this mean I can't take your picture?"

She cocked her head again. "What, so you can sell it?"

"No, I'll keep it for myself."

"Yeah, right. My tits are too good not to share. I would have to have a cut of any sales. And it would have to be priced higher than the others."

"It doesn't really matter how good they are. Or what I price it at. The bottom's dropped out of the market. Everyone's left. No more soldiers, no more sales. I'm ruined."

"Oh," she said, actually appearing to be disappointed. "So what will you do now?"

"I'm not sure. Maybe try something different. Aim for the tourists."

"You're not selling my tits to tourists."

Nicolas couldn't help but smile at this—still unsure whether she was joking or not. "You know, when the Germans vacated the Majestic, they left behind a couple film tins, which I have. They're okay."

"You'll go back to your old job then."

"No, no—they're not Hollywood movies."

"What do you...you mean, pornographic movies?"

"Yes—"

"What are they like?"

"Not very interesting. Just people having sex. There's no storyline. But I still think I can get a regular crowd to pay to watch."

"Did you expect there to be a storyline?"

"Every other movie I've seen has one. Without understanding why people are fucking, it doesn't really make sense. It's like watching animals, and that's not a turn on. There should at least be a basic plot."

"You're quite the expert. You should make your own."

"In fact, I could. I spent last summer as an assistant to Marcel Ichac. He showed me the basics for how to shoot. Like technical stuff. It wouldn't be that hard. You got your camera. You got your film. You got your sound. You got your lab costs. You got your synching. You got your editing. The difficulty would be finding the talent, and, of course, paying for the film. But I think I have that covered. After that, again, troubles: distribution. But I could just play it here at Le Refuge after midnight. No one would notice, since you can enter here through the alley. I've already done it a few times with the German films. People come and ski, but there's not much to do afterwards except drink. You can only do so much of that on holiday."

Eloise stood impressed. "When do you begin production?"

"Oh, I don't know if I'll do it—"

"You must. It'll be exciting."

"Ha, okay, fine. But only if you agree to be in it."

"Be in it? Maybe. Help, sure. Only if it has a good storyline, as you said. You better come up with something special."

"Eh, that's not going to be so easy. What you think is good may be different from what I think is good. What do you like?"

"In porn?"

"No, in movies—in general."

Eloise thought for a moment. It had been a while since she had been to the cinema. "I liked Madame Butterfly."

"Cary Grant?"

She nodded.

"Okay, that's a good one. Then that's what we'll do."

"An erotic version of *Madame Butterfly*?"

"Yeah, why not?" Nicolas said. "It would be easier than coming up with an original plot. We'll just add a little sex."

"Okay, sexy *Madame Butterfly*."

"But we won't call it that." He thought for a moment. "No," he said smiling. We'll call it *Madame Champignon*."

MONDAY

"I'd like to buy your brand, Cham'porn," Josh said, sitting across from Lulu. Josh was every bit the 40-something fashion executive in the mountains: weathered *Redwing* boots, rolled selvage denim, organic plaid button-down over a heather Henley, tortoise shell glasses, and a natural reef knit sweater on the back of the chair. Steam from their coffees wafted upward as she absorbed his words.

Not 20 minutes earlier, Lulu had awoken—having slept through her alarm—to find that she was not only late for her meeting, she was still drunk and had some guy in her bed. *Damn you, Melanie.* The guy would've been too much trouble to rouse and push out, so she just showered quickly and dashed out the door—her hair frozen in places from the winter air, shoulders covered in snow. She arrived at Le Hameau Albert 1er in jeans and a gray Cham'porn hoodie. Everything before her—the white linen tablecloth, the silver cutlery, the words emanating from this random visitor—floated in space.

"You want to *buy* Cham'porn?"

"Possibly, yes. The company I work for, Mediastopheles, is always looking at boutique brands—to acquire or to partner with. We've been looking at your space for a while now and I came across you. Seems worth a conversation."

Lulu bobbed her head. "I see."

For a moment, they each sipped from their coffee. Lulu taking in as much as she could, needing the caffeine to shake herself from a still-inebriated state, so she could properly assess the situation, which triggered deep, inherent skepticism. Here Lulu was presented with the classic trope of Alpine existence: the peasant confronted with the unexpected.

For centuries, the stories of the people of the Alps have revolved around this premise, the byproduct of lives that have historically not been about the freedom to make choices so much as the obligations of survival. While it would be unfair to refer to Lulu as a "peasant," a class of people now largely nonexistent in the Alps, the essence remains.

This is because Chamonix, once a fortress, has long become a valley turned inside-out, a place better known for the access it provides than its seclusion. The tides of modernity, which have ebbed and flowed throughout the decades, moving with the pull of the valley's place as an icon of national and international attention, caused great change.

While this reality may have worn Chamoniards of their superficial coarseness, whilst simultaneously enriching many of them, all the attendant features of the valley's peasant past—the durable values, the work ethic, the hard demeanor, the resistance to external forces—have remained.

And so, if the goal of those who live in such rigorous environments is to attain stability and consistency—to ensure that life runs smoothly in the face of nature or fate, or what the churchmen call the "will of God"—then drama consequently arises when they must deal with that which they are not prepared. And the most significant drama usually results when it comes not from something but from someone, most often a person from beyond the village who forces the peasant into an unusual course of action. And here one was.

Josh, sensing her hesitation, jumped in: "Look, there are still many holes in the picture that is Cham'porn, but what I know is that you move about 1,200 tees, 1,000 hoodies, 1,000 hats, 2,000 bags and other accessories each year, on which you turn annual revenue of about a million Euros, from which you take home about a 20 percent margin—which could be more, but you're based in France, you pay too much for the base merchandise, and you have habit of only charging locals cost."

Caffeine or no caffeine, Lulu was now very awake: "Yeah, that's about right." She wasn't entirely sure how he knew all that, so she countered: "Mediastopheles last year turned $35 billion in revenue, with operating income of about $6.3 billion. You personally oversee a portfolio that amounts for a third of the entire men's outdoor market. Why are you interested in a nothing brand like Cham'porn?"

Josh shot back: "Well, what I also know about Cham'porn is that it has a near-religious following among athletes—in what we call the 'action sports' category—who wear your brand even though you don't sponsor them. Skiers. Boarders. Skaters. Bikers. Everyone. They all wear it." He rolled the base of his empty water glass around and around, creasing the linen. "It's not the type of thing you can build overnight. It takes time for people to form an understanding of a brand's identity. To buy into it." He paused. "But I clearly don't need to explain that to you."

Lulu smiled.

"Or is it just that sex sells—" he said.

Lulu raised an eyebrow: "I like to think that people respond to Cham'porn's values: 'Keep it safe. Keep it local. And leave a little to the imagination.'" She leaned in: "In a culture obsessed with 'pornography'—ski porn, food porn, cabin porn, you name it—we try to be the opposite."

On previous occasions when Josh had swooped in upon a small brand, the owner could barely contain their excitement. From Lulu, he got nothing. No smile. No nervous hands. No obvious questions. He wondered if it was just that he was tired. Josh too was fairly hung-over—except for the fact that he hadn't gone out the night before, only sat alone in the hotel bar polishing off a bottle of Nebbiolo. This was his last meeting before taking a few days off and returning to London. And on the assumed promise of Cham'porn, he had committed those days to being in Chamonix, which did not exactly suit his level of skiing or taste for entertainment. Suddenly impatient to get things going, he dropped all pretenses.

"Look, I'm chasing labels and categories," he looked at her directly. "We sell bags, booze and bling to people who aren't above paying a few hundred Euros a week to ride a stationary bike to nowhere, followed by another 10 Euros to cool down with freshly processed organic cactus juice. Our target customers are a demographic of people with high discretionary income and for whom 'wellness' has become an essential aspect of their luxury lifestyle. The problem is, growth areas are stagnating, and I need new things for people to buy."

"Then why not pick up Grivel or Black Crows, one of the other Chamonix brands? People can hang pricey axes and skis on their wall."

"We've got skis—though the technology is evolving too quickly, year over year. Get on the wrong side of a trend, and you're out a season, stuck with stock. Axes are just decoration—"

"I'm lost on where Cham'porn fits in."

Josh reached down to his bag and pulled out an iPad, on which he displayed to her a series of photos. "These are from London." He flicked through a number of pics. "These are from New York." He kept flicking. "And these L.A., and...Tokyo."

All of the photos showed men and women on the street wearing a Cham'porn-branded item of clothing—some carrying their groceries in open sack bags made for ski boots. "Whether you realize it or not, you've identified a niche for pre- and post-activity athleisure-wear. Or, as you cleverly call it: 'avant' and 'après'," Josh said, identifying the two clothing lines Cham'porn carried: avant-ski and après-ski.

"Athleisure-wear?"

"Pre- and post-activity athleisure-wear. Right now, people are walking around in their high-end workout clothes, just to show off that they take care of themselves. You've managed to create something before and after those workout clothes, but before the real clothes. Not a new product, per se. But a new category. While that's fairly promising, the key for me—and why I really think it works—is because of its association with sex. It's taboo. I hate to use the word 'edgy,' but it is. People are fit. They show it off. They feel attractive. They show it off. They are, as a result, having sex. Good sex. They show it off—discreetly. That's where Cham'porn comes in. It's a nod to something that can't be said."

To Lulu, the notion that she had created a new niche or category or whatever was absurd; however, she recognized that it meant Cham'porn had value, giving her room to maneuver. A glow of possibility arose within her, but she knew she had to keep playing it cool.

"And what if Cham'porn isn't for sale?"

To Josh, this didn't mean anything. He'd been through all of this before. He handed a piece of paper to her. "See if you're interested in that, and how about we meet up later this week."

Up the hill she trudged from Chamonix to her home, a chalet in Les Nants, a neighborhood on the sunny side of the valley. The new snow now stuck with temperatures having dropped. Through the flurry, she could see Chalet Largo, a traditional Savoyard structure, whose roof splayed like an open book, face-down atop stone foundations. While the upper floor was designed to store hay, and half the ground floor would have been where the animals wintered, refurbished it made for superb open-plan house—for both her and Nicolas, who lived together, though on opposite sides.

Nicolas greeted her at the door. He scanned her, as she kicked off her boots: "You're hungover."

"Yep." She walked in zombie-like and crashed on the couch. The fireplace was lit, and music was playing somewhere. "Your friend left. Don't think he was prepared for the snow."

Lulu groaned. Nicolas disappeared and returned with a bottle and glasses. "Here, for you."

"Oh, no."

"Take it. You'll feel better. You know it."

"Come on. Not the gentian."

Yes. I'll take one too...for good measure," he said with a wink, and then handed her the shot, which she downed with displeasure. He then put a large glass of water on the table. Lulu shortly dozed off. He sat enjoying the storm. Outside, the snow continued to fall, and the two of them remained cozy against it all.

★ 1956 ★

"Do you see my feet in the mirror?"

"Yes."

"Do you think they are pretty?"

"Yes, very."

"And do you like my ankles?"

"Yes."

"And do you like my knees, too?"

"Yes. I really like your knees."

"And my thighs?"

"Those too."

"Do you see my behind in the mirror?"

"Yes."

"Do you think I have a pretty ass?"

"Yes, very."

"Should I get on my knees?"

"Yes."

"And do you like my breasts?"

"Yes, tremendously."

"Gently, Max. Not so hard."

"Sorry."

"What do you like more, my breasts or my nipples?"

"I don't know. It's all the same to me."

"And do you like my shoulders?"

"Yes."

"I don't think they're round enough."

Nicolas, watching the silhouette of the audience from the back of the dark theatre, could see that this line—for whatever reason—caused several women to glance down at their own shoulders. The light from the projector betrayed them. *Curious.* He then raised up his own arms and put one around each woman to either side of him, and smoothed their shoulders.

"And my arms, you like them?"

"Yes."

"And my face, that too? Everything—my mouth, my eyes, my nose, my ears?

"Yes, everything."

"Then you completely love me."

"Yes. I love you completely, tenderly, inside and out..." And the two had sex with an ease and a beauty that almost—almost—betrayed the fact that the actors were actually very much in love at the moment they had been filmed.

The scene ended, fading to black, and credits came up. The lights in the theatre did not come on—though someone unseen opened an exit door towards the front, and the crowd shuffled out into the night, quickly and quietly.

Only once the projectionist saw that everyone had left did he raise the lights, and a young man entered with a trash bin and a mop.

Nicolas at this point had already exited the rear of the small theatre and stood in the entryway awaiting his two female companions, one of whom was in the film that had just showed. Nicolas jotted notes in a small pad: things to remember for when making the next one.

In short time, the young man with the mop exited the theatre with his trashcan, and Nicolas said: "Find anything interesting tonight?"

"No, sir. And I shined the flashlight under every row."

"Good man," Nicolas said, and slipped him 10 Francs. The young man moved on happily to his next tasks.

While the desire to keep the theatre clean was foremost, the motivation to get people to go home before finding pleasure became a goal of Nicolas's filmmaking. Create beautiful films, ones with a promising narrative, and inspire people to seek out others to have sex with—not just sit there and watch.

"No masturbating tonight," he said to Eloise, who returned first. "I mean, no signs of it at least. And you saw them, they all rushed out with more enthusiasm than usual."

"How many? I didn't get a count."

"We had..." Nicolas pulled out his pad, "57."

What began as a puerile ploy to touch a girl's breasts had turned into something far more elaborate. The first project, the Puccini knock off, served as an amusing distraction for two youth to pass the quiet time of the post-war era—a period in which the normal rhythms of life returned, along with amplified ennui.

The mayor, the market, the tourists, the church—all put on a good face about how normal everything was and would be. Thoughts of the deportations, retribution killings, the Resistance fighter hanged from the viaduct by departing Germans, or other acts of retaliation by either side were swept away. L'Aiguille du Maréchal Pétain returned to being l'Aiguille de Blaitière. Place Maréchal Pétain became Place de la Libération. And so it went.

For Nicolas and Eloise, the drafting of the script, recruiting of talent, the marshaling of resources, the staging and eventual production of their film gave them a purpose, which was made all the more exciting because of its secrecy— as if they were on a Resistance-related mission of their own. And in a way, they were.

For Eloise, though, there was something more. While boredom, hormones and a conservative father contributed to her nascent rebelliousness, the decision to pursue this particular taboo was shaped by one thing above all: her breasts.

Now, it should be understood that it's not as if they were abnormally large. As breasts go, they were ample but not massive, perky but not floppy, yet aesthetically pleasing and shapely enough to attract attention—predominantly unwanted advances as she made her way through a small world dominated by masculine norms, latent militaristic machismo and the mindless disrespect of transient tourists. If she had been left alone, her approach to sexuality would be no different than that of any other 17-year-old girl. But who in life is ever left alone.

By the time she encountered Nicolas and his dumb stare, she had had quite enough. But instead of fighting or running away, Eloise identified the amateur pornographer—an innocent, awkward and insular young man—as an opportunity to benefit from the great peaks she had been given, both in terms of control and money. At least that was the idea.

Unfortunately for Nicolas, although he found himself with a willing partner, his insistence on maintaining his own level of control—over the production of his first film, and those thereafter—prevented him from acting. Which meant he inadvertently cock blocked himself, a realization he had only once filming was set to begin. There he sat the first day of shooting and watched as Eloise made out with another guy.

Spurned, Nicolas quickly adapted that first script. What resulted was shorter in length and more burlesque than strictly pornographic: no sex, just kissing and a shot of her tits and the other guy's ass. At 15 minutes, the film consisted of a bar scene in which she meets a mountain guide, a marriage scene at the chapel ruins at Lake Gaillands, a "love" scene below Mont Blanc and an ending in which "Madame Butterfly," or in this case, "Madame Champignon," sits silently and waits for her man to return from the glaciated mountains above. He never does.

Not long enough to be a feature, Nicolas showed the short film as an opener for his German movies. The local setting and amateur feel generated considerable amusement for the audiences, whose nervous sexual energy had a chance to be exercised before the main attraction. As one patron noted,

"It returned a little entertainment to the business of pleasure." Nicolas and Eloise considered it an *amuse-bouche*.

Two of these short films a year followed (winter and summer), along with a clutch of foreign admirers—regular tourists who came mostly for the climbing or the skiing, but found themselves in the back alleys at night. Nicolas and Eloise earned enough to pay for talent, cover production costs and take off the spring and autumn—all without raising too much of a fuss with any locals, or their unknowing families.

It worked in a town growingly obsessed with keeping things as normal as possible, since most everyone had long come to appreciate Chamonix's place on the international scene and first considered the bigger picture: its tourist economy. Tourists, happy, entertained and out of trouble, and youth kept busy with creative projects and not wanting for money. What more could anyone ask for.

The only real problem Nicolas and Eloise encountered happened around 1949, when a former churchman—a defrocked priest, a collaborator during the war—found out about the midnight shows. He tried to confront Eloise's father, the former Resistance leader, in Les Bossons one afternoon.

It is often thought that was when the phrase "Les chevaux des Bossons" became verbal shorthand for when things get out of control. What a scene it must have been: a Nazi priest run down by horses that "broke free" from their pen in the golden light of an autumn afternoon. It took a while for the gendarmes to retrieve what remained of the former churchman's body.

With the neighbors in a titter over the equine rampage, the mayor was summoned—and henceforth the bells on the horses. But then he and everyone else simply continued to look the other way, even as pets and people disappeared from time to time, and the films slowly evolved from burlesque to softcore. "The threats are obvious. Just make sure there are appropriate warnings and keep the children away," it was said time and again.

Just like the monkeys: See no evil. Hear no evil. Speak no evil.

It wasn't until Nicolas couldn't source any new German films, as he'd been able to do in those immediate post-war years, that he and Eloise realized they had to make a full-length film themselves, lest they lose their audience. The decade of practice prepared them well, and Cannelle—or, Cinnamon, her stage name—proved to be a star.

To celebrate the opening of their first major film on this night in '55, an ambitious erotic adaptation of Homer's Odyssey, and the seemingly positive reactions, they all went out afterwards. Nicolas ordered Champagne. They shared thoughts and feelings on the final cut. And they had a well-earned toast. Salut! After which Cannelle asked of Nicolas: "So what were you doing in Minorca last weekend?"

"I was asked to judge an ass contest," he said, and the women laughed. "No, really, I was. It was quite something. It was among three beauties. They were actually the ones who chose me to be the judge. I'm serious." He took a sip, and with affected pleasure said: "And they displayed for me their dazzling nudity."

Eloise, while refilling glasses, said laughing: "And the contestants, how were they?"

"The first, she had a gently curving back and two dimples on her round behind. The second, she parted her legs and her snow-white skin became a deep rouge—more cherry-red than crimson. The third was as still as a quiet sea. Her delicate skin rippled gently, shivering involuntarily…"

"Can't you take that somewhere else?" a man at the bar sitting next to them said. "It's disgusting."

"Excuse me?" Nicolas said.

"Your filth, can you please take it elsewhere."

"I do not recall you being invited into our conversation. Perhaps if you just minded your own business, you would be better off."

"I meant all of it," the man said. "I know who you are. You are filth. Those movies, the smut you produce. Can't you take all of it somewhere else? You are a blight on Chamonix."

The bartender, having returned, heard the conversation, turned on his heel and walked away again.

"You don't like our films? Ladies, did you hear what he said—this man who is imposing upon us, this imposer, he doesn't like our art."

Eloise and Cannelle sat smugly, drinking.

"Your 'art'? Your garbage. No, I've never seen your garbage. I cannot speak to them specifically."

"Then it shouldn't bother you. Besides, I don't come to where you work and criticize what you do."

"Fuck off, pornographer. You couldn't if you tried."

"Okay then, how do you earn a living?"

"Honest work."

"Honest, like what? How honest."

"Like building the tunnel."

"The tunnel, the Mont Blanc tunnel? You're going to be responsible for that gash?"

The man nodded. "We dig. That's proper work. Earns good money. Clean money."

"I've changed my mind. I will have to criticize your work."

The man looked at Nicolas confused.

"Your work is filthier than anything I've ever done," Nicolas said. "My money is derived from local work, using local talent, and local creativity. You, you're the one who is actually bringing filth into this valley. That's all that tunnel will accomplish."

"We're building the economy. We're creating jobs..."

"You're going to pollute our valley with foreigners. Just doing the bidding of Paris and a bunch of corrupt Italian politicians. Another Parisian work project to take another piece of Chamonix away from us and give it to the urbanites who visit, leave their shit, and go. But you know what, it's going to be worse. We are just going to become a dumping ground for Europe's trash. Traffic just chugging by."

"You seem to have no problem taking money from that trash. Maybe you can set up a brothel on the highway."

Nicolas quietly took exception to this, because while he was happy to display acts of love and, even better, inspire them, he drew the line at pimping. Time and again, it proved to be something he had to explain. A service he didn't and wouldn't provide.

Staying calm, Nicolas rejoined: "Those who have found their way here, I'm happy to relieve them of their earnings. You could say I am no different than a crystal hunter, sharing our valley's unique beauty, with pleasure. You, on the other hand, are turning our valley into a cesspool. Though, maybe you should head out and get yourself some loving. It might lighten your mood. Or did you intend to be drinking alone tonight?"

The man slapped a few Francs on the bar. "You're sick. You'll rot in hell." He looked at the women. "You too. Whores."

"Yeah, Monsieur Mountain Digger..." Nicolas said, "...as long you keep drilling your holes, I'll keep drilling mine." He smacked Cannelle on the ass. She giggled. The man looked aghast and left the bar saying nothing further.

"Come on ladies," Nicolas said, "let's go find a quieter table."

The next several rounds came and went, and while the encounter with the man at the bar wasn't discussed further, Nicolas seethed. *Honest work. What is honest work.* This went on in his mind while the women talked amongst themselves and, after a while, Eloise and Cannelle became drunk and began to sing a little song:

"...The one who laughs at anything, and says love's a lovely thing," Eloise began.

"Wins men's hearts without fear, and gives without a tear," Cannelle joined.

Together: "To older guys or brave young men, always asking where or when. Likes to please them every day, without going all the way..."

When one becomes aware of politics and commits to taking action in a fight—as Nicolas had done many years before, regardless of his lack of success—it is impossible to shake off those passions once stirred. Nicolas, for one, had retreated during the intervening years to his father's position; however, reading and discussion enabled him to fill in the details of arguments that his father never grasped, only felt. The erotic filmmaker cringed at the Fourth Republic and its ineptitude in dealing with reestablishing France after the war. He became further infuriated by Paris's attempts to interfere in his hometown. He believed firmly that the Savoie region had been unjustly "occupied" by France.

The women continued to sing: "...I see a ship tied to a buoy, then I meet a sailor boy. We sing and we dance; we play with romance. We whirl and we spin, then I say with a grin: that I mean no, it's time to go; that's enough, don't get rough..."

Having now—seemingly—succeeded in his own work, the feature film, that he finally produced, self-confidence grew, along with the money in his pocket. Instead of catering to the values of the French who came to Chamonix, he saw that this was his opportunity to influence them with the values of the Savoie region. If they wanted to build roads to him, he would give them something memorable in return.

Well into their song, each had an arm around the other: "I say, oh, please come back, then I smile behind your back." Cannelle stopped singing, and let Eloise take the line: "But I'm lost on a dream, one that's not a scheme—it's all peaches and cream." Then Cannelle continued: "He'll take me in his arms, and show me that out of thousands, he will know me..."

And together, they sang: "You, you..."

Suddenly the alcohol spoke on Nicolas's behalf: "Damn it, we don't make pornography..."

The two women stopped and looked at him.

"We make..." Nicolas churned, "...we make, alpine erotica." The women continued to stare. A smile came to his face. "Nah, fuck him, we make alpine pornography." He looked at the women who were looking at him. "We do. It's true. What an asshole that guy was!"

The two women burst in laughter.

As she calmed and finished her drink, all while waving over another round, Eloise said: "Nico, what are you talking about, 'alpine pornography'?"

"Yes: Alpine Pornography. That's what we do. It's different from the other shit."

"Different from what other shit?"

"Different from the shit they play in the cities, what we used to show. Most of the actors aren't attractive. They look like goddamned hairy beasts. And that's the women. The guys are trolls. And most importantly, there's no imagination to the scene. Guy, girl, bed, fuck, fuck. That's it. What we do is different. We do Alpine Pornography."

"Okay," Eloise said, amused, "we do the same thing—just in a chalet, on a sheepskin rug, in front of a fireplace...maybe while it snows outside..."

Cannelle, enjoying her drunkenness: "It's true, Nico, that's every movie we've done."

"Not every movie," he thought for a moment. "What about the one in the téléphérique that 'broke down', with the lift operator and the two skier girls?

Both women nodded, then they all thought for a moment. Eloise said: "There was the one in front of Cascade du Dard— you know, the couple on a picnic, and the wife gets mad with the husband; she leaves, and the hiker girl comes along..."

"Oh right," Cannelle said, "and then the wife comes back and it becomes a threesome. I was the hiker girl."

"Yeah, that one."

Nicolas still couldn't think of another one that wasn't chalet-based. "Well, there will be more," and he finished his drink.

"We have entered a new era with our latest film. What if we go out onto the glacier to have some sex?"

"Now?" Cannelle said.

"No..."

"Film on the Mer de Glace?" Eloise said.

"Exactly. People don't want generic sex. Right now, they want something specific and enticing. Something exotic. They want us to fulfill a fantasy. It's more about the idea than the sex itself. That's what we've learned, isn't it?"

The serious turn to the inebriated night had Eloise and Cannelle trying to catch up. Nicolas continued: "They want fantasy and we live in a fantasy world—Chamonix. That's what we have to sell. That's what makes us different. Enables our product to be better." He could see they were lost. "What do people come here for?"

"The mountains?"

"The scenery?"

"No, they come to escape. Look, each and everyone one of them is still try to leave behind the failures of the war. The memories are everywhere, all over their capital, all over their country, but no one talks about them. And now they have even fresher wounds to forget—with the collapse of Indochina—and today, they have Algeria falling to pieces. And they colonized that place well before us..."

Nicolas here wandered onto touchy ground, even for barroom banter well after midnight. The ladies looked around to see if he was risking another confrontation. Nicolas took a turn back to sex. "We need to give them high adventure, not return them to Paris or Amsterdam, Berlin or London. Let's figure out what our films stand for and stick to it. We need to infect them with our culture and our way of life, not the other way around."

"This is what we will call 'alpine pornography'?" Cannelle said.

"I believe so."

"No," said Eloise. "It isn't alpine porn. It's 'Cham'porn.'"

Nicolas looked at her, a grin spread across his face. They all drank to that.

Whilst they reveled in their new identity, a man entered the bar and glanced over to the table, a man Eloise recognized. She downed her drink and said: "Well, it has been a lovely evening. I have to go." It was Michel, the mountain guide she had been seeing.

Nicolas, for all the sex he was associated with and certainly did have, preferred to sleep alone, and took the opportunity himself to leave and so bid adieu to Cannelle, who had anyways been eyeing someone at the far end of the bar.

On the way home, Nicolas reflected on the ideas discussed through a pleasant haze of inebriation—that is, until a flicker of light caught his eye, and he turned to look up into the sky, where a new star shined.

The Mont Blanc massif was not only being penetrated from below. The tunnel Nicolas despised was merely one of a number of ways the sanctity and isolation of Chamonix was being further exploited and exposed.

Just that month a new cable car had opened, the highest in the world, from the center of town to the top of Aiguille du Midi, at an elevation of 3,842 meters. It replaced the old one, with which Nicolas had had his encounter. This was no star on the horizon. It was one you had to fully look up to.

This too had been another long-planned project, a considerably complex feat of engineering that took 45 years to finish at a cost of a half billion Francs. Although he hated it, Nicolas became furious when he found that a Parisian official was required to be present for the lift's opening. Though he still privately gloated a few days after when one of the drive cables broke, stranding its passengers.

The star, which he now realized would be a permanent fixture in his life, soured his state and reminded him of the exchange with the tunnel digger. Nicolas could rage and complain about the tunnel, or the Midi lift, or the tourists, or France itself, but the forces of commercialism were beyond his control. That he recognized. That he felt deeply. That, he said to himself, was why he was just making the most of a bad situation.

Then, from a distance, he saw on the empty street the tunnel digger, who was removing something from the trunk of a car. Nicolas stepped into the shadows and squinted through his anger and inebriation to confirm it was in fact him. It was. Nicolas stood and watched, and after a minute the tunnel digger moved on.

Once clear, and without a thought, Nicolas walked over to the tunnel digger's car, and removed his jacket, button-down shirt and undershirt, which he placed on the hood; and then he put back on the button-down and jacket. He methodically ripped the undershirt into strips and knotted them together into a long braid.

He opened the gas cap to the car and carefully dipped in the cloth, which after a few moments soaked up the fuel. Nicolas then lit it, watched its heat glow blue and white and red, and walked away—only looking back once his shadow was claimed by the fire, which lit up the rear seats. Expecting an explosion, he shielded his face. None occurred. The car just burned and burned, emitting hisses and the pangs of warping metal.

No one came. No one noticed. And after a while, Nicolas went home.

TUESDAY

The lift operator nodded to Lulu, and she and Melanie grabbed their skis and backed into the packed cabin of the upper lift to the Aiguille du Midi. "Sac à dos à la main!" he said to the crowd of about 50 people. "Take off your backpacks, please!" With skiing and climbing gear already jamming the cabin, the crowd grumbled as the two women pressed in, securing the final space by the door. Last on, first off. The doors shut. The moans lessened. The cabin pulled away and ascended to the Midi summit.

"He said he would be back in touch later in the week," Lulu said, pressed against the scratched window of the cabin, without looking at Melanie.

"You thinking about it?"

"Of course." Lulu looked over the clouds now below. She took in the view over the Bossons Glacier, no different from this altitude than that from an airplane.

"Are we going to celebrate?"

"Nothing is done yet—"

"Too good to be true?"

"Maybe."

The massif's steep walls cast long shadows from the low winter sun that darkened the valley. Lulu wondered about the people down there still in bed, missing all that's going on above them.

"And if he's for real?"

"It'll be something. It's always something—"

As the cabin arrived at the summit station, it knocked into the terminus guide poles and clunked its way to a stop. The anxious crowd waited another few seconds for the doors to finally open, and when they did the driver bid them well: "Bonne journée, mesdames et messieurs!" Crisp air snapped at the humid crowd.

Lulu and Melanie clomped quickly through the hallway of the main building and out onto the wood bridge that connects the structures of the Midi—built right into the lofty granite spires of the massif. Workers continued to shovel snow off the bridge into the depths below. The two women hurried into the second hallway, a cave through the granite, lined with cement, metal scaffolding and wires. They walked to the end, and pushed open two large metal doors, into a round tunnel bored through the back of the glacier that clung to the rock, covered with pocked blue ice, and into the white sunlight beyond.

There isn't another place on the planet that offers such immediate access to the level of terrain that Lulu and Melanie were about to ski. The engineering of the Midi and the geology through which they passed only adds to its uniqueness. The contrast of the threshold would be no different than walking the halls of a nuclear submarine, opening a hatch and finding yourself on the moon. Now the only thing before them was a little metal gate with an affixed yellow sign warning of imminent mortal peril.

Opposite that gate a narrow arête extends outward—its width dependent on the weather, though almost always just one or two feet wide. Each side drops off some 50 degrees. To fall off the left is to die. There is nothing to stop a fall except the ground 2,000 meters below. To fall off the right side offers better chances, only a few hundred meters down; however, rocks and open crevasses await. Despite the raw danger, thousands of people take the walk every year, the skilled and novice alike, many of whom had beat Lulu and Melanie up there that morning, and who milled about nervously, making a fuss.

"There is no self-arrest. Only sliding off," a guide could be heard saying to a client.

"But you'll be roped to me."

"Yes, if you fall on one side, I will jump off the other. If that does not do the trick, well, enjoy the view..."

Lulu had seen it and heard it a thousand times before. It was no bluff intended get a rise out of the client. It was the truth, and on occasion it did happen. Lulu, for the countless times she descended the ridge, never had a problem. Just another easy walk in a dangerous place.

Assessing the apprehensive crowd of tourists and others, Lulu and Melanie didn't bother with any last-minute checks or organization. They just made their way directly past those in the ice cave, through the gate un-roped, and right out onto the arête, where they got a look at the line of people making their way down. Third bin, and already they were behind schedule.

"Chemins des écoliers?" Lulu said, indicating a better way, and Melanie stepped off to the right side of the arête and jammed one of her skis in the snow making a platform for it, then clicked in her boot. Secure, she clicked in with the other. Lulu did the same.

Looking back, Melanie nodded to Lulu, then she dropped into the bowl—fast in case the fresh snow sloughed or worse, which it didn't—and then carved out several tight turns, arcing around the inside of the ridge. Lulu was on her heels.

Several of the tourists expressed amazement and a couple guides smiled and shook their heads. They knew who it was: *badass bitches.*

Beyond the headiness of the Midi arête, there are multiple paths of various levels of challenge to be taken down the Vallée Blanche—most of which were first scouted by those hearty, high-altitude soldiers of the world wars. It is a simple irony that although these routes came into existence largely as a result of battle, the toll they have exacted on life only really came after their transition to civilian use.

The access deceives, but the Vallée Blanche isn't a ski area. It is wild, open and uncontrolled. While any outing in Chamonix requires a bit of calculation, the high mountain requires more than cursory estimates to form an understanding of where the best conditions may be—and by "best" that often means "safest," though not always. Anyone can buy a ticket and find their way onto the glaciers—without a soul questioning their motives, perhaps only the PGHM rescuer making inquiries after the fact. So beware all ye who enter.

Lulu was no guide, but no novice either—not that mountains discriminate based on experience. After a lifetime of practice, her assessment process was immediate and, in some ways, always ongoing. She would consider the weather for that month, that week and the forecast for the day. The base of snow. The snow bridges over the crevasses. The orientation of recent storms. The prevailing wind, direction and speed. Whether there's a Foehn wind, or a temperature inversion. The seasonal angle of the sun. The general visibility, in the morning and forecast for later in the day. After that, it was a matter of chatting with friends and others along the way.

Because many alpinists were known to be incomplete in their answers, to throw people off the pursuit of fresh tracks, Lulu would also consult Instagram, where vanity betrayed greed. She followed a dozen or so people she knew and a half-dozen more she didn't, all who regularly went up high. She'd daily scan their posts and stories—often a lot of selfies or ski line shots that inadvertently revealed snow conditions. Given her knowledge of the valley and massif it didn't matter if they added the location. She would know where they were.

The preparation mattered, so she could move quickly from the crowds without attracting notice—a sensibility Lulu took so seriously that when skiing she only wore black: jacket, pants, helmet, gloves. Just another dot on the landscape.

On this day, Lulu and Melanie took a direct route from the Midi to do a "Petit Envers," a path that went skier's-left of the standard Vallée Blanche route, traversing high until they reached the Glacier de l'Envers du Plan, steeper terrain with large crevasses requiring a bit of picking to get around. But it offered some damn fine lines.

This would bring them to the flats between the Seracs du Géant—a massive collision of ice—and the Refuge du Renquin. From there, they would put skins on their skis and cut a fresh track up the Périardes, a large rock theatre within the mountain range, then hang a left up to the Col du Tacul, to which they would have to bootpack. Once atop, they would be greeted with the answer to whether the Glacier du Capucin was in condition to ski or not. This day, it would be.

Without much discussion or faffing, the trip took about an hour and a half, and Lulu and Melanie enjoyed a good rest at the col. They drank coffee from a thermos and ate a bit of sandwich, while pointing out lines and making observations about the condition of the north face of the Grandes Jorasses—one of the most powerful and respected mountains in the world. They also remarked on the entrance of the Capucin, noting a wide cornice hanging from the southeast corner of the couloir—just above where they would enter. But nothing of concern, just common wind-loading from the storm the night before.

While to explain why anyone does this—why anyone chooses to climb a mountain—is a fruitless and clichéd endeavor, it is worth taking a moment to consider why someone skis a steep, glaciated mountain such as this.

Most anyone can appreciate the joy of skiing an open field of fresh powder a kilometer in length—even if you've never experienced what it is like to glide along ridges, over dips, dropping off small cliffs, hopping over crevasses, all amidst hulking, crackled glaciers and thousand-meter-high rock walls. Those who have done it, know. Those who have not, can imagine. It isn't that hard. It is bliss.

Where appreciation becomes difficult is in relation to steep terrain: 40 percent-plus grade slopes, usually in tight couloirs (vertical rock shafts of snow), and usually where falling is not an option. There is a small percentage of people in general who ski at this level; however, in Chamonix there are perhaps more people capable of it than anywhere else in the world—mostly due to the access, and mostly because they've been doing it longer than anywhere else.

It all dates back to 1939, when a strapping young guide named Andre Tournier skied off the Aiguille d'Argentiere with seven-foot wooden skis, leather boots and bindings consisting of cable heel releases and bear-trap toes. The following year, Emile Allais and Etienne Livacic skied the north face of the Dome du Gouter. Then in 1946, Louis Lachenal and Maurice Lenoir skied the 40-degree south face of the Col des Droites. The game was on.

But the difficulty here is not in appreciating the terrain. The terrain demands only respect. It needs not appreciation. The appreciation is required only of the result of the act of skiing the terrain.

If the purpose of skiing virgin powder in "normal" terrain is to turn your brain on, then skiing a steep couloir is to shut it off almost entirely—an act more akin to meditation than sex. Ergo, if skiing powder provides the orgasm, skiing steep provides that transcendence of consciousness that happens right afterwards. Or as Lulu would refer to it "la petite mort"— the little death.

To achieve this requires focus, because the only way to ski steep is to feel the snow and ice you're on by reading it through the vibrations moving across your feet, up your knees and into your core, since you simultaneously need to be visually assessing the forward terrain, while being mindful of what may be coming down behind or aside you—slough or worse—along with whatever is to the sides, rocks or cliffs. To do so effectively is not simply an achievement of skiing a steep path. It is carving a vertical line through a series of tightly controlled turns by way of a rhythm made by harmonizing the body and mind.

That would be the ideal, and of course it sounds lofty—to some probably like complete bullshit. It is not easy, and it is not for everyone. But what can't be denied is that it is as beautiful to experience as it is appealing to watch.

Of course, in this regard, the less than ideal is neither beautiful nor appealing. Though that is not actually death, which of course should be an assumption made going in, but not one carried whilst doing—lest one becomes timid. It may not even be serious injury. It could just be ugliness, derived from sloppiness or hesitation. In which case the result is dissatisfaction and frustration. Sometimes, however, it is just enough to get down no matter what. Sometimes, shit happens.

Glacier du Capucin is a no-fall couloir, steep over 40 degrees—though certainly not nearly the steepest around. When it is in condition, it is a marvelous descent. The path was simple, and one they had taken numerous times. Melanie led off, and although she immediately clipped her ski on a barely covered rock, she recovered without issue and peeled almost a dozen tightly controlled turns in lush, shin-deep powder that stuck well and made for something very elegant to watch. Melanie involuntarily yelped with delight.

Then everything went to shit.

It began with a bird, a black crow, of course. As Melanie set off, it landed just aside Lulu and cawed and cawed and cawed: *Le temps du séisme. Le temps du séisme. Le temps du séisme.*

Lulu didn't pay attention to the crow, just reflexively reached in her pocket for a piece of croissant, which she tossed to the bird without looking, keeping an eye on

Melanie. The crow picked up the food and leapt over and placed it on the end of Lulu's ski. Lulu didn't think much of it, and flicked it back at the bird aside her.

The bird ate the piece and then fell over and fluttered wildly in the snow while squawking: *Le temps du séisme! Le temps du séisme! Le temps du séisme!*

She looked at the bird in fits and spasms on the ground. "What?"

The bird hopped upright: *Le temps du séisme! Le temps du séisme! Le temps du séisme!*

Lulu said aloud what she thought she had heard. "Earthquake weather? What does that mean?"

And then, as Lulu watched, the bird flew up the col toward the cornice, and all hell let loose across the ridge: 1,000 more crows, a black mass swarming through the air. They swooped and rose, dived and swirled in spectacular formation.

And then, together, the crows fell upon the cornice, displacing the snow.

As large chunks above Lulu tumbled and spider lines cracked the couloir's pack—in what seemed to be the slowest of motion—one bird flew ahead of it all, just above the snow right past Lulu, who turned and chased it—moving at whatever gravity pulled: right after that crow, right on its heels, matching its line in sweeping arcs, forgoing any thought of the usual cut turns or careful plotting, just going and going, fast and hard, with smoky debris right on her heels.

The narrow top of the couloir funneled the avalanche, and Lulu pulled hard to stay right toward the rocks, which she straight scraped over with a leap, bringing her into another channel of snow and to where she plummeted into space and landed next to Melanie, who had moved over herself. As they looked up from their state—both implanted into the steep snow—the ground began to roar, with deafening ferocity, and down the fall line the mountain itself tumbled from above.

★ **1 9 6 7** ★

"Who is this? Why is she fucking this black guy? Where the fuck did all this come from?"

"It's a flashback. He's Algerian," said Nicolas.

"To what?"

"To when she was younger and had this, like, amazing experience."

"What does that have to do with this scene?"

"She's fucking this guy, but while doing so, she's thinking about this other guy. So we jump to that. You'll understand in editing."

"This is fucking crazy. You can't put a flashback in a porno."

"Why not? When you make love, do you always exist in the moment, or do you think to someone else, another time, another place? Maybe to some better sex you had. Some lover who was more engaging."

"You should be in the moment. That is the ideal!"

"You are missing it. We're not just capturing sex here. Our film is a part of sex. This isn't just a woman in bed, it's a part of the story of sex. This moment is beautiful. This moment is true."

"This isn't thinking. This is fucking. If you want art, do Shakespeare."

"Ahh, I hate Shakespeare…"

"Now you hate art."

"Shakespeare didn't have flashbacks."

"He didn't have bare-backs either."

"Au contraire, he did—'…making the beast with two backs'…"

"Fine. Whatever. Now what are you doing? What are you doing to the lighting?"

"We need to change it. It's all wrong."

"I set it up myself. It looks fine."

"No, not for her. It was fine for the other girl."

"You're out of control."

"Look, every woman has her most vulnerable part." Nicolas went up to the naked woman, Beatrice, and tapped her all over her body. "It does not make the same sound all over." The director of photography rolled his eyes. "For some it's the nape of the neck. The waist. The hands. But for Beatrice here, in that position, in that light, it's her knee. We need to set up for her knee."

The director of photography looked at Nicolas without expression. "You're killing me, you know this."

"We can't keep making the same film."

"Yes, we can. It is what people want."

"Okay, sure, why people come to see these movies is the same. Like, people will always say 'I love you.' They will always say 'I hate you.' But how they say it, that's what changes. We need to change as well. We need to change how we tell the story of fucking. No more steady cam."

"Seriously, I give up. Make the movie you want."

"I will." And the director of photography threw down his script and walked away to the onset bar nearby.

After his first feature film, "Homer's Odyssey" (cheekily renamed "Boner's Odyssey"), Nicolas decided to stop making the short films and focus on one significant production a year. What followed were erotic renditions of "The Passion of Joan of Arc," "Rules of the Game" and "Battleship Potemkin" (not easy to do in an alpine setting, but Nicolas got it done). His small tourist audiences were dedicated and it all continued to provide him with a basic income and the freedom to explore his artistic vision. Then, in 1959, his fortunes changed when he won an award for his original film "Sexe à Midi."

Eloise had been the one to submit a copy without Nicolas's knowledge. She felt too strongly about its brilliance and, as usual, was right. Nicolas traveled to Paris to collect the award—the second highest in France for the pornographic genre—and he met for the first time his contemporaries, a slick group of mafia-connected filmmakers who churned out movies for international distribution.

It was clear why his film stood apart. Alas, none of what he encountered appealed to him, and he took the bump in earnings and buckled down on his own local work. He didn't need the headaches that came with distribution, since the audiences came to him. Instead, he bought a chalet aside his own in Les Nants and converted it into a private cinema—since the ones in town had become "respectable."

Nicolas now looked at the shot he prepared. An entire porn production right on the Mer de Glace, as they had discussed so long ago. A Bernese Mountain Dog. Sheep skins (always sheep skins). A big brass bed. A complete bar carved right into the ice.

Crystal glasses. Silver trays. A fire pit. And of course plenty of film equipment. The budget for this one had him overextended but he believed in the effort.

"The ice, it's in the way of the shot."

"What do you mean?"

"It's blocking the shot. Look at it."

"The Drus?"

"Yeah, the Drus. I can't get it in the frame. We need to adjust the location."

"We can't. We're running out of daylight."

He was right. The "golden hour" for filming was fast approaching and the set designer had arranged everything with a massive fin of ice as the backdrop, without considering the vista beyond—the Aiguille Drus, one of the most stunning mountains in the valley.

"How much time do we have?"

"An hour, tops. But there's just no way we can scout a new place, pack up, then set up again."

Nicolas did a quick calculation in his head, and picked up the radio: "Pierre, you read me? Over." Some muted discussion followed and then: "He'll be up here in 20 minutes with some dynamite. I'll put a charge on the fin. We'll remove it and save the shot. Can you get some tarps to put over the bed and pull up those skins and rugs?"

"Are you fucking crazy?"

"Do you have a better idea?" He turned. "Beatrice, darling, can you please stop feeding the birds?" He turned to one of the grips. "Can we get these fucking crows out of here!"

"But Nico, they're so cute."

"They're not cute. They're going to ruin the shot."

Pouting, Beatrice got off the bed and walked delicately in her high heels across the ice. She wore a loose, fluffy bathrobe and carried the remains of a cocktail, the contents of which she chucked to the ground. And then she was gone.

Nicolas turned and cocked his head. "Where did she go?"

The director of photography, still flustered from Nicolas's artistic vision, snapped: "What now, who?"

"Beatrice, she's gone. Where did she go? She was just right here."

Nicolas walked over to where she was and saw a gaping hole in the snow, where clearly she fell—right through a snow bridge into a crevasse. Her cocktail glass resting aside it.

"Fuck! She fell in! Call the rescue! Beatrice, can you hear me! Are you all right!"

Within 10 minutes, an Alouette 3 arrived, blowing snow and ice all over the set. It landed, dropped two rescuer workers, and lifted off again. Nicolas pointed to the hole, and the men made quick work of setting up an anchor and climbed down into the crevasse. Ten more minutes passed, and a naked Beatrice—battered and bloody but with nothing obviously broken—emerged in the arms of the man in blue.

As the men affixed her to a backboard and protected her neck, Nicolas saw that one of the men was Michel, Eloise's husband. Once Beatrice was secure and covered, Michel stood up and turned to Nicolas: "You shouldn't be out here." Nicolas nodded. "Do you understand how dangerous this is? She could have been killed."

"Will she be all right?"

"I think so. But she won't ever want to come out on the ice again. I can guarantee that."

Again, Nicolas nodded, and said: "How's Eloise?"

Michel was never a friend of Nicolas, nor an admirer of his wife's former life. "She's well. She's taking care of our son..."

The thumping returned, the helicopter landed, retrieved the men and the patient, and off they went. Everyone else remained, still shocked and standing amidst a destroyed porn set—just as the warm glow of the setting sun cast rays across the ice, no longer white, but hues of red and yellow and orange. An ache gripped Nicolas as he watched the helicopter zip down the valley. How he missed his friend.

That Michel had arrived for the rescue was no coincidence, since he covered most every call those days. The summer the Midi lift opened, Eloise had become pregnant with Michel's child. Despite his faith, he pleaded with her to have it aborted—something she refused to do. His family forever shamed her, and saw the outcome as a personal failing of hers, rather than a fault of his or even "the will of God." Still, they married, the only acceptable solution. She stayed at home, immediately confined by the duties of motherhood— her rebelliousness squashed by the conformity and social conservatism that had not only Chamonix, but the rest of France in its grips.

Michel, however, spent his days deep in the mountains, his first and only true love. The newly formed mountain rescue service, PGHM, gave him cover.

Just as the Companie des Guides de Chamonix formed in reaction to tragedy, so did the PGHM—in the aftermath of the calamity that resulted in the deaths of poor Vincedon and Henry. When the Ministry of Interior swept in to deal with the embarrassment that France had faced, there was little the local community could do but go along and try to control the outcome. After several reorganizations of the mountain safety service, the PGHM was created in 1958. Michel was among the first to sign up.

WEDNESDAY

"Eloise is dead," Lulu said to Nicolas, who looked up from his coffee in the morning sun. He shook his head in a way to ask how she knew.

"A crow?"

She nodded.

"It appears she brought a few friends along." Before Nicolas on the kitchen table sat a laptop, which he spun around to face her. "You're everywhere."

The video, entitled "WATCH: OUT-SKIING A MURDER... OF CROWS," showed, from the perspective of a hovering drone, Lulu below a large cornice watching a mesmerizing swirl of birds against the blue sky, which alone would be worth the viewing. But then, all at once, they landed on the snow, causing the avalanche from which she fled. The drone covered her virtuosic line down the steep, narrow gully and then, incredibly, up over ice and rock to plummet some 10 meters into another gully, evading the crush of snow behind her. The last shot before the avalanche plume blocked the view was Lulu plunked down next to Melanie with a crow on her head. By 8 a.m., it had more than 129,000 views.

Damn you, Melanie. "She must have uploaded that last night. It took us all day to get out of there."

"You're all right?"

"Thanks to that crow. What you don't see is that behind the avalanche were several tons of rock. Had we stayed in that line, we'd have been killed for sure."

"It was a shallow 5.4, right below Mont Blanc," Nicolas said, now pulling up an article about the quake.

There are about five earthquakes a year in Chamonix, though most are barely felt. They are usually only heard; however, they rumble along with a sound similar to that of a massive rock fall or a calving glacier, which sometimes does occasionally accompany them, though not often.

"It had to have been her. I haven't heard anything from Jean-François, have you?"

"He would never call me—"

"I'll go see him this morning." Lulu went to the counter where her phone had been charging: 443 messages, 154 missed calls, and an unimaginable number of notifications on Facebook, Snapchat and Instagram.

In her hand, the phone rang.

"Hello?" It was Josh. "No, I'm fine, thanks. It wasn't that big a deal. Yes, I've seen the numbers. Pretty crazy. No, I haven't checked the online sales. Sure, there might be a bump. Haven't really thought about it actually. People might not even make the connection. Oh, she did, did she? Leave it to Melanie to pimp me out. Definitely it is good exposure. Yep. Yep. Sure, let's meet again. Today's a bad day though. I have a lot going on. Yeah, maybe tomorrow. Give me a call. Hey, I have to go. All right, thanks. Have a good day."

Josh now assumed she was playing hard to get. He could understand that she's suddenly blown up on the internet and had some calls to make. But this type of exposure should be milked. She should be pushing it out more. Maybe she was, he thought. Maybe she was just really into the business right now. Maybe she was smarter than he expected and playing him...

Lulu left Nicolas, as she usually did those days, already into his mid-morning nap. The sky had a low ceiling, but wasn't snowing or raining. By the looks of the glow within the cloud, especially along the edges that hit the mountains, she could tell it was likely pretty clear above. 15 minutes later, she arrived at Jean-François's house.

After a knock, he came to the door in a depressed state. He had clearly been in the same clothes for days, unshaven, hair unkempt, feet bare, body odor she could smell from the door. The formality of a kiss did not occur to her.

"Bonjour, Jean-François."

"Bonjour, Lulu."

"Is Eloise here?"

"I'm sorry, Lulu," he looked now to the ground. "My mother died last month. It's not been an easy time."

Although she already knew that Eloise was gone, hearing it confirmed still gripped her in the gut. "Was...was there a funeral?"

"No."

"Okay then, where is she buried—in the cemetery, on the property somewhere?"

"She's not."

"I'm sorry, Jean-François, I don't understand."

Now he looked in her eyes. His were red and ragged. "It was the horses, Lulu. They took her. What was left, the crows came and carried her away. There was nothing left to bury. She's on the wings now."

In a moment such as this, it might have been appropriate for her to hug Jean-François. She didn't want to. And she wouldn't. She knew he was just one more man that abandoned Eloise, and so his very presence at that moment made her sick. Whatever had befallen Eloise, he must have been responsible in some manner or another. At very least, plain neglect. She took a step back from him. "I see," she said. "And the horses, where are they now?"

"They escaped."

His answers came in such a pathetic and childish manner. "What do you mean they escaped? They're gone?" He nodded, as if it was someone else's responsibility. "Does anyone know? Does the mayor know, the police?"

"They vanished."

"Those horses don't just vanish…"

"I know, I know. I assumed there would be complaints, or sightings or something. They just went up into the forest, I think, and haven't been seen again." She was at a total loss. "Excuse me one moment," he said, and went into the house, retrieved something, and returned to hand it to Lulu. "I believe this is yours. Or, well, it belongs to Nicolas. I don't want it in this house. If you don't want it, I'll throw it away." It was the film tin.

She took it, turned, and walked away without a word—in tears of pain, in tears of anger, in tears of sadness for Eloise as much as for Nicolas and herself.

★ 1 9 7 4 ★

"He was a 'fascinating transitional figure whose unique brand of sophisticated erotic art created a utopian space between the cheap grindhouse sexploitation of the '60s and the full-on hardcore porn of the '70s,'" Nicolas said in the dark while a film played on screen. He looked over to Brigitte, sitting next to him, the only other person in the cinema. "Is that too much?"

"Sounds rather smart for the obituary of a pornographer."

"If I'm not deserving, the work itself must be worthy."

"Perhaps. But does it mean that you were ahead of your time or before it."

The two sat screening an early cut of "Lifterskan," one of the latest pornographic offerings from Nicolas's Swedish acquaintance Joe Sarno. The title translated to "Butterflies", and consisted of a country girl's erotic journey to the big city.

"He's oddly precise here," Nicolas said. "Sex scene, nine minutes of story development, sex scene, nine minutes of story, sex scene—of which there are..." he counted on his pad "...six sex scenes. Why nine minutes, do you think? Why not seven or five or 12? Has he measured for the audiences' tolerance?"

"If he accounted for that, he didn't put much thought into the sex. Maybe a little more aggressive here or there. But it's a lot of the same."

"It's well shot though."

"Yes, good coloring—a nice palette—and quality sound too..."

Nicolas's last two films—"Asses and diamonds" and "Two men and a bathrobe," which came out in 1969 and 1970, respectively—had been panned for being "porn for porn's sake," a criticism he didn't quite know how to take.

Around the same time that Nicolas had taken steps to finally increase his distribution—the pull of Paris had been weak, but the friends he made there were persuasive—a series of events came along to upend his world, not unlike how the end of the war had put a pinch on his fledgling nude photography business. He had to figure out his next steps in a rapidly changing environment.

It had all kicked off in 1968.

As it turned out, the push to create a modern and dynamic France in the post-war era had torn sideways against the country's conservative, stagnating social system. The young people who had been funneled into educational institutions and taught to think modern thoughts now had modern demands: sex.

One fine spring day in May 1968, a clutch of enervated Parisian students had enough with the parietal rules that governed their lives—such as when young men and women could be together in dorm rooms—and staged a protest against the university. Tens of thousands showed up.

In a society in which the birth control pill had only been authorized for sale the year prior, the movement struck a chord, as others identified with such oppression and took it as a symbol of their own broader political and spiritual grief. The student protests grew to hundreds of thousands. And then a general worker strike also erupted—11 million workers, almost a fifth of France's workforce rose up—which altogether brought the country's economy and government to a near standstill.

During the course of six weeks, the entirety of France's social order turned inside out.

The president, de Gaulle, left the capital, buried his family jewels at Colombey-les-Deux-Églises and fled the country fearing for his safety, only to return to dissolve the government and call for elections. Oh, what fear French politicians must carry with them when millions of rioters arrive at the gates of government, since more than a few have lost their heads to enraged masses.

From the Alps, the activity captivated a ready audience. They, the children of the gods—those who sat high amidst great and otherworldly forces—took in all that played out on Paris's stage: the riots, the violence, the speeches, the strikes.

Chamoniards, just like others outside France's urban centers, contemplated the possibilities of civil war and revolution. And while they mused about the many things that might come, they uniquely knew damn well that one thing was for sure: None of it would matter to them.

Life would go on in the Haute Savoie, amidst the creatures, both savage and cursed, the hidden magic of the alpage, and the mysteries of the earth. The glaciers would still calve. The rock fall would still roar. The rhythms of their ways would grind along. And they would, as they'd always done, endure whatever weather arrived.

Sure, consternation existed in some quarters. How could it not? What would all of it come to mean for the French identity that had been regaining its confidence across its territories? For Nicolas though, the events, in all their chaos, represented something wonderful: a clear sign of hope that society after all was not crazy; that there could be openness and expression; that maybe his small efforts to entice those urban insects with his alpine honey helped pollinate the flowers of revolution. "Let the state fall apart!" he would say. "Let everyone make love."

Alas, we often pay for the success of our ideals, and Nicolas for one would pay dearly.

As French society returned to order that summer, slowly, and then all at once, the deflation of sexual repression resulted in fewer people seeking outlets for their angst whilst on holiday. No longer did people feel the need to sneak away into alleys and dark theatres to get a glimpse of skin or an assurance of sexual identity. Vacationers after a while simply didn't require his particular erotica.

But instead of stopping altogether, people—perhaps now increasingly honest with themselves—sought something more, and that something turned out to be hardcore pornography. It was a drought followed by a deluge.

Nicolas's "less is more" approach became overwhelmed by a drive for "more is more," made mainstream by two films, both of which came out in 1972: "Deep Throat" and "Behind the Green Door." These and other American films, featuring graphic sex and punchy storylines, inundated France. Audiences openly went to see them. No longer was it necessary to hide. Porn became chic, and "Behind the Green Door"—the first mainstream hardcore film to show interracial sex—even screened at the Cannes Film Festival.

It then became a race to get into hardcore. "Butterflies" officially came out the following year, along with other films that flushed out the genre—like Jean Francois Davy's "Exhibition," a graphic documentary-style film, and Danille Bellus's "Pussy Talk" (or "Le sexe qui parle"), a story of a loquacious vagina. Nicolas's other domestic competitors, like Jess Franco and Jean Rollin, also followed suit. But he resisted.

It should be no foregone conclusion that someone like Nicolas would have ever stopped for a moment to think about the implications of what he was doing—moral, ethical or otherwise—especially as he plowed ahead non-stop through the heightened state of youth and while driven by need: need for companionship, need for money, need simply for something to do.

But at that moment, confronted with the reality of change, he reflected on a tidy explanation of life events he had conceived for himself, his own version of the path he took to get where he was that day, and he decided that he was more than just an opportunistic iconoclast. If he had come this far by doing his own thing, he would continue to do so—unmoved by trends and the currents of his time.

"The one role we have," Nicolas said to Brigitte, "is to start conversations, to bring things up, to cause people to say 'You know what I saw the other day?' We lose that ability if what we do becomes offensive. We've always skirted the line, but I'm unwilling to cross over."

"Nicolas, I think your work has offended plenty of people over the years."

"You do?" he said. She rolled her eyes. "It's always possible to go further than the last film, to show a little more and to enjoy it a little less. But where does it end? The erotic I know presents sex as something enjoyable. We have for too long lived in a society in which sex is punishment. You weren't supposed to enjoy it, and if you did something was wrong. I want to stick to showing people the simple pleasures of life."

"And if no one comes to watch anymore?"

"Then we can always make horror movies."

Nicolas could see what was happening, but he remained in that moment truly optimistic. He operated on his own terms and according to what values he decided to hold. His rigidity would, however, break him—as would be expected.

He was unaware at that moment, but more change was coming.

To confront the vast inflow of American pornography, the French government would decide to tackle the problem through a series of opposing policies. It ended censorship of erotic movies and moved to protect the French porn industry by subjecting U.S. imports to very high tariffs. But to appease cultural conservatives it also denied domestic pornographers subsidies previously available to all filmmakers and then imposed new taxation on porn. There was no way Nicolas could operate in this environment. He became priced out.

But in that moment, right there in that theatre, whilst he and Brigitte mused about life and took in the latest in hardcore porn, he remained hopeful, believing that ultimately his voice would be heard. He was, in a way, happy.

"We can do as we like," he said to Brigitte, as the house lights came on. "I'm not put off that easily. I'm staying right in this valley, and I'm gonna beat this hardcore racket. I'm gonna show everybody that our work isn't in vain. We have a good vision. It's the only vision we can have—"

THURSDAY

Josh felt punchy. He had drunk his way through most of the week, only skiing a little here and there. The visibility on the valley's moderate terrain had been poor, making it difficult to get out. He had tried Les Houches, the lower valley ski area, but it was too warm and at points raining. He now had his mind fully on business, for he very much wanted something to show for this week. He had been planning for how to deal with Lulu, a reluctant seller, or possibly just a tough negotiator. He knew she must have a price in mind. He sought to apply some pressure.

"Really, this is all just so great. Have you looked at your latest numbers? I bet online sales have gone through the roof," Josh said in reference to the video.

Lulu hadn't checked the numbers. "Yeah, I'm sure it'll make for a nice bump."

"If you had marketing support, you could really make something of this, really push it, you know? Aside from what your friend did, there isn't much brand association. That's too bad. Lost sales—"

"Not really worried about it. Sticking a logo on that video would've killed it." She relaxed back into the couch. "So, you didn't get much skiing in?"

Subject change, Josh thought. *Curious.* "No, not really. The weather hasn't been that accommodating. But you—and I have to be honest here—you really are a hell of a skier. I didn't expect that. Sure, local girl. You must know what you're doing. But all that on the video, it looked really...professional."

"Thanks," Lulu said, not really sure if it was a compliment. "That couloir isn't the most technically demanding. The entrance is a bit funny. The first section is tight. After that it opens up. We just went out to have some fun. We weren't trying to prove anything."

"It must all be so extreme, like one constant rush. You're just hurling yourself down the mountain like that. To go so fast you can outrun an avalanche. I guess that's why they call Chamonix the 'death-sport capital of the world.'"

Lulu bit her tongue. She loathed this expression. "I'd say it's more about risk management to be honest. The goal, every time, is to live to ski another day. To live to climb another day. To fly another day. To enjoy what's there. We're really not looking for out-of-control speed or to put ourselves in dangerous situations."

"Yeah, but you're, like, driven to do it, right? It's all pretty dangerous no matter what. You need that rush. To get out there and go for it. All these 'death sports...'" Josh laughed and sipped his coffee, and, as he did, eyed her reaction.

"You know, it really isn't like that at all."

"Oh, sure. Playing it cool. Just like mulling my proposal. Live fast, die young, isn't that it? Not concerned with all the details."

"Look, I can appreciate that from the outside, you have this impression—the adrenaline, the adventure, the whatever. You're just drinking your own Kool-Aid. It's mostly misperception derived from marketing and advertising, the kind you and your peers push..."

"That I push? What, Cham'porn isn't hardcore? Cham'porn isn't the kind of brand to push the boundaries of taste and reality?"

"No, it's just the opposite. You're looking at it for what you want it to be. You're missing why it's become what it is."

"Bah, you're just pushing another extreme, Lulu. That whole Red Bull attitude..."

"Anyone who goes into the mountains with a can of Red Bull is a joke. Anyone who doesn't take the risks seriously is going to die." Lulu sat up. "What you're missing is that here, there's an ethic behind everything. It's not about what you do. Ski, fly, climb, run. It's not about how well you do it. It's about how you do it. How clean your line is. How clean your climbing is. How clean your product is. People aren't buying Cham'porn because of the sex, because there is no sex. You only want it to be there because you think all skiers and climbers are tribes of happy boys romping off on exciting adventures..."

"Oh yeah, I forgot to tell you. I figured it out..."

Lulu, cut off, blinked and blinked. Had he heard her?

"We need to blow out this whole porn element. We need to blow out the backstory ourselves, make it much more elaborate. I don't know why I didn't see this before. It'll just be a matter of manipulating online search results—"

"Josh, the raw cynicism you have for the very people you are trying to sell products to clearly shows just how far you're out of touch you are with what your consumer wants. That's why you're failing. That's why nothing's working. You should be defending the city spinner, the yoga professional, not exploiting them. Clothing is intimate, and people care about what they put on their body..."

Josh, about to butt in, stopped. Lulu wouldn't let him.

"...That's why people like my brand. This is not some carpe diem, ski-for-the-day, bullshit mentality. We, here, in this place, we're not here to ski for the day. Those who live here—who actually live here—we ski for life. For generations. Our families have become bound with the mountains around us. Our bodies end up in this ground. Our souls haunt those hills. There's a world that exists here, right in front of you, that you can't even see. There's a heritage here, one of myth and madness, and you visitors ride in, do your thing, and head back into your lives oblivious to what's really at work. But it's our lot—to live with that knowledge of both sides of this place, and to live with the inevitable deaths. It's what we owe to those who came before us, who survived the harsh, impoverished hellscape this valley once was, so there could be food on our tables, so we can enjoy it for ourselves today."

The two of them sat silent.

Lulu realized she had crossed a line—not with decorum, but with simply being open to an outsider, someone not from Chamonix. She was right, though. Chamoniards, better than anyone, understand commitment—to place, to each other, to life. Their outlook is geologic, and they know well how impermanent humanity is against everything else. Little time is given to those who don't have respect for that. They will think twice before selling property to an outsider—even to other French, in many cases refusing a high offer from foreigners— and will never, ever show you their mushroom patch. But they will save your life and respect your hard work if you show it. Lulu now sat uncomfortably, her words floating before her.

Josh smiled within, believing that he had cracked her.

"That's all well and good," he said, "but the influence of commercialism is as powerful as the weather. It has the potency of politics and the force to do great things, if you let it. Lulu, you can buzz all you want, but if you're not pollinating flowers, you're not upholding your role in what you describe, in spreading that understanding. We can turn Cham'porn into something worthy."

She wasn't really listening anymore. "Give me more time. Another day or two. I need to sort a few things out."

Josh knew he had her hooked, and conceded easily: "I don't think I have a choice."

She now just spoke in a daze: "Look, I have a friend, a guide, he's British, who can take you out to do a Vallée Blanche tomorrow. It will be a beautiful day, and will give you a real sense of the place. He'll call you this afternoon, just make sure you're there early tomorrow." She then reached in her bag.

"Here." She threw a Cham'porn hat at him, a red tweed Phrygian cap. "Wear it proudly. Go ski. We'll talk."

★ **1977** ★

"The last time I saw him..." Eloise said to the gendarme who had stopped by to see her at the horse pen in Les Bossons "...was a few weeks ago. Is there something wrong?"

"Well, the chalet next to his—the cinema—it burned to the ground. We just want to notify him and ask a few questions."

"Oh my, he doesn't know?" She stood on the inside of the pen next to one of the horses, gently patting its long nose. "Did you hear that? The cinema burned down," she said to the horse. "Nico doesn't know."

The gendarme realized he had just entered a special situation. "Ahh, well, we're not sure. He wasn't present when the firemen arrived, and no one has seen him since. This occurred last night."

"And you don't know what caused the fire? Was anyone hurt?" She turned to the horse and whispered: "I hope no one was hurt."

"No, ma'am, no one was injured. And we don't yet have a cause. The whole place is gone though, right to the ground. Nothing left."

"I'm sure he'll be devastated. He loved that place." She turned to the horse: "Didn't he."

"That time you saw him last. How was he?"

"What do you mean?"

"Like what state was he in?"

"Normal, I'd say."

This was not true—not true at all. The last time she had seen Nicolas, he had been in a bit of a frenzy. She had wandered up to his house in Les Nants, and found him sitting at the kitchen table surrounded by newspapers and books—all over his lap, all over the floor. A young woman was outside sunning herself. He jumped straight into conversation.

"Eloise, the worldwide tourist industry must end its dangerous overexploitation of the environment," he said, and he threw down the paper he was reading.

"Bonjour."

"The tourists, there are too many. They are destroying us. Destroying Chamonix. Destroying the world. It must stop. We are shirking our responsibility of safeguarding our resources. Instead, we've become the great spoliator."

"What's a spoliator?"

"Those who destroy, Eloise," he said. "We must stop the depredations of mass tourism. No more tourists."

She'd have considered his behavior manic if she hadn't known him for so long. His years of frustration from shouting at the world about so many various things had given way to plain rage. She herself had been taking mushrooms regularly these days and so could more than accommodate his behavior, and just listened while enjoying the sun glinting off the dew on the grass.

"Do you know how many beaches in France have been classified as a 'D'?" She shook her head. "Thirty-seven. That's a 'D,' Eloise. Polluted and over-populated. One hundred forty-four more have been given a 'C,' putting them just on the edge. It's all over France. Just like the Lascaux Caves in the Dordogne— closed for the same reason since '72. May never be open again. I never even got a chance to see them. But it's not just France. Same with the Altamira caves in Spain. More prehistoric wall paintings, gone. Pompeii is being ruined. Pompeii for fuck sake, Eloise. How the fuck do you ruin ruins? Vandals, that's how. And weeds. The people who show up don't care. The people who take care of it don't care. All over that country are buildings and antiquities deteriorating due to pollution. And I look out into our little valley, and it's the same."

She swung around to look at the view, and all she saw was a pleasant spring day. He could see she was unimpressed.

"It's invisible, Eloise. Invisible. But it's killing us all the same."

"Well, what are we going to do?"

"I'll tell you what we do. The Brits, they've proposed a tax on tourists, so they stop clogging up London. In West Germany, a bunch of ecologists have called for a stop to development on waterfronts. In the U.S., they're creating a bill of rights for tourism, enumerating tourist responsibilities. But all that's a joke. We need to fight. We need to take the fight to the tourists."

Eloise swung back to look at him. "You want some mushrooms?"

"Yes, I do."

And that was that. She hadn't seen him since.

"Have you ever been up here before?" Eloise said to the gendarme. "Have you ever been introduced to the horses?"

"Oh, no ma'am."

"Want to come into the pen?" She turned to the horse. "Want to meet the nice gendarme? Do you?"

"No. I mean, no, thank you. I...ah, I must be going."

"He's really friendly."

"Thank you for your time, ma'am. If you think of anything, let us know."

"Okay then. Come back any time," and she smiled a dark smile, and he hurried along.

FRIDAY

Now pushing 90, Nicolas had become more objectively handsome than he'd probably ever been in his life. The aging that took its toll on most everyone else treated him rather well—softening the hard features and wrinkling over the inconsistencies. It helped that he had never spent much time in the sun.

Few people saw him these days, however. Only at the market from time to time, where he'd pick up this or that. Often going just to have a chat with Eloise. He made for a humorous sight, a codger kitted out head-to-toe in Cham'porn clothing.

But at this point, almost no one knew who he was, and that suited him just fine. He had had a lifetime of winks and leers, finger-pointing and jeers—periods when he had been considered an outright threat, and for good reason. He had gone from enfant terrible to bête noire to, finally, inconnu. He'd gone from the boy with dirty photos to the dangerous man about town, to, finally, Lulu's grandfather...or uncle...or whatever he was, they said.

On this afternoon, he passed his time at home watching online ski videos made by locals, some amateur, some professional. Most of them Lulu's friends.

He often these days took thrills in seeing young people climb into the craggy mountains and venture down snowy slopes. He would pore over maps of the Mont Blanc range to find the col or couloir or glacier being explored—sometimes the print so tiny he'd have to use a large magnifying glass to read the names amidst the contour lines; sometimes asking Lulu for a little help. Then he'd write his latest find into a notebook with a bygone cursive compelled by a shaky hand—what to anyone would just appear to be a list of families from Chamonix: Devouassoud, Lachenal, Payot, Ravanel, Simond, Tournier, Trappier...

It's how he made up for his regrets. That other world never ceased to exist next to his own, his whole life, a world he could glimpse—and often did, fleetingly—but would never know. Only maturity allowed him the ability to find acceptance in knowing that at his age he was well past those years in which he could only blame himself for not taking the initiative.

Where usually these videos would lead Nicolas to a place of wonder, stoking that old imagination all day, today they led him to a place of reflection on other times that had evoked that same charged feeling of thrill and regret.

He recalled in those early days, whilst he and Eloise were writing that initial script, a night when she stopped by the back room where he stayed before a town dance—all dressed up, intoxicating in appearance and scent. No, he would spend the night working. He didn't know how to dance anyhow. Besides, he'd not been invited, just a youth on the fringe of their small society, never schooled, never socialized. A damn shame, she said, and she put on some music, rolling through the radio stations to find something slow. Together they danced, just for a moment, with Eloise leading a clumsy Nicolas, and then she would go.

He recalled the day Eloise informed him that she was pregnant and that she damn well was too going to keep it. He didn't understand then basic biological limitations. For now, the decision is in my hands, she told him, but for sure someday it won't be anymore, and then I might fear I made a mistake. She clung to that child and that marriage, trusting that it would work out in the way the world told her it would. Eloise would remain steadfast in her devotion to Michel, waiting for him to return to her. She sacrificed her own life before the others.

And he recalled a fearful and fragile Eloise showing up at his door the night of the Montroc avalanche. She swung between sobbing and elation. She didn't have to hide her feeling of liberation from Nicolas. She also didn't have to hide her realization that it didn't matter for her, that now it was too late. In her 60s then, she was stuck in a rut—life in a valley, narrow and tall. She stayed that night, for the only time in their lives, and he held her passionless but caring. She left before he awoke.

From his seat in Les Nants, Nicolas looked on Chamonix—the sun glowed through the clouds, highlighting the layer of wood-fire smoke hanging over the town. She wouldn't be at the market tomorrow, never again. He would not either. His eyes swelled with tears that ran down his face, pouring down on his shirt. Eventually, he fell to sleep in his chair. He didn't see the black crow that came to rest by the window for a time. It looked for food. It looked for him.

Later, Lulu wandered in. He awoke hastily from his nap at the noise.

"Oh, hello. Has your week calmed down?" He tried to seem like he hadn't been sleeping, sitting up in his chair. She pretended not to notice that he had been.

"It's getting there."

"Have you made a decision?"

Lulu puttered about the kitchen, putting some groceries away. "I don't know. I'm just not sure it's right. I'll meet him again tomorrow...maybe. I feel like I'm succeeding with it as it is. But this opportunity seems like success as well. I can't tell which I want. And there's too much other shit clouding everything right now."

"Then why still entertain the conversation?"

"I don't know if this opportunity will come again."

Nicolas got up, walked over to her and kissed her on the forehead. "You can't make any mistakes, Lulu. If you think it's there, go for it. If it turns out bad, let it go. Your commitment should be to yourself and what you believe in, not to someone else's ideas."

She nodded. He bid her good night and went off to his side of the house.

Now, finally alone for the first time all week, the last thing Lulu wanted to do was sift through all that had happened. Though the thoughts and pangs came percolating up to fill the silence and empty space. Avoidance seemed like a much better plan at that moment. She sorted mail, did some laundry, then came across that film canister sitting on the counter. She picked it up, and flicked open the side locks. *Maybe we have a look...*

★ 1 9 8 8 ★

"You blew up the Midi station, didn't you?" Eloise said to Nicolas as he closed the car door.

"Bonjour," he said.

"It was you."

"Do we have to discuss this now?"

"I knew it," and she put the car in drive and pulled out of the Maison d'Arrêt, a low-security prison in Bonneville, a city down from Chamonix towards Geneva. For the next 10 minutes neither of them spoke.

"What if you had killed someone?"

"We could have gone over this while I was in."

"I didn't think it was safe. And I was...busy."

"For five years, you were busy. I suppose I should be pleased at least someone came to pick me up." She didn't look at him or speak, just kept driving. "No one died. No one was hurt," he said.

"You're saying that was an acceptable risk?"

"No one died."

"Damn it, Nicolas, you could have been killed."

"I wouldn't have."

"How do you know?"

"I practiced."

And practiced he had, with dynamite obtained from the pisteurs for avalanche regulation.

One breezy evening in August 1982, Nicolas—emotionless but determined—set out for Switzerland. He drove down the winding mountain road to Martigny, then up the valley, over between the villages of Saxon and Charrot, to a vineyard road called Crettaz-Ballaz. He had scouted the ground. The secluded, single lane offered good access to get to a 50-meter pylon supporting high-tension wires that stood not far from where he'd park, and from where he would have several options for a getaway.

He determined that this type of pylon was similar in size, shape and strength as those that carried the cable car lines up to the Aiguille du Midi. He needed to understand what it would take to destroy one. His knowledge was only good for blowing up the cable cars, and he'd be damned if he was going to fail at his own plan now. But he just hadn't been trained for such a large structure. How much explosive to use. Where to place it optimally. The best distance for detonation.

He discovered it wasn't all that difficult.

The explosion thundered across the valley, and before his ears adjusted to the deafening shock, a shriek of twisting steel met him. The pylon tilted, more slowly than he expected, and dragged down the wires, which sparked and buzzed. Just as the pylon seemed to stop, the top of another pylon, 100 meters away, snapped off, and the jolt reverberated down the line until the first metal structure lay down on its side.

Nicolas escaped into the growing darkness. Not only was he not caught, disgruntled local farmers were blamed for the destruction. They had a history of such behavior, and a recent downturn in the fruit and vegetable market had caused protests, which pointed authorities to the usual suspects. The result emboldened Nicolas.

Well, that is until the practicalities of his main plan came into full view.

The three pylons that support the lower section of the Midi lift are arranged on steep or high ground, making them fairly tricky to get to. No easy access. No easy escape. Unlike the drive-in, drive-out Swiss affair, Nicolas was, once again, faced with a considerable amount of hiking while hauling a heavy pack at night—which, at 18, was one thing, but at 55 was another entirely. He had only ever worked out in his younger years to look good, and that was before the recreational drug use began. Vanity did cling to him; however, it offered nothing that would make his life easier at that moment.

What he really wanted to do was blow up the Mont Blanc tunnel, a logistically easier target and the primary aggressor against the valley in Nicolas's imagination. Although the move would be intended as symbolic—setting up a fight between the town and the national government, while drawing international attention that could not be hidden away—there were legitimate reasons as well: From the tunnel, air pollution pours into the valley, making Chamonix at times one of the most polluted places in all of Europe. In that, the destruction could serve two purposes. But his plan just wasn't going to be. Security was too tight and traffic too heavy.

He had to settle for his old nemesis, the Midi lift, which he rationalized as a direct attack on the tourists; but in the end, he couldn't even accomplish that.

August became September. He plotted. September became October. And October saw a pretty heavy early snow—one that made his plan for the pylon all too treacherous. So he continued to wait, and continued to seethe, all through a bitter cold winter that kept him confined in a near-hibernation state. He'd pass the time taking drugs and, as he had in his youth, watching the same films over and over and over, a mania-inducing cycle.

Finally, in late May 1983, he emerged from Chalet Largot after midnight—a groggy and grumpy old bear stumbling into town—and from the back of his little Peugeot 103 unloaded as much dynamite as he could into the Midi lift base station, right in town. This, he figured, could not be ignored, and if done correctly would destroy the housing, a cable car, and take down the lines. He'd just have to use a lot more dynamite.

While Nicolas intuitively grasped that there would be an exponential increase in kinetic energy resulting from additional sticks of dynamite—as anyone would—he failed to consider that dynamite had changed over the years, to be both safer and more sophisticated. He unwittingly loaded directional blasters that would mostly fail to trigger due to a safety mechanism. He expected a truly mighty roar, but from a distance of 30 meters, Nicolas only managed to knock himself unconscious and cause minor damage to the station—a fact he was informed of upon waking up handcuffed to a hospital bed.

"I basically did them a favor," Nicolas explained to Eloise, avoiding any details about the mishandling of the explosives or time in the hospital. She always assumed he got nabbed for porn-related indecency, and he didn't want to worry her, or further embarrass himself. "Turns out, they desperately needed funds for the lift that the government wouldn't provide. And since no one was injured, I got a lesser sentence on a different charge. They got the insurance money, and some workers got the public blame for mishandling the storage of the explosives."

"I knew you were involved—somehow. And how was it, your time?"

"I spent five years shitting in a hole in the corner of my cell, while two other men watched. I failed to create any change. I failed to create awareness. I have no family. No lover. No career anymore. No one watches my films. No prospects. No pride. I have nothing to show for myself, except sobriety and a criminal record."

"Do you want me to bring you home?"

"No, I need a drink."

"I can understand that, but are you...allowed?"

"Yes, Eloise, I'm allowed to have a drink. I just need to lay low. For a long, long time. No more porn. No more drugs. No more burning things down or blowing things up." He looked out the window to the valley to which he now returned. "Will you join me for one, so I can hear about what you've been up to?"

"I can't. I...I have to get back. Easter weekend and all."

"Right, family. I've heard all I need to. Just drop me in town. I'll figure something out."

Nicolas hadn't been in a Chamonix bar in more than two decades, and didn't bother to search far from where Eloise left him. At 9 in the morning, he entered the first place he found. There was only one other person in there—a young guy with long bleach blond hair hanging down over shaved sides—a smashed Mohawk—wearing a dirty blue and pink jumpsuit. Alone, he sat with his head down, face in a beer. When Nicolas pulled up, the guy looked up with a big toothy smile, one that barely masked fatigue and what appeared to be premature world-weariness.

"Howdy," the guy smiled. "I mean, bon-jour," and lifted his half-filled beer glass at Nicolas.

"Bonjour," Nicolas replied. The bartender came over. Nicolas nodded to the guy's beer and that's what he was served

"Looks like it's just us, enjoying the morning!" the guy said, amused with himself. "Oh, hey, I'm sorry. Do you speak American?" And he laughed again.

Nicolas nodded. "I do."

"OK, cool. Sorry, I know it's early, just I'm a little intense. Was up all night, a bit jumpy. Thought we'd be skiing this morning, so I just kept partying through the night. Turns out, just a bunch of rain. No good for making turns!" And he laughed.

"Rain down here, snow up there," Nicolas said.

"True man. This is a wild place. You live here, you a local?"

Nicolas nodded.

"You must be a hell of a skier if you grew up here."

Nicolas shrugged.

"Ah, all you French are modest about it. Bet you'd been up on some big walls there, skiing and climbing and shit. Stuff we only dream of back home. We'd never be allowed up there."

He reached over with his glass for a clink.

"Oh right, I'm supposed to say, 'santé.' What are we cheers-ing to? What good news do you got. What's the good word, man?"

Nicolas looked into his drink and said: "I just got out of prison."

"Ho shit, man! How long were you in for, when did you get out?"

"Five years. Just this morning."

"Motherfucker," the guy said slowly. "Well, I'll be. That's a fucking long time, man. You know what, I'm supposed to be in right now myself."

The rapidity of the man's speech confused Nicolas. "Sorry, what do you mean?"

"I had a run in with the law. Got pinched. Got caught with some mushrooms. You know mushrooms, right? Yeah, well, you might pick them all over the hills here, but in the good old U-S-of-A they are ill-e-gal. Nabbed me when I was helping a buddy change a flat tire on his car. Statie pulled over, looked inside, and—bam!"

"You did not go to jail?"

The man looked around conspiratorially. "I left the country. Ha! Ran away to France." He finished his drink. "I am looking at like seven years. Can't do it. Just can't do it. That's why I'm here. Well, that and to ski. Love to ski man. Love the bumps. But you all got some fucking gnarly steeps up there too."

"You won't get in trouble?"

"If I go back, yeah, I'm done. Tryin' to stay out of trouble. Tryin'. Ain't easy, man. This place is like a playground, and you know what? I like to play." He laughed again. "But you're free now. We're free. Free like butterflies. Free on the winds. Enjoy that." And he motioned for another round.

For a moment, they both sat silently, but not awkwardly— Nicolas trying to add up what this guy had said so far, and the guy trying to just keep his shit together.

"You know," Nicolas said finally, "butterflies get trapped in the ice sometimes. The winds from the valley, the thermals, push them high up into the mountains. Maybe they want escape. Maybe they have no choice. But sometimes they reach even the summit of Mont Blanc. Sometimes, in the right conditions, they get frozen into the glacial ice, like insects in amber. They keep their color, and in the ice look alive. Then they move with the ice, down and down, unable to escape, pulled back into the valley, until the ice melts and they fall to pieces back into the earth."

"Fuck, man. That's fuck-ing deep. They always die then, even when trying to be free."

Nicolas thought for a moment. "Not always. My father once told me that he had seen butterflies thaw from the glacier and simply fly away. Just trapped temporarily, for some reason. A lot of strange forces at work."

"You like a poet or something?"

"No."

"So what are you?"

Nicolas thought for a beat. "I'm an anarchist. Or maybe, you say, an activist."

"That's cool, man. You an activist for butterflies?"

"Ah, no," Nicolas now laughed.

"What do you fight for?"

"I don't remember. I don't think I knew what I wanted. I only knew how to get it."

"Yeah, how's that?"

"Destroy society."

"I take it that didn't work out so great."

"No, not really."

The guy reached out his hand and the men shook. "Good for you. One way or the other, you have to stand up for what you believe in. Problem is, I believe in skiing, and there ain't no skiing in prison."

"That's all you do, skiing?"

"Yeah, and I guess I'm making movies now too. That's really why I'm here. Some chick broke her back up there, and I'm replacing her in a movie my buddy's filming."

"You make movies?"

"Yeah, I mean, I'm just in them. The talent, you know." And he laughed.

"I've made a few movies up there."

"No shit. Ski movies?"

"Alpine...ah, alpine movies. I tried to do my own thing. They fell out of favor. It's how things go."

"Yeah, it's not easy. My buddy is putting fucking rock music in his. Not like that Warren Miller shit. Trying something different. Like ski porn, or some shit like that. Wonder if anyone'll watch it." Nicolas snorted in his drink, and the guy went on: "You just gotta think for yourself. But be ready for opportunities to come your way, and don't be afraid to take them. That's what I'm learning."

They both sat on that a moment, and then the guy said: "Okay, you're a filmmaker, you have any advice?"

"Sure," Nicolas said, "keep it safe, keep it local and, above all else, leave a little for the imagination."

SATURDAY

Lulu rushed to the Chamonix hospital, where she had been summoned urgently. She had had to shut the store, even though she'd only just arrived.

"Where is he?" she asked a desk nurse, who pointed down the hall.

When she entered the room a cadre of doctors and rescue workers stood around the bed. They looked to her.

"He's with you?"

"Yes, what happened?"

"He was on the ice, the Mer de Glace. He took a nasty fall, but that's not the worst of it. He's only now just regaining consciousness."

She looked down at the bed, where Josh lay, head bandaged and neck stabilized, arm hooked up to an IV. She shook her head. "This is all my fault." She looked up to Miles, her friend the guide.

"He came to stop in the wrong place," Miles said. "The fall wasn't what got him though."

"Weren't you out yesterday? He's just getting to the hospital now?"

The group exchanged furtive looks.

"We were out all night."

"You didn't have a radio, no phone, nothing?"

"We did. And the rescue came. We were just in the ice, deep in the ice, all night trying to get him back."

"Get him back?" They again all gave each other looks. "What?"

"They took him. They took him deep. We had to fight to get him back."

Josh began to rouse, blurry-eyed and groggy. A group of people stood over him all speaking French. He couldn't figure out where he was.

"You're all right. You're going to be all right," Lulu said.

He had to fight his aching head to find the memories of what had happened. Few came. "I was skiing, and…I fell. It was all blue and black and cold." He shut his eyes tight.

The door opened, and the priest from Saint-Michel entered—an old man named Guillaume, who everyone called Père William. Balding and serious, he said hello to the room, shaking hands, and then went to Josh and put a hand on his head. He looked in Josh's eyes, now open, and to the group. "He seems okay."

"Why is there a priest here?" Josh said.

"Relax, my son. You're going to be fine."

Josh now could feel aches all over his body.

The group continued to speak in French, which Josh could not understand.

"Any bites?" the priest asked the doctor.

"No, just a few claw marks. Scratches, really. He was pretty well covered in ski gear."

"I fell in a crevasse," Josh said.

"Yes," Lulu said to him. "You're in the hospital now. You're safe."

"It was so dark down there. So cold. I remember the water dripping on me."

"Are you sure about this?" she asked Miles.

"Ask them," he said pointing to the two rescue workers. They nodded: "He definitely got dragged in there."

"I thought I was going to die down there," Josh said. "I saw such strange things."

"Do you know how many?" Père William asked Miles.

"Two, at least."

Memories continued to percolate. "I think I saw...a monkey," Josh said.

All eyes turned to Josh, and everyone said in rough unison: "Nooo, no, no. No monkeys." Josh pulled his eyes tight again.

In French, Lulu said: "Oh good, now he knows."

A knock at the door, and in walked the mayor, Luc, a chummy, athletic, middle-aged man, who said "Hello" and shook hands with everyone and kissed Lulu cordially. In French: "So is this our latest victim?" The doctor nodded. "He going to survive?" The doctor nodded. "He recall any of it?"

"He's just getting to that now," said Lulu.

"He here with friends, family?"

"He's here to see me. For business. I sent him up with Miles to do a V-B."

"Business, nice," the mayor said. "Expanding?"

"He wants to invest in Cham'porn."

"Oh, really," the Luc said. "To grow the brand?"

"We're still working on it. It's complicated."

"If he wants to invest, create more jobs here that's wonderful."

"He's interested in the pornography."

"Not the clothes?"

"Yes, the clothes, but as a function of its...history. Can we focus on the monkeys, please?"

The mayor thought for a moment. "Does anyone know the last time this happened?"

"Only sightings," Père William said. "A local in November, and that American runner last summer."

"I've never heard of an attack before."

"There have been a few," the priest said. "Some have been claimed as falls or other things. When they disappear."

"Disappear? There have been abductions? You know, you all have to do a better job keeping my office informed of these things."

"It's all written down," Père William said. "Maybe try coming to church some time…"

While the crowd around his bed bantered and bickered, Josh kept recalling the details of his ordeal. First the fall. He had been enjoying himself, following the guide down the glacier, and then, without realizing it, started tumbling into darkness. He'd take a hard hit, come to rest, and then slip and fell further and further.

The suddenness of it left few registered thoughts. His breath left him. His senses left him. When he finally came to a stop, he found himself so deep he could barely make out light from above. He must have been 30 meters down at that point. The glacier cracked and dripped.

To Josh, it felt as if he had broken his left arm. Pain radiated from his shoulder. His lower body was bruised, and he strained to kick off the one ski that remained on his boot. He screamed for help. Nothing. He screamed again and again. Nothing. Now, with eyes adjusted, he could see better where he sat—on a small ledge next to a dark abyss. He scrambled back from it and knocked his ski over. It clattered against the sides a few times, but he never heard it hit bottom.

A sickening despair rose up within him, and his breathing began to accelerate. He screamed again, and again. All that he could hear was the dripping, that incessant dripping. Like rain in his throbbing ears. Sloshing. Ice sliding.

Josh reached for his phone: No Service. "Fuck, fuck, fuck. Fuck me!"

When he could not scream anymore, he sat back against the cold wall, grasping tight his left arm, and he felt it—something else. A presence. He felt he was being watched. But not by something from above. From below, from the darkness. He tried to scoot back further, clumsy in his ski boots. It caused a wincing pain. He couldn't see anything there. Among the dripping and sloshing, he now could hear scratching. And then, trying to squint into the darkness, he saw shapes, maybe, darker than dark. "Oh, come on. No, what is this. Come on. Fuck off!"

He pulled himself into as tight a ball as he could, but the position put him off balance and he slipped out. He grasped for the ice, for something to hold onto. He had purchase but now as he moved, painfully, to pull his leg back in he felt a tug. He turned, and there a hairy arm reaching up from the dark grasped his boot.

The scream Josh let out at this—shrill and from the deepest part of his soul—was the one that final caught the attention of Miles who had been searching for where Josh had fallen in. The creature didn't retreat, however. A second hairy arm came up as Josh tried to yank his leg away. He kept slipping toward the edge. He kicked and kicked, as painful as it all was, just kept slipping, and then another arm, and another, and then the bottom fell out and he fell, weightless into the dark. Toward the light he looked, his last memory was the silhouette of a monkey falling down on top of him.

Now Josh looked around the hospital room with fear. "Who are these people, Lulu? Who is he?"

Lulu looked over, and said nonchalantly, "He's the mayor."

"Why is the mayor here?"

"Oh," Lulu thought. "He does this for everyone. Rest now, please." She could see the look in his eyes and turned to the doctor: "He might need some sedative or something…"

"Look," the British guide said in French, "wild animals, zombie monkeys, whatever they are—if this keeps happening, if this gets out, it'll cause a panic. We've been having too many bad winters. It'll drive business away."

"Worse," said Luc. "Paris will come in and shut us down. The mountain will be off limits for who knows how long. Tourists won't put up with that. And this place will turn into a circus."

"I fear this is our fault," said Père William. "We could try another exorcism."

"With all due respect, father, we all think the church has done enough with its little stunts. It would be nice if we could get cold winters again—"

"Climate change isn't our fault," he said defensively.

"It's that Mary Shelley who cursed us," said a PGHM worker. "She foretold this."

Luc said: "Look, I don't care who's responsible for creating these little monsters. We need to figure out how to deal with them quietly, or at least figure out a way to keep them away from people. How many of these monkeys are we talking about anyway?"

"By our count," said the other PGHM worker, "we're looking at about 150 unaccounted for."

"I think everyone here is incentivized to keep it quiet," said Mayor Luc. "I mean, how the hell we managed to get away with those damn man-eating horses I'll never know."

"There's another problem." They all turned to Lulu. "Les chevaux des Bossons—they've escaped."

"You have got to be joking," Luc said. "When did this happen?"

"I don't know. After Eloise passed away? You'll need to ask Jean-François. It could have been weeks ago. He said he was waiting for complaints, but there's been none I guess."

"We haven't heard anything," said a PGHM worker.

"Nothing odd that we've seen," said the doctor.

Père William shrugged.

"This," said Luc, "may turn out to be another *Annus horribilis* for Chamonix."

Lulu looked to Josh, who was now asleep, and then to the room's window, where outside a black crow came to rest.

★ **1 9 9 5** ★

Of the hundred or so ways to die in Chamonix, the least common is being killed by an elephant. But it happens, and it is just what took Lulu's parents in the summer of 1995.

The previous death-by-elephant was in Sallanches, just down the next valley, in 1957, when a circus elephant swatted an abusive handler with its trunk, breaking most every bone in the man's body, including his skull.

Prior to that, it was in 218 BCE, when the Carthaginian general Hannibal led 37 elephants across the Alps, taking a path not too far from Chamonix. It would be impossible to say exactly who or even how many people those African pachyderms killed, but the Roman writers Polybius and Livy account for dozens.

Indirectly, Hannibal's elephants also resulted in the deaths of Marie and David, who had been rock climbing in the Aiguille Rouge one warm, cloudless summer morning.

Although the crossing of the Alps took place some 2,000 years ago, the sheer audacity of Hannibal's military feat has continued to be celebrated and studied. Which is why several wealthy Russian patrons paid for a young elephant to be sent to Geneva for a conference of international scholars studying the particulars of alpine military exploits. It was an extravagant laugh in the midst of a warming economy; yet when the conference ended, no one quite knew what to do with this elephant on the shores of Lake Geneva.

Though one audacious Chamoniard had an idea.

Without hesitation, the Merlet Animal Park in Les Houches acquired the young elephant so to gain an edge on Madame Champignon's exotic exhibit of carnivorous horses. While they had long ago brought in ibex and chamois to supplement their llamas, the Merlet Animal Park's natural display continued to be no competition for rare, deadly equine. The elephant would change all that.

For several seasons, the "Hannibal in the Alps" exhibit proved to be a considerable draw (effectively irking Madame Champignon). Children and parents alike loved to snap photos of the pachyderm, now named "Hannibal," against the backdrop of snowy Mont Blanc.

But while it was good for business, it wasn't so good for the animal. The park did treat the elephant with superb care, but elephants are social creatures and they require the company of their own species, lest they become bored and lonely. In some cases, they become bored and angry, which is what happened one morning after a night the animal spent terrified during a lightning storm.

Because the escape took place so early in the day, it was several hours before anyone at the park realized what had happened. In fact, it wasn't recognized until the owner received a phone call from a shopkeeper in the center of Chamonix informing him that his elephant had just made its way through and was heading toward Les Praz along the river.

The response was swift; however, Hannibal the elephant proved to be rather elusive. He kept along the riverside footpath until reaching Les Praz, where he took to the hills and climbed the access road to the top of the Flégère telecabine, and kept going up toward Lac Blanc on the Tour du Mont Blanc trail.

Certainly, a PGHM helicopter could have made quick work of the situation. Unfortunately, the numerous emergency calls that were placed to alert the rescue service were written off as pranks, and the animal had to be tracked on foot.

What the mad crowd actually intended to do with the animal once they caught up with it was a different and unanswered question entirely. No one was prepared to deal with an escaped elephant. They just knew they had to get after it.

It was at about this point in the chase, when Marie and David were two-thirds the way up a climbing route called "Les Fée des Druides (The fairies of the Druids)" on Les Chéserys—a long cliff band above the village of Argentière well up the Chamonix valley. As with mountaineering, the dangers of climbing are obvious and the same: falling upon something, and something falling upon you. For Marie and David, these dangers would be no different.

Tragically, as Hannibal the elephant made his way along the Tour du Mont Blanc, confused, afraid and exhausted, with an irate crowd at his heels, he ran out of room to make his escape. Lacking keen eyesight, the poor animal lost his footing on the narrowing and rocky path, and he clear tumbled right off the cliff-side.

Marie and David may as well have been hit by a massive rock fall, and if they had even a moment to ponder what was coming their way they most definitely would have assumed it was that. No, sadly, it was a rogue elephant that took them out.

When the chase group stumbled up to the edge and peered over to see what occurred, the disbelief that engulfed them collectively resulted in only a few people even being able to utter "Les chevaux…" with no one quite able to audibly finish the phrase. The shock of having lost the elephant was too much.

It took another hour for them to climb around and then down to where the elephant came to rest.

The animal did not splatter, as one would assume a body that size would after taking a 30-meter fall. It just resembled a large pile of wrinkly gray flesh—sickening and bizarre all the same.

However, upon closer inspection, the spectacle took on an even more surreal dimension, because out from underneath the hulking corpse stuck two legs, at the end of which was a pair of women's climbing shoes. Also from under the elephant was a length of rope, which the group followed over the rocks and around the trees to about 20 meters away, where they found a man, a climber tied to the end of it, dead.

What are the chances? What are the odds?

In practical terms, informing a child that her parents were killed by an elephant that fell upon them while rock climbing is really no different than informing someone that their loved one had died in an avalanche while reading the newspaper at home in the middle of the afternoon. And actually, from an historical perspective, the odds of either event happening are about the same—though no one recognized that fact at the time.

The peculiarity of the situation consumed all rationalization of what had happened, and unfortunately the disbelief only served to compound the grief. Indeed, upon hearing the news, more than a few people began to say, "Well, at least they died doing something they loved..." but then immediately thought better of it.

For Lulu's sake, and because it has become reflexive behavior in the face of strange events, the people of Chamonix sought to keep the facts of the situation quiet. The death of the elephant and the deaths of the climbers were officially reported as separate events. Had it not been for an Associated Press reporter vacationing in Chamonix that summer, who happened upon the rumor and then confirmed it, they would have gotten away with keeping a lid on all of it.

The article wasn't lengthy, just a four-line item filed under "oddities," but it was picked up by newspapers the world over— the type of story that became watercooler banter and then took on even greater renown as an email forward, something new to the age, with the subject line: "Elephant falls on rock climbers!"

What the people of Chamonix did succeed in preventing from becoming a part of the news was that the three-year-old daughter of the tragically dead parents would be going to live with and be raised by an aged eco-terrorist pornographer. For it was Nicolas, the uncle of Marie, who had been designated as Lulu's caretaker one drunken evening on the basis that he would be wealthy enough to handle the job—and that such a contingency would never be needed.

And that was how Nicolas, at age 67, became a father for the first time.

SUNDAY

"So if we're going to be doing business together, there's a few things you're going to need to understand, as well as a few things you're going to need to respect," Lulu said to Josh, still in the hospital though more alert.

"I don't know if I want to know."

"You've survived a unique experience, one not many people do."

"Are you referring to the fall or the creatures."

"Well, I meant the fall, but yeah, I guess both."

"This is what you had been dealing with all week, isn't it? You weren't playing hard-to-get with the offer."

"Let's just say it's been a strange week, and you've not exactly been a priority."

"We don't have to talk business, Lulu. We can forget all of it. In fact, I'd like to forget all of it."

"I'm afraid you're invested now, Josh. Whether you like it or not. You know too much."

"So it is all real. I didn't just hit my head. There really are creatures in the ice." Lulu nodded. "What are they?"

"All we know is that they came from a plane crash many years ago. Some say they're genetic mutants. Some say they're cursed or undead. Some say they're just a bunch of normal monkeys animated by the forces that exist deep within Mont Blanc."

"What would they've done with me? I mean, if Miles hadn't come after me?"

"Maybe kill and eat you? This we don't know either. It's all a relatively new phenomenon, but one we have to keep quiet."

Lulu could see fear rise in Josh. "You're going to be fine. You're just going to need to keep your mouth shut." She wasn't sure how much sway she would have over him. Maybe just for today, before he finally came to his senses. Maybe he'd been effectively traumatized by the event. Maybe, she bet, this shared secret would be their bond.

"You're going to come to realize," she said, "that knowing more about something, learning that there's more to the world than you've understood so far, won't reduce the extent of the unknown. We're dumber every day, and that's just fine."

"I may have to take a real break from everything," Josh said. "I'm going to need to sort a few things out. Get some perspective on all this."

"Okay, that's fine. Take your time. I don't want you to think I'm taking advantage of you."

"Tell me, Lulu, why have you decided to do this now?"

"Let's just say that everyone, every day, loses a piece of life. So, we may as well make the most of what we've got while we got it."

"What's 'Cham'porn', Lulu asked Nicolas, who was rummaging around a low kitchen cabinet. He stopped, stood up, and slowly turned to face her. He hadn't heard that name in a decade or more.

"Where did you learn about that?"

"Eloise mentioned it. She's been helping with my project. We were trying to come up with a name for the brand. She said it's yours and I should ask you about it."

"She did, did she?" *Damn you, Eloise.* "The name, actually, is hers. I just borrowed it for a while."

"Okay, but what is it?"

"Lulu, you ever wonder what I did for a living?"

"You ran a movie theater, right?"

"Yes..."

"No."

"Yes."

"Oh."

Nicolas reached for a bottle of red wine, then thought better of it. He grabbed the racine de gentiane instead. "You ever tried this?"

She shook her head.

"Grab a seat." He pulled out two small glasses. "We've got a lot to discuss."

4. Les Chocards
Spring

"**B**lack crows are selfish, horrible creatures that have little interest in anything other than filling their stomachs," Misha, a 10-year-old, said before his classmates. "And to be sure, they aren't all black, and they aren't all crow. But they do serve an important role in Chamonix's ecosystem."

Miss Paget approved of the subject of this report, an exercise in which her new student, a recently relocated refugee, was to research a local topic and present it before the class, along with something correspondingly relevant about himself. She nodded along and smiled from the back of the classroom.

"'What people call black crows are actually Alpine choughs, les chocards. They have short, yellow beaks and orange feet. Their bodies consist of fluffy black plumage, which is glossy in the light of day. You'll mostly find them above 2,000 meters, though from time to time they will sneak lower into the valley in search of food or mischief.

"At elevation, the Alpine chough is swift and acrobatic, with loose but deep wing beats. Their agility—of which they have a considerable amount—comes from their tails, which can be fanned into the winds, and their wings, which fold easily, enabling them to soar with the updrafts, right at the face of cliffs, where they build permanent nests.

"Although they are in the Corvid family, which technically makes them crows, they're actually classified as—" Misha consulted his notes "—Pyrrhocorax graculus. This is different from their cousins, the magpies, nutcrackers, jackdaws, jays, ravens, rooks and others.

"The reason they're different has to do with the Alpine chough's selfish behavior, which caused them to change permanently sometime during the last Ice Age."

Misha glanced again at his own scribbles, and Miss Paget, assuming he was done, thanked him for the nice report.

"Now will you tell us something about yourself?"

"But I'm not done. I mean, I will, but I want to tell you what happened to the black crows."

"Oh," Miss Paget said. "By all means, please, continue—" This pleased her, since she was worried he would be reticent as a foreigner to speak before the class.

"You see, the black crows first appeared on Earth about 17 million years ago, when God was busy creating our universe. After having created quite a lot—the mountains and oceans, land, plants, fish, mammals, generally all of it—God then decided to establish a few rules. In seven corners of the Earth, he placed a creature to be guardian of a particular realm— creatures neither dead nor alive. In the Alps, the crows stood guard, just as jackals do in the deserts, or jellyfish in the seas."

The report veered off track into the religious, which didn't fit well in the secular nature of the French system, but Miss Paget continued to welcome the participation. The class appeared to be interested as well to hear where this young Iraqi boy's story was headed.

"The crows, which were then entirely black, did fine weathering the mountains of Europe. Even the Ice Ages, whose great ice sheets advanced and receded, didn't hinder their job: making sure that the dead got to where they were going. The black crows stood as mediators between life and death, consuming the souls of those who passed away and returning them for rebirth.

"Of course, as with everything, there are glitches. Things don't go quite right. And about a million years ago, one black crow became a little too hungry for his own good, just as a new Ice Age began."

Misha now crouched and extended his hands theatrically.

"Seeing his food sources fleeing, the first thing this one crow—we'll call him Black Crow—the first thing he did was to chase off all the other crows. Food was scarce." Misha now pounced around the front of the class, grabbing playfully at his seated classmates. "He harassed and threatened and snapped; pulled their tail feathers and plucked at their eyes until bloody." Misha covered his own eyes, as if they had been injured. "He was a mean one, who wouldn't even await the death of a dying creature before gobbling it up and returning it to the cycle of life."

Miss Paget didn't have the heart to interrupt Misha, though she couldn't recall any time any student went on so much.

"As the ice continued to grow he found less and less to eat, Eventually, he began to starve, all alone, facing a frozen eternity until the temperatures changed once again.

"But just as Black Crow was at his bleakest moment, he stumbled upon something astounding: Frozen butterflies!"

Misha flapped his hands around through the air, imitating the erratic flight of butterflies, and then clasped his hands in a frozen stance. The students too looked in amazement at the performance.

"Tens of thousands of them, locked in the ice, stored perfectly to be pecked out and eaten up. Hope restored Black Crow enough to dig, and dig he did—eating and eating until he became once again a horrid, selfish creature.

"There was just one problem for Black Crow. The butterflies had made a deal with God. Instead of being forced from their homes by the Ice Age, they had come to an agreement to freeze themselves in the growing ice and endure as long as it lasted. Because this particular Ice Age was not a natural occurrence. It was punishment, but not for them.

"Black Crow didn't care. Here, he figured, was a perfect food source, and he lived fat and happy on the butterflies—entirely ignoring pleas from those not yet entombed.

"Unheard by Black Crow, the butterflies cried foul to God, who, despite a usual ambivalence towards such Earthly matters, took issue with Black Crow's bad behavior. God sent down a gust of frigid wind that froze Black Crow's feet to the ground.

"'Help!' he cried. 'I've become stuck.' No matter how hard he tried to pull himself free, flapping his powerful wings, he could not budge. Ice grew around him. No creatures came to his aid—certainly not the butterflies or any of the few other insects that friscalated in the winds.

"As more time passed, Black Crow became weaker and weaker—his pleas and efforts to be freed lessened—and the number of creatures to which he could call out grew fewer and fewer. The great Ice Age had now expanded fully.

IN THIS DELICIOUS GARDEN

"Then one day, Black Crow—barely conscious—heard a voice.

"'What have we here?!' said one of the Children of Paradise, who had been trekking across the glacier. 'It appears we have a crow, frozen in the snow.'"

"Black Crow, although exhausted and terrified of the Children of Paradise—he knew of them—roused and begged for help.

"It might seem like an obvious ask, but the Children of Paradise—young adventurers who were as mischievous as they were creative—had problems of their own. And everyone, including Black Crow, knew it.

"The Children of Paradise had been let free to play here on Earth, a place where God assumed they could be kept in line. It wasn't to be. The Children of Paradise saw no reason to be confined by rules."

Miss Paget couldn't stop him now.

"The Children considered gravity and laughed. They'd find ways to scale the vertical peaks, then fling themselves off and fly in defiance of the ground. They'd look into the deep, dark, airless waters and plunge to the bottoms of the oceans just to gaze at all the life there. When they came up, they had no fear of the waves, which they glided upon freely. Heat, cold, wind, weather, none of it mattered. All of it could be played with. All of it had potential.

"God intended for them to do God's work on Earth, and God became angry. 'If you continue to defy the rules set forth," said God, grasping for a threat, 'you'll be banished from the cycle of life.'

"But the Children responded with a resounding 'whatever', and rather quickly, they discovered the price they'd pay for their desire to play.

"Upon the death of their Earthly form, their souls—that which was the essence of their beings—now had nowhere to go. The souls would remain on Earth, unreturned to their home. And so their souls were forced to wander the valleys and mountains, ocean and rivers, deserts and plains. Eventually, they took refuge wherever they could find it: in the rocks, in the snows, in the trees, in the sands, in the clouds, and even in the mushrooms.

"God believed the Children would come begging. But that's not what happened.

"The Children of Paradise—as mischievous as they were creative—simply saw this new situation as another area to exploit for fun, and found that they could cause hilarious troubles for their friends and family who still lived. Their souls, now inhabiting the Earth itself, caused rocks to fall, avalanches to descend, and great waves to rise up. To them, it once again became something of a game, now between the living and the dead.

"Annoyed even more, God sought new ways to stop their fun, and unleashed momentous floods, caused enormous volcanic eruptions, sent down comets and asteroids and caused a great Ice Age—the one that led to the deal with the butterflies and Black Crow's predicament.

"'This,' the Children of Paradise said, observing Black Crow's bizarre and desperate situation, 'could only be God's doing. You are being punished for something. What have you done?'

"'Nothing! I did nothing. I am just trapped. Help me, please.'

"'Fine, we'll just leave you to fate, since fate is what found you here.'

"'Okay! I admit it. I did wrong. Don't leave me. Help me—if not, I'll be stuck here on the ice for all of eternity. Please, please, please help me.'

"'Explain yourself,' the Children of Paradise demanded, and Black Crow confessed to his rebellion.

"Upon hearing his tale, the Children of Paradise acknowledged Black Crow's repentance but remained skeptical. Black Crow's once matte feathers now glistened unwashed of oils. The black of his beak and legs had drained of their color. His tail feathers, once straight and mighty, were now splayed and crooked. He appeared honest and repentant, having stared down an ugly eternity twice now. Still, they had doubts: 'If you are set free, then you'll just go back to eating up the little creatures and tormenting the others, and they'll just be angry with us. We don't want that. We have enough problems with God.'

"'I promise I won't. I promise I'll behave. I promise. I swear.'

"Black Crow could see the Children were going to say no, and with desperation said: 'I'll do you a favor in return. I know how God traps you. I can get you out of it.'

"Now Black Crow had their attention. 'Upon your death, I'll carry your souls to the afterlife, where they can return to the cycle of life. Right on my wings you will fly. You can escape God, and be free here to enjoy the Earth.'

"To his horror, and without warning, the Children suddenly lit him on fire.

"'It's the only way,' they said, and he cried and cried in anguish, feeling betrayed. His feathers burned and burned. And finally, truly broken, Black Crow's tears, which became heavier and heavier, served to extinguish the flames. As they did, the Children smiled with satisfaction. Black Crow emerged a new bird, and, in return, he set the Children free."

Misha smiled at the class, which sat stunned.

"Thank you, Misha," said Ms. Paget. "That was, really…
unexpected. A very thorough report on les chocards." She
paused before asking: "Do you have anything you'd also like to
share about yourself now—quickly, I mean. As we've run out
of time."

"But I did," Misha said. "That was about me. The bird. The
Children. This is my faith. These are my people."

××

"You need to call this man, this doctor…" Chloé said and
looked down at the notes she had taken "…this Dr. Albert
Reinhardt." She lay in bed, propped up against pillows,
holding an iPad and reviewing various papers that rested on
her pregnant belly.

"Can't you do it? Can't you just call him?" Luc said from the
bathroom. He rinsed his razor under hot water.

"Honey, I'm not a government official. I doubt he'll even
take my call."

"But you're a physician. Don't you have some doctor club
code word or something?"

Silence. He didn't see the annoyance on her face, but he
could feel it. "Okay, just leave me the number, and I'll try to
call later."

"And there's nothing else, no other information from the
crash or the laboratory?"

"Nothing."

She too had now become frustrated by the mystery.

Although Luc very much wanted to forget the monkeys after
his visit with Josh in the hospital, he recognized the potential

they had to get out of hand. Anomalies and abnormalities could never be written-off as nothing or assumed that they would take care of themselves—no, not in Chamonix. And, as mayor, he stood as one of the few people, if not the only one, with the authority to delve deeper into the "official" side of the matter. Unfortunately, there remained little to go on.

For an hour every night, after his staff had gone home, Luc would descend into the basement of the Mairie and rummage through aged metal file cabinets and dusty old bins. He didn't trust his staff with the task—not because they wouldn't be diligent, but because they'd most certainly question why he cared about a plane crash from so long ago. He didn't want to lie to them, and telling the truth meant risking the exacerbation of a matter that would be all too ripe for the small town's circle of Saturday morning gossips.

The search became for him an exercise in patience, but after a month, it evolved into something of a daily period of meditation—one more job he had to undertake, but one that had to be performed in isolation and therefore offered refuge from his other work: meetings, handshakes, ceremonies, phone calls and, of course, paperwork. This was the only time he had to himself.

So focused he became while looking for whatever sign of monkeys he could find in the bins and bags and binders that stored evidence from the crash—hundreds, if not thousands of files, copies of bureaucratic filings demanded of the French government on the situation— that Luc almost flipped past what became a turning point: in the center of a blank piece of paper, a nameless business card affixed at corners by brittle, yellowed tape:

Department of Developmental & Molecular Biology
Albert Einstein College of Medicine
1300 Morris Park Avenue, Bronx, New York 10461

Luc took a photo of it with his phone, and continued on with his search, finishing out the hour, and then headed home to share his finding with Chloé.

Aside the obvious intrigue of this particular matter, she recognized that this search gave her husband time to decompress, away from complaints about the air pollution, complaints about regulations, complaints about the tunnel, complaints about the new parking fees, complaints that there are not enough bike paths, complaints about too many bike paths, and on and on. She heard it all.

Not working due to the late stage of her pregnancy, Chloé delved into the mystery—something Luc had first shared with her the summer before Josh's encounter, and kept her filled in along the way. She had in fact assisted with chasing down a number of leads.

For instance, she ruled out yetis. Unlike other mountain ranges, like the Himalaya, the Alps did not have a tradition of abominable snowmen. The European mountains were too populated by humans for large animal life to go unnoticed and unidentified, and anyway the Great Wars had killed off or driven away most everything else.

As for the monkeys being some gothic monster, while Mary Shelley had been inspired to write "Frankenstein" while on a trip to Chamonix—and while the most critical scenes did take place on the Mer de Glace—the subject matter had not drawn on actual sightings or lore. Chloé had gone so far as to track down Shelley's notes.

She had also contacted the Chamonix priory and inquired of the churchmen, who insisted vehemently that an exorcism cannot be "undone," that it was impossible to provoke the Devil like that, and that the event that had taken place years earlier was just a stunt. Their overly adamant protestations, however, did not sit well with her. Her science-trained mind decided just to let it go, though she certainly enjoyed remarking openly to anyone about the untoward role of the Church in Chamonix's climate change history.

Many ideas and possibilities floated up, and she and Luc pondered them night after night. "I may just give birth to a monkey," she said to him with a wink one day. "At this point," he said, "I wouldn't be surprised."

But here, with this business card, they turned a corner.

The 1960s, it turned out, had been a boon for non-human primate research—at the height of the Cold War, when funding poured into medical and biological studies. Albert Einstein College of Medicine had, in 1964, become the first medical school in the U.S. to establish a Department of Genetics, a distinction added to a year later by it also becoming one of the first General Clinical Research Centers funded by the National Institutes of Health (NIH). What could they have been working on, Chloé wondered. It turns out, a lot.

When Luc awoke that morning after he had found the clue, he saw that Chloé was already awake—in fact she had never gone to sleep. She stayed up, uncomfortable in her own body and anyways incapable of rest, though pleased to have a relevant distraction with which to bide her time.

"They should not have been getting monkeys from India," Chloé said, upon seeing her husband stir.

"What?"

"The plane. I haven't been able to figure out why this laboratory would've been acquiring monkeys from India. By '66, there's no reason for it."

She then proceeded to explain to her half-awake husband that after the Second World War, the U.S. had undergone a process of standardization for its diverse forms of laboratory "labor;" that most "monkeys" were in fact rhesus macaques, due to their close association to human anatomy and metabolism; and the most prized of the rhesus macaques, in terms of quality and genetic consistency, came from India.

"The problem," she said as he arose to get himself ready, "is that India banned the export of rhesus macaques in '55. Too much controversy with animal rights activists. They made exceptions when experiments weren't for military or space research. But any NIH lab at that time would have been getting their specimens from either..." she looked at her notes "...Cayo Santiago or one of the National Centers for Primate Research. That can only mean they were smuggling them in."

"How much sleep have you had? I'm going to assume none."

She turned her iPad to face him, and there in an old news photo from Le Monde, of a group of serious-looking men assessing Air India wreckage that had been retrieved from the mountain, stood a shy-looking guy with a pipe, wearing a dark jacket with a logo on it—a logo from the Albert Einstein College of Medicine. "You have to call this number," she said, reaching out to him a piece of paper.

Now having shaved, showered and dressed, while sitting on the end of the bed, he asked: "Even if I get through to someone, and that someone happens to be this Dr. Reinhardt?"

"Reinhardt's the only one left I could find. His name is all over a number of monkey studies published from that period. His abstracts line up. Like this one: 'Cerebral concussion in the monkey' or 'Cardiovascular effects of experimental head injury in the monkey'.... They're 'impact studies,' the few non-vaccination studies involving macaques, and they stop after '66."

Chloé had done her medical training in Paris, where she had been raised. She spent a year doing research at the Mayo Clinic in Minnesota and spoke English fluently. She found it almost nostalgic to dig through technical research papers, having long since resigned herself to general medicine in order to be with Luc in Chamonix. "If those monkeys actually survived that crash," she said, "it would make sense that they would've been intended for studies like these."

Then she actually looked at him. "Why are you wearing a tie?"

He didn't usually wear a tie. Despite demanding a lot of its mayor, Chamonix is still a ski town and formality for the sake of formality is viewed as pretentiousness. A collared shirt would do, with a sweater or fleece in the winter, or just a polo when it became warm. (Lulu once gave him a Cham'porn hoodie, which he never wore...)

"Meetings."

"About the refugees—"

He nodded.

"Who with? Wait, don't tell me, the troublemakers."

"No, they come next week. And they're not troublemakers. They have a voice, and have influence among the voters. I have to hear them out." Chloé rolled her eyes. "Today it's the regional heads, with some locals, who probably want to lodge some complaints. This whole thing, it's like air pollution: Everyone's for action, but no one wants to do anything themselves."

"Okay, if you have time," she said. "The main questions are on the paper. I wrote them out for you." He leaned over and kissed her. She looked at him tenderly: "Can you bring home some Tanpopo ramen tonight?"

He smiled. This was a good sign: Japanese food. She had gone through several weeks of terrible heartburn and would only eat neutral, boring foods—which he also had to eat as a token of their shared burden.

She noticed: "Maybe it's because I'm overtired. It's just what my body is telling me it wants."

"No problem for me. I'll check in with you this evening to make sure it's still on your menu."

×××

Springtime is when everything falls down in the mountains. While snow storms will continue at higher elevations, where they do all year round, the bulk of the winter white that pads the peaks fades to gray as it softens, slides and recedes, destabilizing the steep walls of Chamonix.

Standing on a glacier, any glacier—though particularly the Mer de Glace—one will see and hear in a matter of minutes the geological process taking place. The snows, warming in the sun, release in cascades down couloirs and chutes. From cliff sides, rocks clack and boulders conk. By late afternoon, tiny rivulets almost invisible in the morning become muddy torrents—flows that will again calm over night as the warming-cooling cycle repeats itself until there's little left to sacrifice to gravity.

All of it eventually merges and moves down into the middle elevations, below the rock and permanent ice, where vegetation is able to grow, to an area where after the spring-melt one will find the evidence of winter's violence—entire fields of trees uprooted by avalanches, streams no longer on course, whole mushroom patches missing from the alpage, and yes, even the dead, thawing bodies waiting to be discovered, human and animal alike.

Further down into the valley they continue, the now rich waters, eventually feeding into the Arve, which is channeled straight through Chamonix. On the opposite side, this river runs out of the valley for 100 kilometers until it merges with the clear waters of the river Rhône in Geneva.

The Genevois have long griped about how the dirty churn of the Arve—milky green with glacial fleck—corrupts the transparent Swiss waters. They contemplated what sins the people who lived at its source must've committed to be given such filthy rot. Their Protestant minds, of course, would never have been able to imagine what truly lurked up yonder, and they certainly weren't going to find out for themselves.

And yet these swollen waters, causing havoc on high and irritating all those below, serve an important purpose: They signal that the season has changed and work needs to be done. After the last major snow has fallen, after the ski lifts— one by one—have closed, after the last of the visitors have left, and most restaurants and hoteliers take a break, that's when the real Chamonix emerges, like animals creeping back into the woodland after a threat has passed.

For long before winter could be enjoyed it was just that: a threat. Chamoniards toughed it out, remaining largely inside thick-walled, small-windowed houses, eating root vegetables, stale bread and cheese. The times may have changed. Commerce has brought wealth, and politics have steered investment. But the habits of life, guided by the seasons, have not.

Only about 10 weeks stand between the end of one tourist season and the beginning of the next, and the town while trying to take a breather must also begin to prepare. Cleaning, sweeping, dusting, airing out and opening up. This particular spring turned out to be busier than usual. The weak winter had been tough on the town's economy, and everyone had to work that much harder to lock in summer bookings.

Even Lulu, who normally just closes up shop for interseason, had been plunged into the corporate acquisition process with Mediastopheles. Josh had managed to sell the deal internally; however, still suffering the after-effects of his fall, he decided to take some additional time off and left Lulu at the mercy of the lawyers.

Nicolas had also come to require more attention, not that he asked for it. His sadness at Eloise's loss grew, and Lulu spent more and more time with him over dinner and just trying to keep him distracted with life: movies and books, music and art. And for her, an additional stress emerged.

It came one night after Nicolas had retired, and she herself had almost fallen asleep at the kitchen table while reviewing business documents and contracts.

That familiar chime.

She turned her head to get a better sense of whether it was actual, or just the faint echo of memory ringing in her head—one of those unexpected remembrances of Eloise that percolated up to cause a sharp, fleeting pain. But there it was again. It seemed far off. And gone. As if on the wind. There for a moment and then— There it was again.

She stood up from the table. Was it coming from inside the house? She walked slowly to the stairs and listened upwards. Nothing. And then towards the cellar. Nothing in any of the rooms, and then she returned to the kitchen. Nothing.

Lulu shook her head. She must be going— There it was again. To the door she walked and opened it.

The light from the kitchen fell diagonally against the garden, and she went out to the edge of the deck, where there, emerging from the darkness, stood three large horses.

She froze.

Hot breath from their nostrils rose through the light. If she ran for it and threw herself into the house, it would buy her a minute or two on the animals. She could hide. Not if they charged the door. Not if they got inside. And what about Nicolas? She had nothing to defend herself with either. She just stayed very still.

Lulu kept her eyes on the middle horse, a step closer than the others. She flinched when it turned its head—down to the side into Lulu's backlit shadow—and its glassy eye met hers. It recognized her, she thought.

The horse shook its head, and Lulu heard and then saw the bells—three of them, in the horse's mouth, their leather straps clinched in its teeth. The horse jangled them again. And then with a quick snap, tossed the bells toward Lulu's feet. She didn't move. She didn't look at them. She kept her eyes on the animals.

The ones either side of the middle one turned slowly, and they floated with an even trot into the darkness. She couldn't see where. Night consumed them. Did they mean to flank her, while her attention stayed with the middle one, just a leap away? They had proven to be just that cunning.

Stillness prevailed while she and the horse remained fixed on one another, though all she could see of it was the wet gloss of an eye, not anything behind, if there was anything at all there. Then, it let out a snort and receded without a sound into the dark.

Lulu's eyes darted all around, and she tried to listen for anything—a crunch or breath, a snort or the snapping of a twig. Nothing.

Slowly, she crouched to the ground. She reached out and collected the bells with trembling hands, her fingers fumbling inside the castings to keep them from chiming.

Then ever so steadily, she inched backwards to the house, pausing again and again to listen, and once inside pressed the door shut and turned out all the lights.

Her back against the door now, she took giant breathes. "Fuck. Holy fuck." Then she realized, and whipped around to check the door latch. It was locked. She slid down against the door again, to the floor: "Fuuuuck."

×××

"They're not Muslim."

"Then they're Christian?"

"No, Yazidi."

"Yah-what?"

"Yazidi."

"If they're not Christian and they're Arabs, then they must be Muslim."

"But they're not Arab."

"They're Jews?"

"No, not them either." Luc hesitated at mentioning Arab Jews or bringing Persians into the mix; it would just further muddle his already messy talking points.

"And they come from the Middle East—where did you say, Iraq?"

"Yes. Look, they're not any of what you're thinking, which is precisely why they're here. Yazidi, it's like Zoroastrianism..." That was a mistake; he could see this word didn't register... "Just another minority—not Muslim, not Christian, not Jew. Something different. Ethnically, they're Kurds—Kurdish Yazidis."

"Kurds, where is that from?"

"Where are they from—technically, this family is from Iraq, but the Kurds don't really have a single country where they live. They're a nation of people split into a number of countries, countries at war. But you could say they're mountain people, like us."

"They're not like us, Luc. Why are they here?"

"Basically, everyone is trying to kill them, since they're a hated minority in the region." He oversimplified the issue, but he did not want to say it's because they worship the Devil—or so the Islamic State believes, which is, in a way, true.

"Everyone hates them, and you want to bring them here? How do you know we'll like them? What did they do to anger everyone?"

Ah, there it is. Walked right into that one. "I don't think that's a fair question."

"Why is that not fair? Why is it not fair to question who they are? Maybe they're the problem. Maybe they caused all of these issues in the first place. Now you're bringing them—and their problems—to us."

"That is not what this is about. They are an oppressed minority that had to flee their home, flee their village, flee their country. They're displaced. Had to run for their lives—from the Islamic State, from problems much larger than themselves. Problems they didn't have anything to do with." He realized he didn't actually know. "It's the right thing to do to provide shelter for these people."

"That still doesn't answer why they're here, in Chamonix, and not any one of a million other places in the world."

"Why does it trouble you so much that we're hosting a single family—just one family, four people...." Yes, turn it around.

"What's troubling is you foisting these rejects on us. You're creating a dangerous situation for our town, for our community, just so you can please a bunch of people in Paris. That's what's troubling."

"How is this dangerous?"

"They bring their problems, from Iraq or Calais, wherever. They bring their drugs. They bring their way of life, which is not our way of life. They may even bring terrorism right to our door."

"They're facing genocide..."

"Fine. You can play the sympathy card all you want, but the parents, they'll need work. They can't just sit around sponging off the system. Who's going to give them jobs?"

Luc paused. "Shit, that's a good point."

"You don't know? "

"No, no idea. Do you know?"

While Arthur, Luc's assistant, shuffled through the stack of papers on his lap looking for an answer, Luc said: "Don't you think this is all a bit aggressive?"

Luc had been sparring with Arthur all morning, trying to get his arguments down in preparation for his meeting later in the week with representatives from the Front Républicain—the troublemakers to which his wife referred.

Unlike the locals, who remained reticent to speak out for or against the refugees, the Front Républicain, a political party, would be different. This right wing French nationalist group saw Luc as a liberal target to promote their anti-immigration policies. That's something he knew. "Effers," he called them.

A year earlier, Luc's announcement that Chamonix would heed the call of Paris to accept refugee families that had been turned away from a camp in Calais had been met with a cool response from townsfolk. At the Saturday market, talk of the idea consisted of either gripes about the practical aspects: where they would stay, what would they do, how long would they be here; or a generally hazy optimism about it being a feel-good humanitarian gesture. No hint of ideological judgment rose to the surface, at least any that reached Luc.

"And that," Luc told Chloé at the time, "is what really bothers me. They're either not taking my offer as a serious one, or they're hiding." He had all too often been present for conversations rife with blatant racism against Algerians. He knew how rigid the townsfolk could be against the British. And he even felt himself the long simmering resentment Chamoniards held for Paris. No community was immune to such fears or bigotry. But where was it now?

"Maybe they're just not buying into your bluff," Chloé told him. "Rest assured, they'll still use it to criticize you—'all talk, no action'—when it doesn't happen." He responded with a sheepish look. He knew she was right.

Luc's had been a rather calculated decision, to make a grand offer publicly to distinguish himself—even taking a vocal stand against the president of the Auvergne-Rhone-Alpes region, who had called upon the communes to disobey the state—so to gain favor with Paris in order to negotiate on other matters, like air pollution and housing subsidies. Here, he walked a fine line.

Despite Chamonix-Mont-Blanc being Chamonix-Mont-Blanc, the mayor still had to fight tooth and nail to gain the attention of the national government. But he knew well that to do so sometimes required getting the attention of a larger audience.

Not just another small town in France, Chamonix could command the world's attention if it needed. And he did so with his announcement, generating news in Belgium, Germany, the UK and the U.S., making the bet that he could ride the goodwill, while his offer would be overlooked by Paris for larger, better-resourced cities normally selected first in such matters.

After a year of hearing nothing, he assumed he was in the clear. Not so. Just a month earlier, the same day he learned of Josh's encounter with the monkeys, a call came: not one, but two families would be arriving. It turned out his bluff had been called, not by his fellow Chamoniards, but by Paris—and just months away from the town's mayoral elections.

He immediately leapt into action—drawing up talking points, issuing statements, rallying his fellow town officials, conducting outreach. But it all seemed too easy. Arthur continuously monitored Facebook groups and chat forums, which held a mix of discussion, mostly dominated by people from outside the valley. Very little was remarked by those in Chamonix.

The known unknown for Luc remained the same as always, that which lurked in the town's dark shadows. The insidiousness of the quiet, to him, could only mean the people of Chamonix would wait and express judgment at the ballot box.

Luc, now done with his sparring and no longer paying attention to whatever Arthur was saying, looked up to the two portraits behind his desk: Charles de Gaulle—the great politician and adamant realist, who certainly would not entertain notions of settling immigrants; and Jean Moulin, the revolutionary—who fought for French values, "liberté, égalité, fraternité," but was betrayed, and murdered by the Gestapo.

These silent gentlemen offered little in the way of advice or example, their images long since consumed by hagiography and political marketing. He needed a fresh view on the matter, to at very least confirm that he was doing the right thing in accepting this family, despite his dubious intentions.

The vibration of Luc's phone broke his thoughts. A text from Chloé: "How about egg rolls and stir fry vegetables?"

OK, tonight she wants Chinese. Not something they hadn't had in a while, but he was again pleased at the change. He reached for the phone to make the order and noticed Dr. Reinhardt's number. Not today, he thought. Not today.

×××

Lulu dropped a burlap bag on the desk. The contents clanked. "Is Luc in?"

She had initially tried to find Jean-François, but after several calls and a drive out to his place, she gave up—consumed with the seemingly endless details of her business negotiations.

When Nicolas happened upon the bells one morning, he nearly lost his mind, and she knew she needed to take more immediate action.

"Bonjour, Lulu," said Arthur, who poked at the bag on his desk. "What do we have here?"

"Bonjour, Arthur. Bells."

"Bells?"

"Horse bells."

He gave her a look of non-comprehension, and she returned it with a look that said: *Yeah, bells, moron—horse bells, get it?*

To which Arthur then said: "Oh, horse bells...oh, bells. Oh shit, those bells..."

"Yes, those bells. Is Luc in?"

Arthur pushed the bag away to the edge of the desk using a pen. "No, he's out today. Meetings up in Argentière, and then he has a lunch and a number of events."

"You know when he'll be back?"

"Not likely today, and his schedule is pretty packed tomorrow."

"Okay, well, make sure he gets these, and tell him to call me."

"Hey, Lulu—" She turned. "Have you heard about the refugees, the ones coming to live in Chamonix?"

"Sure."

"What do you think?"

"It's good? I haven't given it much thought, to be honest."

"Okay, thanks." And she left.

Several days later, Luc stood in the doorway of the rectory of Saint-Michel, shaking hands with Père William: "I'm here to learn about the Jews."

"You've got the wrong house," Père William said. "Try up the road. All we've got here is red wine and stale bread."

"Damn," Luc said, rubbing his neck. "Well, it's about time for an apero anyways. Shall we?"

As the men sat down at a table in the rectory's kitchen, a younger man, another churchman, brought in an old scrap book, leather-bound with brittle matte black pages; photos and yellow newspaper clippings stuck and stuffed within. Père William gently opened it and flipped through. The young man then poured a couple glasses of wine and left the bottle for them.

"There were almost 40 children," Père William said. He pointed to a sepia photo of a group of happy looking kids playing in a field—some, just toddlers, a couple as old-looking as 13 or 14 years of age. Lacking context, it would appear to be any other image of a summer camp in the Alps.

"They stayed in Chamonix for almost two years, starting in the summer '42. Most of them didn't arrive to go into hiding. Most came to go to camp, but just had nowhere else to go by the end of the summer—no parents, no relatives, no home. All gone. Eventually more arrived as the situation in France worsened."

He flipped to another page that showed a group of women. "Here, these two are the women that ran the summer camp, in a chalet up in Les Bois. By the end of that summer, the 'camp' converted into a 'home' for children who came from supposedly war-torn areas of France. The country was so split up then. Eventually, they relocated the operation to the Hotel de la Paix, when the winter arrived."

"What about the Italians and the Germans that were here. No one knew?"

They were kids, and they were French. They looked and acted like any others—though they weren't allowed to practice their faith or have any outward expression of it. Anyone who asked was told their parents were atheists. The kids definitely had to play along over the holidays. Names were changed. Levy became Laroche. Simple things—mostly under the direction of the Resistance. They could easily create false papers for them, and the home itself covered a lot of activities."

"I can't imagine what the kids went through."

"Between the duplicity and the sacrilege, those children were as afraid of the Germans as they were of their own god."

Luc, now turning the pages himself: "And no one sold them out, incredible."

"Oh, they had their troubles." Père William said, filling Luc's glass. "There was this counselor in charge of the boys. What was her name? Sister Claire Brawzy, Brozy, Brozsky..." He reached to turn over a few pages in the book. "Here, Brazitzky. That's her. Sister Claire Brazitzky. A German nun, but anti-Nazi. Sister Claire devoted herself to those children. In retrospect, it's possible she knew more about their fate than she let on. If it weren't for her connections, life would have been a lot more...difficult. Basically, since all this was one big religious ruse, she helped smooth the way with priests in the area. But wouldn't you know it, there's always a troublemaker."

"One of our own?"

"No, a Catholic priest visiting down in Servoz. She knew him fairly well, actually, since he was German. And she gauged pretty well where his sympathies lay. She largely kept everything hidden from him—until, one day, she ran into him on the street in town here around Easter. She had a number of the kids with her. Oh boy, he peppered them with questions about Jesus and faith. You can imagine how it was—none of them knew anything. It was a disaster. Of course he became suspicious. Of course he wouldn't let it go."

"What'd they do?"

"Pretended they were Protestants instead. Much easier."

"No, about the priest."

"Oh right. Well, it wasn't immediately clear whether he was upset at their poor education in the faith—something I can appreciate—or whether he actually saw through the whole charade. He started making visits to the home, and asking all sorts of questions. He spent a good amount of time up at the Majestic, so who knows what he was sharing with the Nazis. The problem was that if the children's home was outed, then the Resistance would be as well. He put the entire operation in jeopardy."

"Did they confront him?"

"Well, Sister Claire immediately went to Michel Tarbot, the local leader of the Resistance. You knew his daughter there, Eloise, who just died. Tarbot was never one to fool around. He actually threatened to kick out the children, since they looked to compromise everything. He assumed it would be easier to take the risk on moving them than give up all his work. But Sister Claire persisted. Allegedly, she obtained evidence to show that the priest was a spy. True or not, we'll never know.

She wasn't one to fool around either. And she definitely played on Tarbot's allegiance to the church.

"So the story goes, when Tarbot learned of this, about this Nazi priest, he went after him. At that point, the war effort was not looking good. The French were being humiliated at every turn. The Allies doubted the ability of the Resistance to be organized and contribute, and arms were drying up. Tarbot sure wasn't going to give up one of the strongest positions in the region just for some kids.

"One night he got that Nicolas, who was working at the photo shop, and went down to Servoz with a couple big guys. When that old German answered the door, they barged right in. Got him to the ground, stripped him down. At gunpoint, put him in a frilly dress and had him kiss a picture of the Pope. Nicolas took a bunch of photographs. Tarbot swore that if the priest ever talked, he'd distribute copies across every village in the Haute Savoie."

"That's one way to defrock a priest."

"It was more like a frocking, actually..."

"Did he ever cause any more trouble?"

"Tried to, but you already know what happened to him."

"You mean—"

"Les chevaux des Bossons..."

"Les chevaux des Bossons." They clinked glasses.

"But it's not what you think." Père William refilled.

"The horses didn't kill him?"

"They finished the job," Père William said.

"Tarbot?"

"As Tarbot told it, the priest slipped and fell, knocked his head, bled out and the horses went for him. Certain witnesses claimed otherwise."

"And in the end, all because of Eloise…"

"Non, non. She became the excuse. The issue was much bigger. It wasn't until after the war that everyone learned of what happened to the parents of the kids. During that summer, that first summer, thousands of Jews had been deported from internment camps in Drancy, Beaune-la-Rolande, others places, and all sent to Auschwitz. Most of them, they were gassed upon arrival. For a man like Tarbot, whose only concern had been defending his home, when he learned of it, the guilt of his own self-centeredness crushed him. And the realization of just exactly what had been jeopardized by the priest—not the Resistance operations, but the lives of those children—well, he became despondent. Avoided everyone, even his own family. He also saw what ruin he made of Eloise's friend Nicolas, almost killing that young man with that stupid scheme to blow up the Para. After a time, he just went to live with those horses. When the Nazi priest turned up in Les Bossons years later to out his daughter, he, well, lost it."

"Killed him?"

"Shot him dead."

"And the horses did their job…"

"Exactly. Didn't take much blood for those animals to go to work."

"So the whole story about the horses getting loose?"

"All made up, just a version of the truth, since they did get loose—well, were let loose. The mayor, the gendarmes, all played along. Tarbot had paid too many dues to be done up over an issue like that. People die in the mountains all the time. Good people, bad people. For all sorts of reasons."

"And the bells—"

"A gesture to quiet concerned neighbors. The horses do have a history. You know, as mayor, it's what you have to do sometimes: Play along. Politics and all—"

Luc thought on that, thought on all of it for a moment, then said, "You know, if it was up to some people, we'd be putting bells on the refugee family that's coming to stay with us."

"You're facing that much opposition?"

"From places I didn't expect, and not getting support where I thought it would be. For a town that sheltered 40 Jews." He shook his head. "It's disappointing. I don't even have 40. I have four. But you'd think 400 were on their way, at least by how the Effers are treating this."

"And you've heard a lot of negative comments from people in town?"

"I haven't heard any comments from people in town. Yeah, some odd remarks here and there. Little things on Facebook. But largely, everyone is quiet on the matter."

"We are a quiet people sometimes." Luc shot him a look. Père William said: "Tell me, are you more worried about the reception of these refugees or about the effect they may have on the upcoming elections?"

"I made the decision. I had it ratified by the counsel. I'm standing by it."

"What took place so many years ago, sheltering those children, it may seem simple now—simple in terms of the moral imperative, simple in terms of the actions that had to be taken. But it wasn't. It was risky, since the stakes were not well understood. Or the outcome. As for why, ultimately, they did it? Children are children. They should be protected. It had little to do with their religion or some heroic act."

"But no one went out of their way to criticize the effort..."

"It's because it was a small group of people who were involved. Most people may have known but looked the other way. They remained quiet. Sometimes that's all you need." "These people are being murdered, their mothers and daughters raped. It's all over the news. It isn't some rumor, or something we're going to discover down the road. Now people—the Effers—are going to come here and try to get me tossed out of office because of it."

"What you describe, it's happening far away. We've all become entirely desensitized to such violence. I'm obviously as sympathetic as anyone. I served in Algeria. But we're inundated with images of battle and bloodshed. I see a good number of hypocrites every Sunday morning, Luc. I don't see anyone who isn't deeply compassionate when it counts. There's just a big difference between having bombs bursting in your backyard and bombs bursting where you would assume they would be anyways. And it's much more complex.

"In the '40s, we had Christians and Jews. What do you have now? You have Islam and Christianity, Judaism and Hinduism. In Kurdistan alone, you have those, plus Babaism, Yezidism, Yazdanism, which has its own sects of Yarsanism and Alevism. And there are the Shabaks, another Muslim sect, and Turkmen Shiites, not to mention the Chaldeans. People aren't going to understand that.

"They won't understand that these people are Yazidis, people who claim to be descended from the original inhabitants of the Garden of Eden."

"It shouldn't matter, we're French. Why is everyone so attached to questions of identity when the fundamental issue is about social justice—"

"Luc, stop with the talking points. If you go high and mighty, you're going to lose your audience. No one cares about nobility of purpose, especially in a down economy. Trust me, I sell them on a zombie-god called Jesus every Sunday. I understand why you have fear, why you're suddenly sensitive about a world in which you're about to bring a child and what it's capable of, but don't get lost.

"These people will come and you should at least hear them out. They do, for good or bad, represent the opinion of many French, and do so for a variety of reasons—some good reasons. You need to see if those reasons live in this valley. You cannot do that by demonizing them the way you perceive they demonize others. Go with an open mind. You may learn something about the people of Chamonix."

Luc agreed he would. For the first time, he admitted to himself that he had made an unforced error, and his fears had gotten the better of him.

"One last thing, Luc. Before you go," Père William said.

"Sure—"

"Could you ask your wife to ease up on my guys with respect to the climate change issue? We can't have people believing the Church is responsible for the bad winters. I mean, that's ludicrous," and he laughed nervously, "but sadly people are beginning to believe it."

"You are the ones who brought the Devil to the glacier," Luc smiled. "I'll see what I can do. But you know how scientists can be."

"Where did these come from?" Luc shouted from his office.
"Lulu. She stopped by with them the other day," Arthur said.
Shit. "Any message?"
"Call her."
"Any immediate message?"
"Call her."
"She leave a number?"
"No."
"Can you get me a number?"

Luc had never actually touched a horse bell before. Gently, he pulled one from the bag. In his hands, it seemed larger than it appeared around the neck of a horse—from a distance. And it was rough. And weighty. He held it out by its chewed, weathered leather strap; the clapper banged, making a resonant dong that he let reverberate, even though it caused a salty feeling to turn over in his stomach.

For the mayor of any other town, such a thing would seem, at least, weird—not just the bell, but its purpose, why it existed in the first place, and how it may have come to be on his desk. This bell, this situation, it was not abnormal, however. Not to Luc. Not to any mayor of Chamonix before him. He didn't question it. He only wondered what would come next, as if contemplating the path of a storm.

As he did so, he glanced over the dossiers on his desk: housing, education, training, health, seniors, environment, air quality, transportation, energy, tourism. Where did these old bells fit in?

To arrive at the office and at this question, Luc had taken a meandering path through the main streets of Chamonix from a meeting he had had at the train station. He walked down Avenue Michel Croz, where outside the bar Elevation at 10 a.m. sat a handful of young foreigners, mostly Brits: dirty looking fellows pressing each other with stories of spring skiing exploits. They wouldn't recognize the mayor by face, let alone name. These types usually lived in Cham-Sud or way up in Argentière. They would roll into town for a season or two. The money would dry up, or friends would leave, and so would they.

A little further down, past a number of restaurants now closed for a few weeks, he bid good day in English to a couple women bantering in front of a Swedish-owned salon. He then glimpsed a discarded aluminum can in one of the new planters across the street, went over, plucked it out and tossed it in a nearby trash bin.

Luc looked up to see in front of him the old photo shop, now a tourist gallery for artistic mountain prints. He smiled and kept moving toward the McDonald's, within which he saw a good number of young people hunched over their phones, likely just there for the free wi-fi.

Now in the pedestrian area, he scanned the desolate walkways in front of the shops, mostly open but empty: Timberland, North Face, Icebreaker and a curious "luxury" décor store named Rock & Ice, which had nothing to do with rock or ice.

Not ready to go straight back to the office, he turned toward Quai du Vieux Moulin, but heard voices behind him, down Quai d'Arve. The view above the voices grabbed his attention first: Mont Blanc, obscured by a bank of billowy clouds; below it and before him on the street, a gaggle of old locals smoking cigarettes, drinking beers and arguing as old men do—about what, about sports, about the weather, about refugees, per chance?

Luc carried on. Along the Quai, he stopped for a moment to examine the reconstruction of the retaining wall along the river below the old fire station once stood. At the end of the Quai, he turned up Rue des Moulins, noting that the Cham'porn shop was closed. New graffiti appeared on the walls of some of the buildings. Luc frowned and took photos. Further up, now on Rue Joseph Vallot, he noticed some initial preparations for the Mont Blanc Marathon and posters announcing this year's UTMB.

Luc wound around to the Mairie, saying hello to a few people he passed. Before stepping into the building, he turned and looked up to the Aiguille du Midi, the cloud bank now bruised and moody, a world apart—like the alpage or the champs. And then there, as he looked directly at the rock, a plume of white poured down from the clouds, an avalanche, that hit ledge after ledge—a magnificent sight that lasted but a moment, seen likely only by him.

Perfect, he thought, though not for any obvious reason.

You see, anyone could be forgiven for mistaking the normality of the town's goings-on, but Luc saw more, if only because he paid attention: the tobacco-cut marijuana the young men were smoking at Elevation; the dominance of English spoken across town; the presence of a nefarious alcohol-infused "energy drink" littering the street; the young people desperately tethered to the internet inside a dingy fast food restaurant instead of being outside; a notorious recidivist drunk driver day-drinking when he should be locked away, saved only by his family name; the radical change in climate literally undermining the town's center; the foreign corporations absorbing that which once was local; the distant avalanche that he hoped had been triggered naturally and that no one else had to experience. And now—right there in his office, right here in his hands—the bells: more or less as dangerous as anything he had just seen. They were not weird, just more storm to prepare for.

Luc pushed around the files on his desk, now distracted. He should be reviewing the proposals for wing-suit regulations, the new takeoff and landing sites, trajectories and flight plans. He should read the latest notes on the study conducted about the valley's winter air pollution, which presented a scheme to improve housing insulation. He should call the Foreign Ministry liaison to get more information on the refugees before they arrived.

Instead, Luc picked up the phone. He called Lulu. No answer. He called Jean-François. No answer. He sat quietly thinking, tapping a pen on his desk. Then he reached for the phone again, and as he did saw the number for Dr. Reinhardt.

Luc should not have been surprised that someone answered, that that someone was Dr. Reinhardt, or that his wife, a wizard of research, had found a direct line.

"Reinhardt here. Who's this?"

"Hello, ah, Dr. Reinhardt. This is Luc Berger. I'm the mayor of Chamonix-Mont-Blanc, the ski station in France."

"Is this a joke?"

"No, no, sir, it's not. I apologize for the randomness of my call. I'm really not sure how to..." Luc scrambled to find the notes his wife had given him and fumbled to find the best words in English.

"It's about the monkeys, isn't it?"

Luc, excited to have found Chloé's paper, stopped. "How did you know that?"

"Why else would you, the mayor of Chamonix, be calling me?"

"Yes, well, I have a few questions, if you have time."

"I'm retired now, Mr. Berger. So yes, I have some time. Not a lot of time. But remember, my involvement with that crash was more than 50 years ago. I'll tell you what I can."

So little of this Luc had discussed aloud with anyone other than his wife. He realized that all he was about to say seemed rather absurd just on his lips. He decided to hedge, "We recently found some remains of one of the monkeys, in a cage that had melted out of one of the glaciers."

"Remains?"

"Yes." Luc felt that since this was technically true, it was all right to claim.

"Not a whole monkey?"

"No."

"Then the lab wouldn't need to see it. They're well past all that by now."

"Sure, but I do have a few questions about it still. Just answers I need to complete for some paperwork. You know, bureaucratic requirements."

"That's fine, Mr. Berger. What can I help with?"

Luc looked at Chloé's note. "Okay, thank you. I guess to begin, why were you importing rhesus macaques from India, since their importation had been banned over a decade earlier?"

"Is there some problem?"

Damn it, Luc thought. He should have gone in more gently. "There's nothing wrong, sir. No inquisition. It's just for the file. Some things we noticed to be missing. Since it's a dead animal, we need to be sure. Again, bureaucratic paperwork. Filling in blanks." Now he'd done it.

"Okay then, we weren't."

"You weren't...?"

"Importing rhesus macaques."

"Then who was?"

"No one. Those creatures, that monkey you have, it's not a rhesus macaque. They were...something else."

Luc scanned the other questions, all of which were now irrelevant.

"What were they?"

"Another type of primate, something akin to the rhesus. Something tougher. We had secured special permission to export them from northern India. I'm sure the laboratory has the paperwork for all of it. You'll need to contact them for it..."

"Tougher? Why tougher?"

"The studies we were conducting—mostly related to cerebral trauma..."

"Impact studies."

"Yes, impact studies. We were not getting the results we needed. Not getting what we thought would be reflective of the human experience. So we tried to obtain an animal more proximate in cranial durability to a human. More, how should I say, robust."

"Did you go to collect them?"

"I don't recall who made the arrangements, but back then placing an order for a specimen wasn't exactly like it is today. More like a game of telephone. We were sent several specimens. Trial and error. Most of them didn't work out, but one did. It did very well. You have to understand, this is ugly work, Mr. Berger. But that particular creature—that specimen—it performed admirably. Despite the behavioral issues, we decided to order an entire batch for study."

"Behavioral issues?"

"Because they are considered sacred in India, primates tend to be domineering, undisciplined and bad tempered. That we had always known. But the first of the new batch that we had obtained was far worse than the usual. We thought it was an anomaly, which is why we went ahead with obtaining more."

"Those were the ones on the plane."

"Yes, that was a setback."

"And their robustness, that's why they survived the crash?" No response. "Dr. Reinhardt, do you think that's why they survived when nothing else did?"

"Mr. Berger, there are all sorts of reasons why those creatures could have survived that crash. It could have been the design of their cages, or how they were stowed in the hold, or just plain luck. It's impossible to say, just as I told your government a long, long time ago."

"Did you ever get more of them?"

"We did."

"How did they behave?"

"I couldn't say."

"Did you not work with them?"

"I did."

"So...you can't say, or you won't say."

"They had to be destroyed, Mr. Berger."

"Destroyed, why?"

"Like I said about the first one. We discovered that they were not...normal. Not like anything we had ever seen. Not like anything I've ever seen since, thank god. They were treacherous to handle and, to be honest, near impossible to kill."

"Maybe that's why they're still alive," Luc said, more to himself than to Dr. Reinhardt.

"What did you say, Mr. Berger?" Now Luc didn't respond. "Did...did I hear you correctly? Did you say they're still alive? You said you found a carcass."

Shit, caught. "We're not sure what we found."

"Do you have it? Have you trapped one?"

"No, just sightings. Really, we're just not sure."

"I see," Dr. Reinhardt said with urgency. "Mr. Berger, you listen to me. If you do capture one, if you trap it, you must burn it—incinerate it. Immediately. It's the only way. If it is still free...well, then god help you. God help all of us. I thought they had all been destroyed."

"Wait, why do you say that? What's going on with these monkeys?"

"I'm an old scientist, Mr. Berger. Only an old scientist will admit freely that there are some things out there that even science cannot explain. That our study of something may bring us no closer to understanding the world. Sometimes some things bring us farther away. That's all I can say."

"But why? Can't you tell me at least where they came from? So I can find out more?"

"They came from northern India. Sikkim. Nothing more. I must go."

Luc scrambled to write that down. "Okay, but if I have any more questions..."

"I can't answer anything more, Mr. Berger. Listen, I hope everything works out on your end with your paperwork. Goodbye."

"But I—" and the phone line went dead.

Immediately Luc called Chloé to explain what happened, and immediately she got to work on the new information. It didn't, however, lead to much. By the time Luc arrived home that night—with Thai food, this time—all Chloé had been able to produce was a tiny item from the Saturday edition of The New York Times on December 30, 1967, entitled "Fire Damages Lab in Bronx:"

ience for who is retiring Jan. 1.
with the Justice G. Robert Witmer of
ties, the Rochester, designated tempo-
in which rarily to the Appellate Division.
en dress-
cade had **Fire Damages Lab in Bronx**

    A fire yesterday damaged a
and even research laboratory at the Al-
potential bert Einstein College of Medi-
al White- cine and hospital at Morris
for the Park Avenue and Eastchester
an form Road, the Bronx. A spokesman
ence has said the blaze, confined to a
le world small, unoccupied laboratory on
e of the the third floor of the Ullman
emporary Research Building, caused no
injuries.

Had Luc spoken with Dr. Reinhardt in person, he would have seen the scarring, which ran from his neck to his hands. But he hadn't and never would. It turns out the fine people of Chamonix are not the only ones who try to shape the news in order to avoid drawing attention to that which they would rather be left unknown. Because this article, located on page 24, tucked in between an appreciation for Paul Whiteman, the "King of Jazz," and a notice about the New York State

Governor's designation of appellate court justices, left out some important details.

While the fire itself caused no injuries, it had resulted in deaths—specifically, those of 80 primate specimens; specimens flown in from India that could not be controlled, would not be sedated and which had viciously attacked Dr. Reinhardt and his colleagues, who in their desperation to prevent the creatures from escaping, set fire to their own laboratory. It proved to be the only thing that worked.

×××

Monkeys and horses didn't occupy Luc's mind as he sat, days later, in the council room of the Mairie. Bigots and fascists did.

Arthur had pulled together biographies for each of the attendees of this meeting, and while Luc sat listening to preamble and pleasantries, he tried to recall the background of each of them.

Here we had Jacques, the eldest by far, descended from parents resettled into France after Algerian independence in the '70s. He served as the "local," having moved to the industrial outskirts of Cluses, just 30 kilometers from Chamonix. Joining him were two representatives from the "rust-belt" in the north of France—Julie and Margot—disaffected socialists that demanded more from the state to protect their livelihoods in dying domestic industries: washing machine manufacturing or something.

There also sat a well-dressed, well-groomed young man, Fabian, barely out of university, from "peripheral France," as he called it. He took the most logic-based approach to his arguments, likely having just read some articles on the topics he discussed. His experience couldn't've been anything. Yet Jacques let him go on at length. Fabian complained about how Uber, bike-share schemes and co-working spaces had left "real people" high and dry, how globalization has passed them by and how foreigners stole their jobs.

Luc sat quietly and listened politely while pretending to take notes. In an odd way, it reminded him of the group of wingsuiters with whom he had met a day earlier. They lobbied the Mairie about the new regulations regarding valley flight paths. As agenda-driven groups went, they also proved to be a set of irascible individuals, to whom Arthur referred as the "extreme fringe of extreme athletes:" a recovering alcoholic American; a free spirit Norwegian with relentless body odor; and an obsessive-compulsive woman from the Romandie.

But where the wingersuiters spoke fluently and with passion—almost to a philosophical extent about their code of personal responsibility and how they savored life—the group now in front of Luc so far possessed a disaffected nonchalance, like they didn't really need to work to convince him of their points, as if assuming he understood them. He didn't. Though not because of some superior liberal morality or noble drive to protect others. Their thinking just didn't apply to a place like Chamonix.

Luc, however, did pep up when Fabian spoke of the need to eliminate Halal options from public food programs and eventually from all restaurants. Luc wondered if any restaurants in Chamonix offered such a thing. Might be something new for Chloé's ever-changing appetite. He knew the Indian restaurants offered a Jain menu at times. Wasn't quite to his taste though—vegetarian but no roots or garlic...or flavor—and he smiled at the thought of it.

At this point, Jacques could see the group had lost the mayor, and decided to change course. "Monsieur Berger, ultimately, we're here as a courtesy to inform you of our intentions. We will be staging a protest in the main square outside here."

"A protest, okay," Luc said, looking up. "I expect you've filed the requisite paperwork for holding a manifestation?" He looked to Arthur, who shook his head not knowing.

"We haven't, actually. We'll be showing up illegally. A technicality, you know."

"And you're informing me of this because..." Luc stopped. "You want to be arrested."

"We hope it doesn't come to that but if it does, so be it. We invited the media to be in attendance. We'll also have our own cameras. It's fine. We don't want you to worry about whether you think the police will cause a scene. Let them do what they do. It's fine."

It's not fine, Luc thought. "How many of you will be in attendance?"

"We expect a considerable turnout."

"You'll be bussing people in?"

"I don't want to reveal everything, but as I'm sure you know, the people of Chamonix are not as happy as you may think about having these Middle Easterners here."

"You expect a significant turnout...of locals...during inter-season." Luc smiled and turned to Arthur who played along, smiling. Luc tried hard not to betray any sense that he actually was surprised by this news.

Fabian said: "We've done a bit of outreach online and generated a lot of awareness about our intentions—ahead of the arrival of these foreigners."

Luc again shot Arthur a look, but Arthur feigned ignorance of what Fabian spoke of.

"What exactly is your goal here?"

"Ah yes, I suppose you are wondering why we choose to torment you so," Jacques said with a smile. "We wish simply to make an example of you, of Chamonix." He pronounced the town's name "Sham-mon-neeks." Luc hated this. If all that had been stated thus far had only revealed their ignorance, then this one thing, this mispronunciation, right at that moment betrayed their true intentions.

"What kind of example do you intend to make of Chamonix?" Luc said, enunciating the local pronunciation of the name.

"Don't the people of France have enough troubles in their lives—the poor economy, the lack of jobs, the price of housing—without having it all be corrupted by foreign interests? Without having their barely-affordable ski holidays to one of the prides of France distorted by politics and outsiders? You've said it yourself, M. Berger—'open to others but protective of your own.' Those are your words, aren't they? How protective of your own are you when you're inviting these people into town?"

"Outsiders? Everyone in this town—including myself—is an outsider." Technically true, but technically false. Still Luc didn't care.

"It starts with one family, M. Berger. You're being kind and generous. Very Christian of you. But then it ends up like Calais. You don't need the drugs or deviant behavior, or, God forbid, the possibility of terrorism. Think of the businesses,

M. Berger. You also don't need the negative publicity. Maybe if you change your mind right now we can have a different type of event tomorrow—one celebrating France and the French identity."

"Outsiders, death, drugs, terrorism—you clearly don't know Chamonix. You're turning an act of compassion into a photo op for racial intolerance. That's pathetic."

"We've seen the statements you've made. But we thought we'd give it a try. You now own this issue. We're going to do everything we can to make sure every mayor and town councilperson from Bordeaux to Strasbourg knows it. Because if anything happens to this town—or anyone in it—because of those outsiders, your neck will be on the line. And not just at the end of your term..."

"My neck?"

"This town has convicted one mayor of manslaughter because he didn't warn of an avalanche. What do you think they will do to you when there's a terrorist attack?"

"One family. Their religion doesn't even have enough people left to have an extremist wing." Rage grew within Luc, and he gripped the arms of his chair, and tried to at least seem calm about the whole thing. But Jacques continued, and as he did Luc boiled inside; a ringing accompanied the man's words.

"Either way, M. Berger, you will be replaced. And that's at least something we thought would help open your mind about this situation. Because that is what this is all about: being replaced. They come by way of this Muslim migration. They take our homes, they take our jobs. All of this is made worse by the fact that they have a very strong culture and civilization. That means our language gets replaced. Our religion gets

IN THIS DELICIOUS GARDEN

replaced. Eventually—eventually, M. Berger—our population gets replaced. It is the way of history, as we have seen it.

"And I would say that the French race, or, if you'd rather, the French people, in all its dimensions—ethnic, cultural, civilizational—is especially menaced. We are fast losing our own territory. Our culture and civilization are quickly becoming just one among others. Chamonix will go in the same way. It will be replaced. Like Las Vegas has become a replacement for Venice. Or rollercoasters are replacements for your Vallée Blanche. And everything else is being replaced by mass production. I think it is perfectly awful, yes, because I think the dignity of man is that he is not replaceable. The nightmare is 'the replaceable man,' the man who is just something which can be replaced by someone else or something else at any moment. It looks like that nightmare may be you. Replaced.

"So you say one family now, M. Berger, but you're opening the door. Only someone with the brain of a butterfly would believe it will end there. There will be more, others, always looking to take what you have. And you're just giving it away. Before long, you'll discover that Chamonix-Mont-Blanc has become Chamonix-Mosque-Blanc."

"What did you just say?"

"You heard it exactly."

"Okay, thank you. I think we're done here." And Luc stood up.

"We still have to go over the..."

"No, we're done. I understand quite well your requirements. I don't want to take up any more of your time. And it would be a shame for you to miss seeing a bit of Chamonix while you're here. After all, none of you are actually from here." Then Luc became overly polite. "In fact, maybe I can help arrange something for you. Something local, something very Chamonix." He pronounced the "x" with emphasis. Luc turned to Arthur. "Can you give Jean-François a call? Ask him if he found the horses, maybe bring them out for some guests of ours. Some special guests of ours. They would benefit from a good, close look at les chevaux des Bossons."

✕✕✕

The sun sets several times a night in Chamonix. At the valley floor, the white light of day first vanishes behind the Aiguilles Rouges or the Aiguillette des Houches, depending on where you're standing. The sky will remain blue, though dusk has now flashed in town and a coolness nips the air, brought up by the flow of the River Arve running through the center of the valley. The Arve henceforth controls the night.

The second setting is when the sun falls behind the Fiz, a mountain one valley over above the town of Servoz. The shadow in Chamonix center will darken a shade, and Mont Blanc, up to the Plan—that balcony upon which dear Nils once ran into his monkeys—remains lit. It is that high up. At this time, the Bossons Glacier turns bright white contrasted against the growing shadows of the granite aiguilles all down the range, which sharpen in relief.

Ten maybe 15 minutes later that same layer will begin to pinken, and only the summits remain in the stark light—that is, until the sun falls behind the Jura, a range on the western side of Geneva, 100 kilometers away. At this point, yellows and reds absorb into the gray granite, and the snows high up relinquish their white until morning. A spectrum of intense hues makes the coldest of rock and ice glow like embers.

Another 10 minutes passes and the yellows are gone, pushed out by the reds to make room for an array of violets that now soften the rock and snow. But this is when the clouds, the only thing above the mountains, take their turn with the sun's rays, which are now setting thousands of kilometers away on a distant horizon, maybe the western coast of France, maybe the Atlantic Ocean.

At this point—when the whole massif and sky are ablaze and the dying light is consumed by night creeping upward from the valley floor—even the eldest, most jaded of Chamoniards will stop and take a look at the magnificence of color and wonder at the world in which she or he lives.

Weather permitting, to observe any moment of this nightly display is to be enthralled—for it is one of the singular instances when a human's relatively limited ability to perceive can grasp fully the enormity of Mont Blanc, all 3,800m that rise nearly straight up from the valley floor. It evokes emotion and shortens the breath.

To observe the entire sunset, from beginning to end, takes more than an hour, and is a rare and distinct pleasure for anyone in the position and who has the time to do so. That is, unless you're watching it from your kitchen window while on an unending conference call with lawyers in London and New York, who have proven themselves very capable of sucking the beauty out of everything, including one of nature's most impressive sights.

Lulu had put the speaker on mute. She grew tired of listening to others bicker over the details of the transaction she had agreed to with Mediastopheles. Now they beckoned her to make a decision on...

"What was it? Sorry, the line cut out. Mountains, you know."

Eyes rolled on three continents. *Sure, right. We're doing all this for you, you know.*

"No problem," someone said. "We will need you to make a decision on the address of the subsidiary. Cham'porn the brand will now also become Cham'porn SA, a wholly-owned subsidiary of Mediastopheles, Ltd., which is a U.S. corporation."

"Okay, well, I'll get back to you on an exact address then. My shop is leased."

"You don't own the property?"

"No."

"Any property?"

"None."

With that the conversation turned to assets, and by the end of it Lulu left the call with a raw, disturbing sense of her own worth. According to the assessment, all she really carried in value was intangible—a brand, an idea, a notion of a way of life that she had expressed through pictures on t-shirts and a logo. For that, this corporation would be willing to give her a few million. She, however, had to remain involved, because they—admittedly—didn't understand what Cham'porn stood for. She kept that to herself, but she knew if she was going to succeed that would have to change.

×××

The refugee family stood in silence in the home of Albert Berger, a stout, powerful Chamoniard of about 80, who had gone to fetch them cold drinks. Albert, Luc's father, had spent his life applying Chamonix-honed climbing skills to the great mountain ranges of the world, and, after retiring as a guide and semi-professional athlete, he rebuilt his family home—a structure more than 150 years old on property the Berger's had been on for almost as three times as long.

Although each member of the refugee family looked over the elaborate carpentry of the home's interior, typically intricate woodwork designs of the Haute Savoie, none of it left much of an impression—their interest only a rough assessment of the latest place they had arrived at, knowing that they wouldn't be there for long. Understanding what they saw did not add anything in real terms to their ability to survive, so they appreciated the artistry only as exercise in their freedom to do so.

The same went for Albert's many pictures—dim photos of rescue helicopters, of climbers on the top of peaks, of travelers bowing before lamas surrounded by prayer flags, of Albert and his late wife. Little registered other than the understanding that this man would help them, not hurt them, and a benign presence is all they sought.

"Normally, we have beautiful sunsets from here," Albert said pointing to the large windows fronting the living room. He placed a tray of glasses and a pitcher of juice on a table and vanished once again. The family looked at each other, and, as if his voice had been a signal, they all moved to sit and continued to wait quietly. Their lives had become all about waiting, but waiting in peace for them had become a luxury.

Albert, meanwhile, bustled about in the kitchen. He had been unsure of what they ate, and had passed on the idea of serving a fondue or raclette or any of the traditional regional dishes made up of meat, cheese, potatoes and bread. He didn't want to offend them by assuming they'd eat anything. But they would have. In any case, he went straight down the middle, if not a touch overboard with his desire to be balanced, and offered steak and fish, potatoes and rice, vegetables and salads, and even a vegetarian curry.

When Luc had asked him to put together a dinner, Albert had been all too happy to help, to have something to do, to feel useful. It would give him something to talk about with his friends, since his days of sharing stories of being in the mountains had passed and fodder for new tales had dwindled. Like the refugee family, he too felt as if his life had become all about waiting—though for him, the luxury lay in the opportunity for the unexpected.

Into the kitchen Luc arrived without a knock at the backdoor. Quick pleasantries with Albert were followed by: "Now go see to the family. They're in the other room."

When Luc entered, he found the parents bickering quietly in a language he could not understand and the children, two boys, nearly asleep in chairs. Upon seeing him, they all stood up, and for a moment it became awkward, no one quite sure what to say in what language. Luc looked around for someone who wasn't there.

He realized immediately his mistake, assuming that a minder or government chaperone would accompany them. But why would they need one? They're adults with a now-legal status in the country. Despite heightened concerns about their very existence, an Alpine Taxi had unceremoniously dropped off the family in town earlier in the day, just like any tourist, and now here they stood, the very real manifestation of a document that Luc signed more than a year ago.

"Bonjour," the husband, Aslan, said in heavily accented French, while reaching for an opposite-handed shake. He held his right hand, fingerless, close to his chest. Aslan thanked Luc, on behalf of his family, for the generosity and kindness in providing a new home for them.

All Luc could say in returned was: "You speak French?"

"Yes, of course. You forget, the French have a long history in the Middle East," Aslan said.

Luc apologized for the misunderstanding, for his being late, and for the absence of his very pregnant wife. He then welcomed the family to Chamonix and introduced his father and Arthur. Some practical discussion about their arrival, their stay, their housing and the children's schooling followed, after which they sat for dinner.

Although a rigid politeness reined at first, the dinner became increasingly convivial thanks to Albert who, by default, filled wine glasses and asked the types of personal and potentially risky questions Luc would not. This was why Luc chose his father as host, though he made faux apologies, for him anyways.

Aslan assured: "We don't mind. We don't eat pork. We do drink alcohol. And we're happy to tell you our story." By dessert, he and his wife had become comfortable enough to share so much that Luc had begun to regret his desire to know more.

"After four days on Sinjar, without food and with only a few sips of water from shallow springs," Aslan said, "we knew we had to go. The heat sapped us of our sanity, made worse knowing killers waited not far away. They would either starve us on that rock or murder us as we ran..."

Gerus, his wife, interjected: "We had to spit into their mouths—" she pointed to the children "—to try to get them some liquid. We ate broken sticks and cloth that we could find. How quickly we became savages. We felt death would soon come to them, to all of us."

Aslan continued: "We had only so much energy left, only so much strength. So we decided to risk our children's lives and try to escape. What mercy met us, we do not know, because as we ran into the night, no one met us. No soldiers. No one at all. And we were amazed to find that after going only three hours beyond where we were, we were nearly in Syria.

"Gerus still had her phone and we called relatives when we found a signal. They helped us cross over, but they were in a dire situation of their own. We spent our last few dinars on a taxi back to Dohuk—a Kurdish city in the north—which was again easier than we expected. It was like there was no border. But none of this made us safe, only more confused, like it was a trap."

"We thought the Islamic State would only stay a short time in our village," Gerus said. "We thought the Kurdish fighters would succeed in beating them back. But the Peshmerga, they used up all their bullets." She looked down. "All these groups at war and no one had any easy means to kill one another. Toothless wolves, they just circled one another. We couldn't wait to find out who would grow teeth first. We passed several days living under a highway bridge, uncertain where to go or what to do. Local Kurds brought us mattresses, bread and cakes, and some brought cooked food. They wanted desperately to go home—" She nodded again to the children "—there is no more home, we had to keep telling them."

Her husband nodded and said: "We could never go back to our village, or we'd die." And with his fingerless hand, he made a cutting motion across his neck. "We could not rely on neighbors. They either died or fled. The Yazidis scattered to the wind. Anyone else was too afraid to shelter us. We could not rely on family, because they also either died or fled. So we too left. The four of us walked—and ran—about 250 kilometers from Dohuk to Kızıltepe in Turkey. It took three days. At a Lassa station...you know, for petrol...we caught a ride. And then we hitchhiked two more days to Ankara. From there to Paris, and then Calais. We had planned to go to London. We have relatives there. But no. And then to Sweden. But again, no. So here we are. With you."

Luc could see that his father and Arthur had become rapt by Aslan and Gerus's tale, one honed by numerous tellings. From border guard to police officer to humanitarian aid worker, it clearly had served well as a tool by which the family gained the sympathies of others in order to get away, to stay together, to survive.

Luc didn't feel cruel for looking at their story with some amount of realism. He didn't bother to ask any specific questions—about how Aslan had lost his fingers, about where the money or means came from the get from Ankara to Paris. All of it just meant to him that they were clearly willing to adapt to survive; however, were they in fact one of his "own?" Could they learn to adapt to live in this place?

It would be conceivable, Luc thought, that once they walked out the door that evening, he may never see or hear from them again. That, in a sense, would be ideal, that they integrate neatly into Chamonix's community. But how likely would it be for them to harmonize with Chamonix?

It is France. Jacques the Effer was not wrong about that. They must eat the bread and cheese, drink the wine, speak the language, be discrete in their religious practices. And yet, there was so much he didn't and wouldn't know about them— their traditions, their norms, their mannerisms, which may or may not make them a target for derision and ridicule. But then, he had already made them into a target, an example of what "refugees" would be seen as by the public. They were vulnerable and a potential threat.

Maybe this Aslan was a thief. Maybe his wife a whore. Maybe the children would cause trouble, get into fights. Maybe the family would end up serving as a beachhead for others, those less tolerable, those 400 more who would come. Maybe, maybe, maybe.

All the same, even if they accommodated what France asked of them, how would they be shaped by the Alps? Deep down, this, Luc knew, was what really concerned him. Whereas the French sought to hold everyone to the rhythms of culture, Chamonix's peaks demanded something more: The great forces manipulated the senses; there was no choice in how a person changed because of them—a reaction as involuntary as when facing a wild animal.

He heard Alsan's words: "...the Yazidis had long entrenched themselves in the mountains of Kurdistan to preserve their heritage and way of life..." but Luc wasn't so sure how that would work here.

Luc's own family had come to the Chamonix valley to find refuge from conflicts between the Swiss and Italians. Nature here protected them because they were willing to endure that which their tormentors would not. The obligations of survival never made for easy life. The forces that protected them, threatened them all the same. They changed as a result. Their traditions evolved because their priorities evolved.

This Yazidi family and their traditions would undergo the same change, but not as a result of nature, as a result of politics and commerce, those other forces that guide life. They had different obligations of survival. They may find safety, but would they ever find joy? Would Chamoniards let them?

Then his thoughts morphed from fatigue. Luc lost entirely the conversation at the table. Instead he thought of his grandfather, his father's father, a man never known to be joyful—just tough and resilient. He made sacrifices, just as each generation did, to create a better life for the next. He wouldn't care about refugees, as long as they didn't cause trouble. What then would his grandfather care about? He'd care about the wingsuiters, people just throwing themselves off cliffs for the fun of it. Is that what he made sacrifices for?

Misha, one of the boys, the elder of the two, interrupted Luc's passive thoughts—as if he had been listening inside Luc's head: "Our grandfather knew joy. He threw himself off a cliff on Mount Sinjar so he would not be a burden to us. He was joyful to do so. I remember him as joyful. We are grateful for his sacrifice."

Startled both by what the boy said and how it carried with what he had been thinking, Luc looked at Misha agog, and then to the others at the table.

Gerus and Aslan glanced at each other, and to Luc they nodded. Yes, what he said was true: "A number of the elders did this. We had to move quickly and for them it was a faster death than waiting on the animals below."

Misha then said, "This is the way of Tawûsê Melek. Our grandfather was not born with wings to fly, but since he had faith, we know he had wings to soar to heaven. Falling down and rising up are one in the same."

"Tawûsê Melek," said Aslan, "this is the central figure in our religion. You say, a 'bird-angel?' What he means is that there are no opposites. Good and evil, they are fluid and interchangeable to us. A fire burns but it also provides illumination. Gerus's father died in order for us to live."

Luc thought on this a moment, and he looked to his own father, and then turned to the boy: "In Chamonix, we also have a sacred bird in our mountains: the black crow. We believe that the souls of those who have died ride on their wings, and that's how they are transported to the afterlife."

"We saw these birds," said Misha, with a happy flash of recognition. "At the Midi today. We went up there. They were at the top. I tried to touch one!"

"Yes, those would be them," Luc said, relieved by the new direction of the conversation. "When you see them, it is good luck to toss them a bite to eat, some bread maybe." He winked at the boy.

"I also saw the monkeys," Misha said.

Luc shook his head not thinking he understood. "I'm sorry?"

"You have the monkeys..."

Luc looked at his glass, wondering if he had had too much wine.

"Forgive him, Monsieur Luc. The journey was very traumatic for him. He is very tired, and, along the way, he has hallucinated many things. He had been dehydrated, starving at points. Besides, he can be as mischievous as he is creative."

Luc looked to the boy and their eyes locked.

The world around the two of them fell away. No sound. No light. Just the words of the boy who said in an even voice: "All treasures and hidden things are known to Tawûsê Melek; and as he desires, he takes them from one and bestows them upon another. It is the way of the world. The monkeys have been taken from one and given to another. Let them be. They have their work. They have a role to play. They won't hurt those who don't hurt the mountain. They will find their own way home."

Luc and Misha remained transfixed with one another for what seemed an eternity. Later he described to Chloé what had happened. Luc admitted to visions that accompanied Misha's words: Luc had seen the glaciers advance and then melt away; the mountains grow and then tumble; even their child, a son, be born, grow old, and die—all the Earth would undergo great change, just as it had, and the people, they would fade away. Emotion swelled within him.

The boy dropped his gaze, and Luc looked up to Albert and Arthur, and then to Gerus and Aslan. No one appeared to have heard Misha's words. No one noticed the exchange. They carried on, oblivious to what had just happened. He looked back at Misha, who had now turned his attention to a bowl of fruit salad on the table, reaching to scoop from it—seemingly unaware that he had just shattered Luc's world.

"You'll have to excuse us, Monsieur Luc," Aslan said. "It is late, and we do not want to keep you from your wife. We should also get these boys to bed. Again, we are eternally grateful for your generosity—"

Luc, stunned, moved trancelike as everyone made their way to the door.

As each of them said their goodbyes, Misha held onto Luc's hand. Before leaving, the boy tugged at Luc, who leaned down and fought a sudden, desperate urge to ask the boy about what happened to all the people in his vision. Instead, he just looked at Misha without a word, and waited for whatever would come. "Merci" was all Misha said, and the family went into the night.

With the click of the door shutting, Luc snapped back to the present, and as Arthur came up to him to say how well he thought the evening went, Luc abruptly asked: "I need to speak with Dr. Reinhardt, the scientist I told you about. Call him until he answers. This is very important. As soon as possible."

Arthur looked at him, confused by the unrelated command, and said: "I meant to tell you earlier, Luc. Dr. Reinhardt...he's dead. He died last week. And Jean-François, you asked me to call him as well. He's dead too."

"Wha-what?"

"I meant to tell you, but there's been so much going on."

"How?"

"I don't know. It was just some woman who answered Dr. Reinhardt's phone. She said he killed himself. And Jean-François, well, it looks like the horses. There have been others as well."

✕✕✕

Often tourists remark of those lost on Mont Blanc: "Why didn't they just come straight down? You can see the summit from town." Well, the answer is simple: One can also see the ground from an airplane, but that doesn't make an unscheduled return to Earth any easier. As the rules of mountains go: It's always further than it looks. It's always taller than it looks. And it's always harder than it looks.

Such is life in the Alps.

The ability to see the lofty destination of Mont Blanc's dome, or any other peak, from a position of relative comfort, is deceiving. As is the converse: being able to look upon the warmth and safety of the town thousands of feet below while trapped skyward or icebound, unable to move or think.

The obstacles are many. Massive fields of snow and ice. Crevasses. Unscaleable cliffs. And the distance itself must be covered on exhausted legs or with frozen hands. If the landscape alone is not enough to make diminutive the stature of man, there is, as previously mentioned, the weather, which can distort visibility, light and temperature.

There are also the invisible, non-obvious obstacles—those that creep in: the sun and the altitude. They sap energy and morale, slowly and imperceptibility, until one becomes incapacitated, whether physically or mentally. The strongest can be reduced to nothing if they lose their will to go on. Even in perfect conditions, the invisible will burn those with a lack of experience or preparation.

Upon that very first summiting of Mont Blanc, as Jacques Balmat and Michel-Gabriel Paccard basked in the glory of their ascent, Balmat—so overwhelmed by the brilliance of the sunlight upon the snows—proclaimed while looking out over the lands that would be France, Italy and Switzerland: "Whichever way I look, I see only tears of blood..."

He meant this literally. Snow-blindness—or photokeratitis—is basically sunburned eyes, inflamed cornea due to excessive exposure to the sun's UV rays, exacerbated at every angle by the snow. But on the eve of a century of increasingly contentious wars—conflicts of territory, of religion and of economies, those which would culminate with the Great Wars of the 20th century—more prescient words have been rarely been spoken.

Paccard, a doctor not a poet, replied: "That is because you cannot see. The sun has risen, and the swelling of your eyelids has rendered you temporarily blind."

Exposure to these types of alpine conditions result in a prismatic view of the world, and as a result offer an endless supply of lessons and metaphors, which elsewhere—in places less distorted—can be applied to attain clarity and certainty.

They mostly involve the duality of nature: the fragility of life and ability of humans to endure the most inhospitable conditions; the emotionlessness of wilderness and the odd luck one can be afforded by the randomness of nature. In all, it grabs us quite by the throat and forces us to assess what's really important or shakes us to our core, and does so on any number of levels.

A trail runner plucked from a glacier may carry with him second thoughts about going back onto the ice; a tourist plumbed from the depths of a crevasse may stop working so much and spend more time with family and friends; a wingsuiter who watched his best friend collide with a barn may turn his entire life upside down, destroying relationships and turn to excessive drug use. Not all of the outcomes are positive.

Most people who visit Chamonix come and go, unaware of such undercurrents, only skimming off the top a scene, an experience, or maybe just a token—that sunset, a taste for skiing, or one of Lulu's t-shirts—not considering that they could have temporarily lost their vision, plunged to their death or are wearing around the mark of an aged eco-terrorist pornographer. They may arrive and leave with assumptions intact about unknowable things.

For those who have been immersed in this environment, their whole lives, the locals, whose families are sewn into the fabric of the place, what they carry with them as a result of living in this faceted world is a comfort with the unanswerable Unknown, and a familiarity—though never an ease—with the scars.

×××

The Unknown, the Yazidi family, that had occupied Luc's mind for months, now revealed its scars: Aslan's fingerless hand. Luc questioned why he hadn't asked what happened. He wondered why his father hadn't either. Politeness, maybe. A desire to comfort his guest and not bring up what clearly would be a horrible memory. Or, unfortunately, just cynicism.

The hand recalled for Luc another man he had known without fingers: Maurice Herzog, who had sat in the very seat— both actual and elected—that Luc occupied at that moment.

Maurice, along with steep skiing pioneer Louis Lachenal, both from Chamonix, had together in 1950 been first in history to climb an 8,000m peak: Annapurna—which continues to be today the deadliest mountain in the world; one in three people who have attempted to climb it have perished. Before Everest's summit was reached and before the Moon landing took place, it served as a singular human achievement.

Maurice and Louis themselves barely avoided death on that mountain any number of ways, and while they escaped with their lives, Maurice left behind fingers and Louis left his toes.

While certainly one of those creeping and invisible obstacles, frostbite was no mystery to these men.

Upon setting out for Annapurna's summit, wearing thin leather boots and realizing the implication of numb feet, Louis asked of Maurice: "If I go back, what will you do?"

"I should go on by myself," Maurice said.

Louis knew that to go on meant the loss of his toes. But he also knew that turning back meant the loss of Maurice's life. "Then I'll follow," Louis decided.

It proved to be a heroic gesture, and certainly helped secure not just the summit but the return home for both men. However, few average people know of Louis Lachenal. He vanished, along with the monkeys in the lab and the escaped elephant, similarly papered over by an alternative recounting of history.

Maurice told a tidy tale of his trip up Annapurna in a best-selling book, writing himself as the hero of the expedition. He received a Gold Medal from the Société de Géographie, served as a member of the International Olympic Committee and became a grand officer of the Legion d'Honneur. Charles de Gaulle appointed him as Minister for Youth and Sport, and later he became mayor of Chamonix.

Louis received no such accolades. He just went back as best he could to his life, without his digits, and watched as Maurice soared, kept aloft by the combined forces that dictate life in the mountains: commerce, politics and nature.

Maurice had secured exclusive rights to the Annapurna story for the first five years. No one else on the trip could publish a word. Cementing that tale were the French government and the Club Alpin Français, which badly sought to make a mark in the Himalayas to redeem the nation's self-esteem after the war and a long period in which the country had been overshadowed by the mountaineering exploits of Germany, Austria and Britain. And then, just as the embargo on the Annapurna story was about to be lifted, Louis died.

He took the lift up to the Aiguille du Midi in 1955 to ski the Vallée Blanche with some friends. He followed the same path that Josh took, in fact; the very same that a thousand people go each year. The last sign of Louis were ski tracks that led out over a low slope. In the blue light of day, there opened a small hole, down which he fell, not too far from where Josh took his own plunge.

There is no doubt that for a second, Louis's friends all looked around, either in disbelief or shock, and felt the gravity of the situation. Mountains don't play favorites. Wind whistled, water trickled and black crows came to have look.

Maurice went on to edit for publication Louis's journals about the Annapurna expedition—in a way that further reinforced his own claims. Unlike mountains, people do play favorites.

As Luc contemplated the many hands without fingers he had seen in life, he rubbed over his own, nervous about what he now realized he had done. Through his arrogance, he had invited not just refugees, but judgment; the whole matter would now become a test of the values of the people he served. The world would see that at the rally. This would not be about him. Not at all. It would be about Chamonix.

Although the people of the mountains, especially those of Chamonix, have always been poor, they have been compensated with the gift of perspective. They sit up high next to the gods with a clear view of life below, watching the machinations of culture and civilization, as if it all plays out on some great stage. Chamoniards have long watched the burlesque of Parisian politics, mocked it and moved according to the stronger natural forces.

But the stage itself had now turned on the audience. The actors waited for those in the cheap seats to take direction. They look to Lulu's viral video as an example of adventure, to Nicolas's movies as an example of love, to Maurice's tales as example of heroism. And Luc feared that the forces that guided life had also been turned on their head—that commercialism and politics had crept in and blinded those who normally look to nature. Would people no longer be able to tell the difference between fingers lost to vainglory and those lost to war?

Luc looked at his own hands again, and a doubt rose that perhaps they were the wrong hands to guide the people. He slammed a fist on his desk so hard that one of the horse bells, which had been sitting on the corner, jumped up and landed on the floor with clank.

Luc's phone chimed. It was Chloé: "Pépé Luc, how about Annapurna tonight ☺"

✗✗✗

Luc sat in an old, uncomfortable wooden chair—one more decorative than practical, the only one the Indian restaurant had for those waiting for their pickup order. As he shifted in his seat repeatedly, he smiled politely to the young man behind the register, who seemed nervous—and who conveyed this nervousness to the kitchen—at having the mayor waiting too long for his food.

"Just a minute. We want to make sure it is hot, hot. Not cold for you when you get home."

Luc thanked the young man for the third time, and, as he did, the husband and wife who owned the restaurant entered the front door. What a surprise, how pleased they were to find the mayor patronizing their establishment. He hadn't been there before, had he?

"No, Chloé—my wife—she's pregnant, and we don't really go out that much."

Small talk ensued, the usual about business and the weather. At a moment of awkwardness when the conversation dragged, as the owners clearly intended to wait with him, Luc asked: "Just curious, but why did you name the restaurant after Annapurna?"

"In honor of the mayor of Chamonix, of course," the wife said, very pleased with her answer, and the husband smiled too.

"Right, of course," Luc said with a forced smile of appreciation, and sought to change the subject. "Look, this may seem like a strange question. And please, forgive my ignorance of Indian geography. But where your family originates, are there a lot of...monkeys?"

The couple laughed. "Well, we come by Mauritius, but in India, of course. Monkeys inhabit large portions of the country, Monsieur Mayor. They are like brothers to the Indian people. As you know, Buddhists and Hindus hold animals to be sacred."

"Right, right," Luc thought. "Again, forgive me if this is a strange question, but did they ever get collected for medical research—around where you're from?"

"It was very common a long time ago, yes. My grandfather's cousin, he used to do this. Made good money. It is now very unpopular. Very unpopular."

"Rhesus macaques, right?"

"Oh yes, those are the ones. They were the best for the laboratories."

"Were there other species, other types of macaques or anything..." he paused "...more robust? Stronger, like invincible?" He realized how stupid this sounded, and the husband and wife exchanged a glance, unsure if they heard him correctly.

"If you want an invincible monkey," the husband said, "you would have to catch a rachyyas." He smirked, and his wife laughed, which made him laugh.

Luc shook his head. "What is a rachyyas?"

"A Kanchenjunga rachyyas," she said. "It is a demon that looks like a monkey. The Sikkimese Buddhists believe they protect Kanchenjunga. They work on behalf of the Dzö-nga, the mountain spirits. This is what makes Kanchenjunga as dangerous as Annapurna. All who climb must respect the Dzö-nga, or else." She made this last statement with extreme seriousness, but then broke into a smile.

Luc looked at her stone faced. Although she joked, what she said was true.

When the first Westerner circumnavigated Kanchenjunga in 1899 to scout possible routes to the summit, he reported: "...the mountain is guarded by demons for the express purpose of defense against human assault; so skillfully is each comparatively weak spot raked by ice and snow batteries, it is impossible to believe to be without intent."

Upon the summit rests a crown of seracs, which release avalanches without notice and offer few lanes for safe ascent. Only a few dozen people have ever successfully climbed Kanchenjunga. Those who have had to make promises to the local shaman not to actually step foot on the summit, which would be an offense to the Dzö-nga. Most have abided, many have not. The results are telling. Usually, the fatality rates for mountains decrease over time. Not for Kanchenjunga, where the number of climbing deaths has increased.

Those who have lived through deadly expeditions claim to have seen the rachyyas first hand—a terror amidst the snows, possibly a stress-induced vision or maybe just evil itself. The local Buddhists say they emerge as result of the disrespect shown by the visitors, and the Dzö-nga set them loose. So serious the problem became that in 2000, the Indian government banned expeditions to Kanchenjunga, a prohibition that remains in force today.

"It's a joke, Monsieur Mayor. They are not real." The couple suddenly got nervous, thinking they offended him. But then the young man came through the door with Luc's order: "All ready, nice and hot!"

×××

On a cloudless night the aiguilles of the Mont Blanc massif can appear darker than the sky, and their sharp, triangular shape make them seem like teeth. To Luc, who looked up at them now as he walked across an empty parking lot, food in hand, they made him feel as if he was right in the mouth of a monster. The frozen tongue of the Bossons Glacier unfurled into the valley, and a cool breath floated up from the waters of the river Arve.

And yet, after a shudder at this notion, which caused him to stop, he looked out to the stars, to the universe beyond those teeth, and thought how much colder and worse it must be out there. At least here, he knew that life in the mouth of a monster, forever facing oblivion, constantly reinforced one's priorities—his wife, his child, his life, the town—all to be considered in every decision he made. Nothing to be taken for granted amidst the, he smiled, weirdness of it all.

Among the constellations, Luc then recognized Chamonix's star, the Aiguille du Midi, and became further reoriented. His eyes now adjusted to the darkness. The fangs returned to being granite spires, and gray glaciers became recognizable as ice. The only monsters left were the rachyyas, which he realized must be scrambling around up there somewhere.

And that's when he heard it.

A snort and then the clomp of a hoof. Luc turned, and in the night three horses emerged from the shadows.

✕✕✕

When word got around that the mayor hadn't shown up to represent at the immigration rally, an event he provoked all on his own, ire grew amidst certain quarters of Chamonix. For good or bad, he should be handling it. Arthur became frantic. He couldn't reach Luc. As a result, a number of people turned up out of curiosity to see what would happen, some turned up out of anger. A dozen became a few dozen, and then 100 people met 100 more—all gathering below the statue of Jacques Balmat in the sunny, late spring weather.

Without any formal organization, the sudden manifestation wheeled around town, a mob in search of a purpose, and it shuffled through the streets toward the Mairie looking for the Effers: would-be rioters at the gates of government. Police had been organized and once the crowd saw them mulling around in front of the Post Office, it went to meet them. Who were they protecting?

As the crowd moved into the Post Office square, a voice over a megaphone could be heard, shouting "On est chez nous!" ("We are at home!"), though to most the words were inaudible. The people, now motivated, moved away from the police toward the voice. Chanting rose up. Whistling. Cat calls.

And then, out of nowhere, an ugly din echoed across the square and the crowd became dead silent.

The sharp ringing of a bell—a bell everyone knew—pierced the air. Its tones became louder as silence swept back through the crowd. Everyone looked around, trying to identify from where this horrible sound came.

"There. Look!"—a sight as surreal as the mob itself. Luc on horseback made his way through the crowd, which gave him a wide berth, so shocked they were to see the mayor up high, clanging one of those bells—a sound so distinct no Chamoniard could mistake it. A mixture of fear and amazement rose up within them. What craziness was this!

Luc, who wore a tricolor sash, worked his way along, all eyes on him and the horse. Giddy whispers went through crowd: "Un cheval des Bossons...les chevaux des Bossons!"

The surprise that met the crowd was only matched by the relief that overcame Luc when he saw the signs people had made: welcoming the refugees; telling the Effers to go home; declaring Chamonix a valley open to all. He waded through the people, from the Post Office square into the small canyon of buildings that led to the Mairie, and directly in front of him Saint-Michel.

Luc could now see standing on the steps of the church about 10 people facing the crowd—four of which were the FNers he had met the other day. Although they clearly sought to lead a crowd, it appeared more like they had been cornered. The eldest, Jacques, held the megaphone, but he was too dumbfounded at the sight of the mayor on a horse to use it.

Luc moved in between the Effers and the people, and turned circles on the horse while ringing the bell over his head. He looked at all the faces, some smiling, most just in awe. He saw Arthur upon a lamppost in front of the Mairie, his free hand upon his forehead: "Incroyable!" he mouthed.

Luc, satisfied he now had everyone's attention, stopped ringing the bell and shouted out: "It's a good day to welcome a new family to Chamonix!"

The crowd roared with approval. The police moved quickly to reposition themselves.

Luc looked back at the Effers who now appeared frightened, whether by the crowd or the horse or himself, Luc couldn't tell. But he turned the animal and trotted over, bringing its face close to them, and looked over them, despite their elevated place on the steps. The police kept their distance from the horse.

"You appear to be outnumbered," Luc said.

Unsure what to do, Jacques took up the megaphone and clicked the button to speak. The device emitted a metallic squawk, spooking the horse, which jerked its head and snapped at Jacques, who in turn let out a yelp, dropped the megaphone and ran. The others similarly backed off, and the crowd, knowing what the horse was capable of, fanned backwards quickly.

The horse calmed down as Luc led it back around to face the crowd.

"There is a narrow path between responsibility and conviction," Luc shouted. "But as Chamoniards we know how to walk a fine line." He pointed to the Aiguille du Midi, and some chuckles rose up through the crowd. "Our town is on a border, one that has changed many times over the last few hundred years. Does this make us French, or Italian or Swiss?" The crowd stayed quiet. "Does it matter? Foremost, we're Chamoniards. We're defined by our own history, our own actions. They wish to make an example of us." He pointed backwards to the Effers. "No, we're here to set an example for them."

A voice from the people shouted: "Plus Americain que les Americains, hein John Wayne!" ("More American than the Americans, right John Wayne!") And crowd laughed. Luc gestured, as if doffing a cowboy hat.

The crowd clapped and laughed, and Luc turned back to the Effers, dismounted the horse and handed it off carefully to Arthur. Now face-to-face with the 10 Effers, Luc said: "Yes, I do say often that we're 'open to others, but we first take care of our own.' You, in this case are the 'others.' You're welcome to stay and say your piece. But make no mistake, you are not 'our own,' you are certainly not 'home,' and your ideas—that craziness you spout—will not replace our ideas of right and wrong."

The Effers stood defiant in front of the church, until Père William came out with a few fellow churchmen. Between the church and the Mairie and the people, the Effers clearly saw that they had been outflanked. They milled around talking amongst themselves and eventually wandered away. The crowd had anyways begun to disperse. The show was over, and people had to get back to work.

×××

The good and the bad both get buried in Chamonix. Without willing witnesses, most things just disappear, whether into the ice or into history—though as is now well established some things do reemerge after a spell.

Accounts of the rally have been gleaned only from the whispers in the Saturday market. No tourists attended that day, it being interseason, and the Effers failed to document their own embarrassment. A few photos did pop up on social media, but most of those in attendance just assume to let the whole matter go.

After all, it happened pretty quickly. So caught up in the surprise and emotion of the event, most people hadn't even noticed that the animal Luc rode in on didn't quite glide like a cheval des Bossons. "So where did you get that horse?" Arthur asked of Luc later. "The Merlet Animal Park," Luc said with a wink. "I swapped for three chevaux des Bossons. They finally have a home."

This nonchalance to extremes should not be confused with apathy. It is just the way of people who live in the mountains, particularly those who live in these Alps. Aspects of life here may be strange to outsiders, but here is established a clear understanding of what in life truly matters: birth, death, hard work, and looking out for one another. Perspective therefore becomes the only currency worth having, especially in a world increasingly bankrupt of compassion. It is the argument Chamoniards would make, just as they'd insist that gestures of welcome deserve neither praise nor reproach. But you may be hard pressed ever to get them to say anything at all.

Acknowledgements

In This Delicious Garden; or,
Les Enfants du Paradis

The title is taken from John Milton's "Paradise Lost" (1667), and is the completion of the line Mary Shelley used as the epigraph for "Frankenstein; or, The Modern Prometheus" (1818), which she conceived while on holiday in Chamonix, and where her novel's most enduring scenes take place.

> *Did I request thee, Maker, from my clay*
> *To mould me Man? did I solicit thee*
> *From darkness to promote me, or here place*
> *In this delicious garden?*

The "garden" is clearly an allusion to the Garden of Eden, which as an idea people look to as a haven, but one that contains certain perils. How did the original Chamoniards first come to see this dangerous valley as a place of refuge? How did the Yazidis, a people thought to be the "original children of the Garden of Eden", also later come to find the same thing? Yet how much death has been realized in the garden of Chamonix by outsiders who believe they can either remake themselves or live life to the fullest?

The second part of the title is taken from a film of the same name by Marcel Carné and made in France during the German occupation in 1945. The phrase translates literally to "children of paradise", but is best read as "children of the gods". The phrase refers by Carné to those in the cheap balcony seats of a theatre who sit high up and look down upon and judge both the actors on the stage and the upper classes in the floor seats.

By including this second title, I am in format echoing Shelley's title (the original English-language novel of Chamonix) and asking: Have Chamoniards—seemingly aloof and self-possessing—acquired some moral high ground as a result of their proximity to death and literal perspective on the world? If that is the case, has it over time been perverted by the politics and commercialism of the outside world? Or, is their quiet position (and desire to thrive like anyone else) not resulting in any judgment at all, but the mark of a deep and enduring sympathy for their fellow man?

The following sources have been consulted and, in some cases, directly referenced. Annotations with in the text have been omitted for the sake of the reading experience.

Kanchenjunga

"Mont-Blanc : enquête sur les secrets enfouis des disparus de la montagne" (2017) by Mathieu Delahousse
L'OBS
https://www.nouvelobs.com/justice/20170323.OBS7051/mont-blanc-enquete-sur-les-secrets-enfouis-des-disparus-de-la-montagne.html

"Literature's Arctic Obsession" (2017) by Kathryn Schulz
THE NEW YORKER
https://www.newyorker.com/magazine/2017/04/24/literatures-arctic-obsession

"Le terrible destin d'Air India" (2006)
14 HUIT MILLE
http://enfant.de.solo.free.fr/14huitmille/airindia.htm

"The Little Ice Age history of the Glacier des Bossons (Mont Blanc massif, France): a new high-resolution glacier length curve based on historical documents" (2011) by Samuel U. Nussbaumer and Heinz J. Zumbühl
SPRINGER SCIENCE+BUSINESS MEDIA
http://www.geo.uzh.ch/~snus/publications/nussbaumer_zumbuehl_2012.pdf

"Malabar Princess" (2004) by David George
PISTEHORS
http://pistehors.com/news/ski/comments/malabar-princess/

"L'avion 'Constellation' qui a percuté sur le mont Blanc garde toujours ses secrets" (1950) posted by André Signoret
ASIGNORET.FREE.FR
http://asignoret.free.fr/malabar.htm

"Crashs au Mont-Blanc de deux appareils d'Air-India à destination de Genève" (2005) by Jean-Claude Cailliez
PIONNAIR-GE
http://www.pionnair-ge.com/spip1/spip.php?article87

"1950 - 2016: The Malabar Princess Has Not Yet All Revealed" (2015) Jean Voruz
CONSILIUM PHILATELIAE HELVETICAE
http://www.airindiacollector.com/uploads/8/1/0/8/81084928/rpsl_india_malabar-princess_opus_e[2]_copy.pdf

"Chamonix celebrates the 150th anniversary of the golden age of mountaineering" (2015)
PETZL FOUNDATION
https://www.petzl.com/fondation/projets/chamonix-1865?language=en#.WG9rA1MrJhE

"Monte Bianco" posted by Wikipedia
WIKIWAND
http://www.wikiwand.com/it/Monte_Bianco

"So you think you know Chamonix" (2016) by Katy Dartford
KATYDARTFORD.COM
https://katydartford.com/2016/12/08/so-you-think-you-know-chamonix/

"Why Is Mont Blanc One of the World's Deadliest Mountains?" (2012) by Lane Wallace
THE ATLANTIC
https://www.theatlantic.com/international/archive/2012/07/why-is-mont-blanc-one-of-the-worlds-deadliest-mountains/260143/

Les Chevaux des Bossons

"The Mushroom Hunters" (2007) by Burkhard Bilger
THE NEW YORKER
https://www.newyorker.com/magazine/2007/08/20/the-mushroom-hunters

"The Secret Lives of Mushroom Hunters" (2013) by Nick Davidson
OUTSIDE MAGAZINE
https://www.outsideonline.com/1918991/secret-lives-mushroom-hunters

"Mushroom picking 'more complex' than expected" (2014) by Catherine McLean
THE LOCAL
https://www.thelocal.ch/20140908/mushroom-picking-proves-a-challenge

"Most Poisonous Mushrooms" (2013)
PLANET DEADLY
https://www.planetdeadly.com/nature/poisonous-mushrooms

Le Peloton de gendarmerie de Haute Montagne de Chamonix
PGHM
http://www.pghm-chamonix.com

"Suivi du dispositif paravalanche de Taconnaz" (2014) by Hervé Bellot and Florence Naaim
IRSTEA
http://www.irstea.fr/la-recherche/unites-de-recherche/etgr/suivi-du-dispositif-paravalanche-de-taconnaz

"Le Glacier de Taconnaz" (2013) by Julien Zannoni
GLACIERS ET CLIMAT
http://glaciers-climat.fr/Taconnaz/Glacier_de_Taconnaz.html

"Quand PARIS-MATCH retraçait le drame VINCENDON-HENRY...
comme la plaque au cimetière de CHAMONIX" (2014) by Michel Guerin
UN MONDE DE PAPIERS
https://unmondedepapiers.com/2014/09/06/la-plaque-vincendon-
henry-du-cimetiere-de-chamonix-et-le-paris-match-qui-en-parle/

"The Martyrs of Mont-Blanc" (2004) by David George
PISTEHORS
http://pistehors.com/news/ski/comments/0665-martyrs-of-mont-blanc/

"France's Wingsuit Graveyard Claims a Ninth Life" (2016) by Lauren
Steele
MEN'S JOURNAL
https://www.mensjournal.com/adventure/frances-wingsuit-graveyard-
claims-a-ninth-life-w436204

"Mont Blanc shrinks 38cm, new height is 4810.06m" (2013)
CHAMONIX.NET
https://www.chamonix.net/english/news/mont-blanc-shrinks

"How Hard is it to Become a Mountain Guide?" (2015) by Brooke Sutton
ADVENTURE JOURNAL
https://www.adventure-journal.com/2015/10/how-hard-is-it-to-become-
a-mountain-guide/

"Imperiia: Mapping the Russian Empire" by Center for Geographic
Analysis
HARVARD UNIVERSITY
http://worldmap.harvard.edu/maps/886

"How Fungi Saved the World" (2014) by Andrew Tomes
FEED THE DATA MONSTER
http://feedthedatamonster.com/home/2014/7/11/how-fungi-saved-the-world

Sex, Drugs, Rock & Snow

"Chamonix-Mont-Blanc en 1939-1945" (2012) by Karine Létang
ANONYMES, JUSTES ET PERÉCUTÉS
http://www.ajpn.org/commune-Chamonix-Mont-Blanc-74056.html

"A University Professor Wants You to Look at Porn for Science" (2017)
by Lisa Power
VICE.COM
https://www.vice.com/en_us/article/qkbyb5/a-university-professor-wants-you-to-look-at-porn-for-science

"How Anna Nicole Smith Became America's Punchline" (2017)
by Sarah Marshall
BUZZFEED
https://www.buzzfeed.com/sarahmarshall/the-american-dream-created-anna-nicole-smith-and-then-it-kil?utm_term=.lpWkmWoop#.tyx1oBZZQ

"LVMH Confirms Acquisition of Bike Brand and That Makes a Lot of Sense" (2016) by Julie Zerbo
THE FASHION LAW
http://www.thefashionlaw.com/home/lvmh-to-buy-a-bike-brand-and-that-makes-a-lot-of-sense

"Why Louis Vuitton's Parent Company Wants to Buy High-End Bike Brand Pinarello" (2016) by Jen See
MEN'S JOURNAL
https://www.mensjournal.com/gear/why-louis-vuittons-parent-company-wants-to-buy-high-end-bike-brand-pinarello-w445606

"Volcom sells Electric brand" (2016) by Danielle Wightman-Stone
FASHION UNITED
https://fashionunited.uk/news/business/volcom-sells-electric-brand/2016031819818

"Candy: Taking the wrapper off a Texas legend" (1976) by Gary Cartwright
TEXAS MONTHLY
https://www.texasmonthly.com/articles/candy/

"Brigitte Bardot had 100 lovers" (2014) by Caroline Howe
MAIL ONLINE
http://www.dailymail.co.uk/news/article-2791264/brigitte-bardot-100-lovers-including-women-four-husbands-fame-led-despair-tried-end-life-four-times-abandoned-child-reveals-new-book.html

"The French way of work"
THE ECONOMIST
http://www.economist.com/node/21538733

"The French are wide awake to the joys of life" (2009) by Celia Walden
THE TELEGRAPH
http://www.telegraph.co.uk/comment/personal-view/5280355/The-French-are-wide-awake-to-the-joys-of-life.html

"Battle of the Vallée Blanche"
RAMPART TOURS
http://www.ramparttours.com/tours/vallee-blanche/

"Massif du Mont-Blanc: Le combat du col du Midi, 17 février 1945" (2013) by Laurent Demouzon
TVMOUNTAIN.COM
https://www.youtube.com/watch?v=EXZvBQUcZlk

"DEUX PYLONES DYNAMITES : 1 million de dégâts" (1982)
CONFEDERE
http://doc.rero.ch/record/134833/files/1982-08-24.pdf

"Mont Blanc: Le Bataillon du Mont-Blanc et les engagements dans
le massif" by Laurent Demouzon
MÉMOIRE DE ALPINS
http://www.memoire-des-alpins.com/historique-des-troupes-
alpines/1944-1945-2/bataille-des-alpes/mont-blanc/

"Chamonix : souvenirs de bataille dans la montagne" (2014)
by Philippe Cortay
LE DAUPHINE
http://www.ledauphine.com/france-monde/2014/07/13/souvenirs-de-
bataille-dans-la-montagne

"Golden Age of Porn"
WIKIPEDIA
https://en.wikipedia.org/wiki/Golden_Age_of_Porn

"Glen Plake is Still Punk" (2016) by Liam Doran
POWDER MAGAZINE
https://www.powder.com/powder-radio/glen-plake-still-
punk/#jWGVckolqFtS20C4.97

"SKI Magazine's Interview With Glen Plake" (2017) by Kim Beekman
SKI MAGAZINE
https://www.skimag.com/ski-resort-life/interview-with-glen-plake-2017

"Glen Plake: Soul Man" (2000) by Steve Casimiro
SKIING MAGAZINE
https://www.skimag.com/uncategorized/glen-plake-soul-man

"Auguste and Louis Lumière"
WIKIPEDIA
https://en.wikipedia.org/wiki/Auguste_and_Louis_Lumi%C3%A8re

"Head and Shoulders Above the Rest" by Terry Marsh
FRANCE TRAVEL GUIDE
http://www.france-travel-guide.net/Haute-Savoie.html

"Discover the historic province of Savoie" (2012) by Pierre Guernier
FRENCH MOMENTS
https://frenchmoments.eu/savoie/

"Living and Writing the Peasant Life" (1987) by Gerald Marzorati
THE NEW YORK TIMES
http://www.nytimes.com/1987/11/29/magazine/living-and-writing-the-peasant-life.html?pagewanted=all

"Avalanche Handlers in Chamonix" (2014) by Paul Streetly
STREETS 23
http://www.streets23.com/avalanche-handlers-in-chamonix/

"Recommendations to deal with Snow Avalanches in Europe" (2003)
edited by Javier Hervás
EUROPEAN COMMISSION JOINT RESEARCH CENTER
http://www.unisdr.org/files/1483_avalancherecommendations.pdf

"The Evolution of the French Language" (2013) by Melissa
TODAY I FOUND OUT
http://www.todayifoundout.com/index.php/2013/12/fascinating-history-french-language/

"Egalité! Liberté! Sexualité!: Paris, May 1968" (2008) by John Lichfield
INDEPENDENT
http://www.independent.co.uk/news/world/europe/egalit-libert-sexualit-paris-may-1968-784703.html

"Quand la France s'ennuie…" (2008) by Pierre Viansson-Ponté
LE MONDE
http://www.lemonde.fr/le-monde-2/article/2008/04/30/quand-la-france-s-ennuie_1036662_1004868.html

"When Did Porn Become Sex Ed?" (2016) by Peggy Orenstein
THE NEW YORK TIMES
https://www.nytimes.com/2016/03/20/opinion/sunday/when-did-porn-become-sex-ed.html

"Le secours en montagne, un peu d'histoire…"
AVALANCHE NET
http://www.avalanche-net.com/secours/histoire.php

"Glen Plake: The Biggest Moments in My Life So Far" (2016)
FALL-LINE SKIING
http://www.fall-line.co.uk/glen-plake-biggest-moments-life-far/

"When Graham Bell met legendary ski filmmaker Greg Stump" (2016) by Graham Bell
THE TELEGRAPH
http://www.telegraph.co.uk/travel/ski/interviews/graham-bell-interviews-greg-stump/

"Notes: Tourism Under Attack" (1977) by Robert J. Dunphy
THE NEW YORK TIMES
http://www.nytimes.com/1977/08/28/archives/notes-tourism-under-attack.html

"Skiing the Steeps" (1981) by Peter Miller
THE NEW YORK TIMES
http://www.nytimes.com/1981/01/25/magazine/skiing-the-steeps.html

"The Oral History of the Money Shot" (2016) by Mark Hay
VICE.COM
https://www.vice.com/en_uk/article/qkbwd5/an-oral-history-of-the-moneyshot

"International Exposure: Perspectives on Modern European Pornography, 1800-2000" (2005) edited by Lisa Z. Sigel
RUTGERS UNIVERSITY PRESS

"Swedish Cinema and the Sexual Revolution: Critical Essays" (2016) edited by Elisabet Björklund, Mariah Larsson
MCFARLAND & COMPANY, INC.

"Eiger Dreams: Ventures Among Men and Mountains" (1990) by Jon Krakauer
LYONS & BURFORD

"The Ski Gods" (2010) by Nick Paumgarten
THE NEW YORKER
https://www.newyorker.com/magazine/2010/03/15/the-ski-gods

"This Is Softcore: The Art Cinema Erotica of Radley Metzger" (2014)
FILM AT LINCOLN CENTER
https://www.filmlinc.org/series/this-is-softcore-the-art-cinema-erotica-of-radley-metzger/

"Porn Before It Was Chic: An Interview With Radley Metzger on Sex and Cinema" (2014) by Hillary Weston
BLACK BOOK
https://bbook.com/film/radley-metzger/

"Porn for the Young Moderns" (2010) by Mark Olsen
LA WEEKLY
http://www.laweekly.com/film/porn-for-the-young-moderns-2167902

"The Implacable Progress of 'Porn'" (2007) by Tim O'Neil
POP MATTERS
https://www.popmatters.com/the-implacable-progress-of-porn-2496232586.html

"A Murder of Swarming Crows" (2012) by Snow Bird
GARDENS & WILDLIFE
http://www.gardensandwildlife.com/2012/06/29/78/

"Jobs for the Savoyards"
ALPS FAIRY
http://www.alpsfairy.com/jobs-for-the-savoyards/

"New Energy at Versace, Ralph Lauren and Emporio Armani" (2017) by Guy Trebay
THE NEW YORK TIMES
https://www.nytimes.com/2017/06/18/fashion/mens-style/versace-armani-ralph-lauren-milan-spring-2018.html

"Small Brand Shoutout: Black Crows" (2015) by Catherine Lutz
POWDER MAGAZINE
https://www.powder.com/stories/small-brand-shoutout-black-crows/#06jsfOeDKmRSxtzx.97

"The Alps: A Cultural History" (2006) by Andrew Beattie
OXFORD UNIVERSITY PRESS

Les Chocards

"No escape from Mount Sinjar: The forgotten Yazidis" (2016) by Olivia Ward
THE STAR
https://www.thestar.com/news/world/2016/02/15/no-escape-from-mount-sinjar-the-forgotten-yazidis.html

"À Chamonix, le Maire ne veut ni élonges ni oppropre" (2017)
AMNESTY INTERNATIONAL
https://www.amnesty.fr/refugies-et-migrants/actualites/a-chamonix-le-maire-ne-veut-ni-eloges-ni-opprobre

"Eric Fournier : «Notre ambition est d'avoir une vallée ouverte sur les autres mais protectrice des siens»" (2014)
LE JOURNAL DES PROPRIÉTAIRES DU PAYS DU MONT BLANC
http://www.jdpmontblanc.info/article/eric-fournier---notre-ambition-est-davoir-une-vallee-ouverte-sur-les-autres-mais-protectrice-des-siens,15379.php

"Les Jeunes agriculteurs manifestent en bloquant l'autoroute" (2017)
LE DAUPHINE
http://www.ledauphine.com/vaucluse/2017/07/05/les-jeunes-agriculteurs-manifestent-en-bloquant-l-autoroute-orange

"Accueil Effectif a Chamonix d'une Famille de Refugies Irakiens"
MARIE DE CHAMONIX
http://chamonix.fr/index.php/actualites/625-accueil-effectif-a-chamonix-d-une-famille-de-refugies-irakiens.html

"Kurdish Religions"
THE KURDISH PROJECT
https://thekurdishproject.org/history-and-culture/kurdistan-religion/

"Mont Blanc, Mon Amour" (2017) by Martha Miklin
BEST OF THE ALPS
https://www.bestofthealps.com/en/d/chamonix-mont-blanc/christian-mollier-mont-blanc-mon-amour/

"Winter has come" (2017) by Carolyne Larrington
1843 MAGAZINE
https://www.1843magazine.com/culture/the-daily/winter-has-come

"National Front"
ENCYCLOPEDIA BRITTANICA
https://www.britannica.com/topic/National-Front-political-party-France

"Where France's National Front is on the rise" (2017)
THE ECONOMIST
https://www.economist.com/blogs/graphicdetail/2017/03/daily-chart-1

"France's National Front Finds Support Among Millennials" (2016) by
Lauren Chadwick
NBC NEWS
https://www.nbcnews.com/news/world/france-s-national-front-finds-support-among-millennials-n697681

"The Long History of French Military Intervention in the Middle East and
Africa" (2015) by Ryan McMaken
MISES INSTITUTE
https://mises.org/blog/long-history-french-military-intervention-middle-east-and-africa

"Rhesus macaque"
WIKIPEDIA
https://en.wikipedia.org/wiki/Rhesus_macaque

"French priest helps expose IS group's Yazidi genocide" (2016) by
Benjamin Dodman
FRANCE 24
http://www.france24.com/en/20161115-holocaust-bullets-french-priest-desbois-yazidi-genocide-iraq-islamic-state-isis

"For Refugees on Mountain, 'No Water, Nothing'" (2014) by Alissa J. Rubin
THE NEW YORK TIMES
https://www.nytimes.com/2014/08/10/world/middleeast/chased-onto-iraqi-mountain-there-is-no-water-nothing.html

"The Cornhill Magazine, Volume 28" (1873) edited by George Smith, William Makepeace
SMITH, ELDER & CO.

"Earth and Sea" (1875) by Louis Figuier
T. NELSON AND SONS

"The London Lancet: A Journal of British and Foreign Medical Surgical, and Chemical Science, Criticism, Literature, and News. Volume 1" (1851) edited by Thomas Wakley and J. Henry Bennet
STRINGER & TOWNSEND

"'You will not replace us': a French philosopher explains the Charlottesville chant" (2017) by Sarah Wildman
VOX
https://www.vox.com/world/2017/8/15/16141456/renaud-camus-the-great-replacement-you-will-not-replace-us-charlottesville-white

"Kangchendzönga: Secular and Buddhist perceptions of the mountain deity of Sikkim among the Lhopos" by Anna Balikci Denjongpa
UNIVERSITY OF CAMBRIDGE
http://himalaya.socanth.cam.ac.uk/collections/journals/bot/pdf/bot_2002_02_01.pdf

"No Room at the Top" (2000) by Bruce Barcott
THE NEW YORK TIMES
http://www.nytimes.com/books/00/06/04/reviews/000604.04barc.html?mcubz=1

"Were 'Devil Worshipper' Yazidis There for the Birth of Human Culture?" (2014) by Michael Smith
VICE.COM
https://www.vice.com/en_us/article/gq8mxx/yazidi-gobekli-tepe-is-172

"The Longest Ski-run in the World" (2015) by Justin Cartwright
1843 MAGAZINE
https://www.1843magazine.com/content/places/justin-cartwright/shadow-mont-blanc

"Irak : les Yazidis de France sortent du silence" (2014)
LE PARISIAN
http://www.leparisien.fr/paris-75/irak-les-yazidis-de-france-sortent-du-silence-23-08-2014-4081671.php

Flamm, E. S., Ommaya, A. K., Coe, J., Krueger, T. P., & Faas, F. H. (1966). Cardiovascular effects of experimental head injury in the monkey. Surgical Forum, 17, 414-416.

Ommaya, A. K., Hirsch, A. E., Flamm, E. S., & Mahone, R. H. (1966). Cerebral concussion in the monkey: an experimental model. Science, 153(3732), 211-212.

"The Macaque Connection: Cooperation and Conflict between Humans and Macaques" (2012) edited by Michael A. Huffman, Anindya Sinha, Sindhu Radhakrishna
SPRINGER

"Behaviour and Ecology of the Chough and the Alpine Chough" (1972) by David Holyoak
BIRD STUDY
https://doi.org/10.1080/00063657209476345

"The Children's Home in Chamonix"
YAD VASHEM
http://www.yadvashem.org/yv/en/exhibitions/childrens-homes/chamonix/index.asp

"Everything You Need to Know About Grackles, the Horny Devil Bird of Texas" (2017) by John Nova Lomax
VICE.COM
https://www.vice.com/en_us/article/gv3qe4/everything-you-need-to-know-about-grackles-the-horny-devil-bird-of-texas

"How the French debacle in Algeria shaped the rise of Marine Le Pen — and what America can learn from it" (2017) by Steven A. Cook
SALON
https://www.salon.com/2017/04/30/how-the-french-debacle-in-algeria-shaped-the-rise-of-marine-le-pen-and-what-america-can-learn-from-it/

"The Conquest of Kanchenjunga" (1955) by George C. Band
SPORTS ILLUSTRATED
https://www.si.com/vault/1955/10/03/597924/the-conquest-of-kanchenjunga

"A Demon In The Drift: Kate Bush Interviewed" (2014) by John Doran
THE QUIETUS
http://thequietus.com/articles/07364-kate-bush-interview-2

"Kanchenjunga"
WORLD HERITAGE ENCYCLOPEDIA
http://self.gutenberg.org/articles/eng/Kanchenjunga

"Who's Fueling Conspiracy Whisperers' Falsehoods?" (2017) Clyde Haberman
THE NEW YORK TIMES
https://www.nytimes.com/2017/04/30/us/retro-report-conspiracy-theories-kennedy-trump.html

"Charles de Gaulle : « Colombey-les-Deux-Mosquées »" (2015) by Alain Peyrefitte
LES OBSERVATEURS
http://lesobservateurs.ch/2015/09/28/charles-de-gaulle-colombey-les-deux-mosquees/

"The Future of Europe Hinges on a Face-off in France" (2017) by Lauren Collins
NEW YORKER
https://www.newyorker.com/magazine/2017/05/08/the-future-of-europe-hinges-on-a-face-off-in-france

"Philippe Gaussot et la Libération de Chamonix"
GAUSSOT.EU
http://www.gaussot.eu/textes/liberation.html

"History of Savoie Mont Blanc area"
ALPS FAIRY
http://www.alpsfairy.com/history-of-savoie-mont-blanc-area/

Films

"La Roue" (1923), Abel Gance
"The Passion of Joan of Arc" (1928), Carl Dreyer
"Madame Butterfly" (1932), Marion Gering
"Swiss Miss" (1938), John G. Blystone
"L'Assassinat du Père Noël" (1941), Christian-Jacque
"L'Assaut des Aiguilles du Diable" (1943), Marcel Ichac
"Les Enfants du Paradis" (1945), Marcel Carné
"Les Étoiles de midi" (1958), Marcel Ichac
"Lola" (1961), Jacques Demy
"Le mépris" (1963), Jean-Luc Godard
"Les Tontons flingueurs" (1963), Georges Lautner
"Papillon" (1973), Franklin J. Schaffner
"Claire's Knee" (1970), Eric Rohmer
"The Blizzard Of Aahhh's" (1988), Greg Stump
"The Royal Tenenbaums" (2001), Wes Anderson

Music

Sex Pistols, "Anarchy in the U.K."
The Ramones, "Blitzkrieg Bop"
Fugazi, "Waiting Room"
Brasstronaut, "Mean Sun"

Any updates to the references and all related hyperlinks can be found at www.chx.xxx/references

Merci

Special appreciation goes to **Sunil Iyengar, Chuck Conconi, Sam Seifman, Jamie Hunt**, and my many friends in Chamonix and beyond who helped with editing and feedback: Tom Adams, Rob Alpen, Jennifer and Jacques Belissent, Johannes Bokesten, Lisa and Miles Bright, Nicola and Giles Broom, Charlie Davies, Hilary and Trevor Dugan, Eva Eskilsson (and Wolfgang), Michael Gaspar, Catherine and Chris Gribben, Sioban Healy, Andy Hoffman, Asa Johnson, Cheryl Jones and Malcolm Mcnaught, Bonnie Millette, Jane Kenyon, Anne Lasseman-Trappier, Samantha and Matt Lauer, Emma Lawrence, Dee and Jean-Baptiste Leclercq, Ruth Martin, Chelsea McCarthy, Ryan McCarthy, Paige McClanahan, Enzo Merluzzi, Fay Mackman and Naoimh O'Hagan, Megan and Neill Pearman, Dr. Ellis Slack, Jim Steen, Ben Tibbetts, Nadia Verlyck, Monica Zugan, and many others. For the encouragement: Colleen, Kyle and Christine, Roz and Ron, Pete, and Nate and Kelly. And I sure do hope Linda Becker gives me a Roscoe for this one: is, am, are, was, were, be, been, being.

In addition, thanks to **Annapurna, Bighorn Bistro, Elevation 1904, Hibou Deli, La Maison Carrier, Moody Coffee Roasters, La Tanière, Tanpopo, Monkey Bar**, and **Les Vieilles Luges** for feeding the insanity, whether you knew it or not.

About the Author

Seth Thomas Pietras is a writer and specialist in communications and public affairs. He splits his time between Geneva, Switzerland, and Chamonix, France. When not at work, he's ski touring, mountaineering, or trail running. Yes, he has seen the monkeys.

www.sethpietras.com / @alpineseth

MEDIASTOPHELES

Printed in Great Britain
by Amazon